Totally Bound Publisi

Per:
The S
Sharing
In

Collections
Naughty or Nice?: Santa Daddy
Sun, Sea and…: Sun, Sea and Satisfaction Guaranteed
Dark and Deadly: Show Me Something Good

Perfect Taboo

IN HIS HANDS

HANNAH MURRAY

In His Hands
ISBN # 978-1-83943-799-1
©Copyright Hannah Murray 2022
Cover Art by Erin Dameron-Hill ©Copyright April 2022
Interior text design by Claire Siemaszkiewicz
Totally Bound Publishing

IN HIS HANDS

Dedication

This was a hard book to write, and I couldn't have done it without my support system. So I dedicate it to them — they know who they are. And to anyone out there who sees their secret desires on the pages of this book.

Special thanks to my niece Shelle and her husband Lindo, who double checked my Portuguese. They speak it every day, and since it's been thirty years since I lived in Brazil, they had a lot to correct!

Content Warning

In His Hands features a taboo kink called consensual non-consent—CNC. This is sometimes referred to as 'rape play', and some of the scenes in this book contain the appearance of both physical and emotional violence in a sexual context.

I want to assure you that every sexual encounter you'll see on these pages is one hundred percent consensual, and at no point is anyone raped or assaulted. But people who play with CNC want it to feel real, and I've written it that way. It may be a difficult and triggering read, especially for survivors of sexual assault or trauma. I am a survivor of sexual assault, and at times this was a very difficult—and yes, triggering—book for me to write.

I encourage you to care for and prioritize your mental and emotional health while reading In His Hands. And I hope, in the end, you'll find Cade and Olivia's love story—and their happily ever after—to be as beautiful and valid as I do.

For more detailed content warnings for In His Hands, and all the books in the *Perfect Taboo* series, please visit the Books Page of my website, www.hannahmurray.net.

"It's easy to fall in love. The hard part is finding someone to catch you." ~ Bertrand Russell

Chapter One

Olivia stared at her boyfriend in disbelief. "Are you serious?"

Kyle raised one blond eyebrow, which unfortunately added a layer of smug condescension to his Generically Handsome White Guy face. "Do I look serious?"

"Yes." His usual affable smile was missing, his mouth pinched tight. "You look very serious."

"Well, then." Kyle took out a pen and tapped the thick sheaf of papers on the table between them.

"You're telling me if I don't sign that, we're done."

"That's what I'm telling you."

This didn't make any *sense*. "I don't want a Master/slave relationship, Kyle. You know that."

He laid the pen on the table. It was the fountain pen she'd given him for his birthday last month, she noted. It was made in Germany, by some company that was apparently the world leader in fancy fountain pens, and had cost almost as much as her share of the monthly rent. It had a black lacquer finish, gold trim, and a gold nib that squirted ink all over her fingers every time she used it.

"It's not about what you want, but rather, what you need," Kyle said, and Olivia narrowed her eyes. He only used words like 'rather' when he was trying extra hard to be taken seriously.

"I don't need a slave contract — which, by the way, is not in any way legally enforceable." She paused to take a calming breath. If she started yelling, he'd just shut down, and they'd never get anywhere. "I need you to talk to me. I don't understand where this is coming from."

"There's nothing to talk about." He leaned back in his chair and folded his arms, his expression shuttered. He looked the way he did when he was trying to bluff his way through a crappy hand at the poker table, or when someone disagreed with some political talking point he was repeating. Like he knew he was fucked and wanted to walk away, but his pride wouldn't allow it.

She knew that pride. It was stubborn and immovable and her biggest obstacle to figuring out just what was behind this ridiculousness.

She switched tactics. "Kyle, this is something we have to talk about. You can't just spring a contract on me like this."

"Actually, I can." He arched an eyebrow again. "I'm the Dom, and I make the rules."

That was such pile of verbal crap that she momentarily lost the power of speech, and while she was gaping at him, trying to figure out what the *hell* he was thinking, he stood up.

"I have to pick up Andy for the game." He crossed the room and scooped his keys out of the bowl on the table next to the door. Her bowl, her table. "I expect that contract to be signed when I get back."

The bafflement and shock that had held her frozen since he'd first tossed that contract on the table was fading, replaced by an incredulous fury that made her feel like she was breathing sulfur. "Or?"

"Or you can pack your things," he replied calmly. "It's your choice."

He twirled his keys around his finger—another nervous tell—opened the door and walked out.

Olivia stared at the closed door for a moment, then looked down at the contract. It was at least twenty pages, held together with one of the bright pink binder clips she kept in the kitchen junk drawer to use on bags of chips or frozen vegetables. Kyle's name was in bold type at the top, right in front of the words, "hereafter referred to as Master", and her name, bolded but not capitalized, right before "hereafter referred to as slave", and the remainder of her disbelief disintegrated in a flood of pure rage.

She stood up, shoving back from the table hard enough to make it wobble, and stalked to the bedroom. She pulled her suitcases from the back of the closet, laid them on the bed, and began to pack.

She worked methodically, rolling her clothes to minimize wrinkling and maximize space. When the dresser, the closet, and the nightstand on her side of the bed were empty, she walked across the hall to the guest room-office to gather the clothes she had stored there.

There wasn't a lot—the cocktail dresses she rarely had occasion to wear, a formal gown she'd bought on a whim when a local dress shop had gone out of business, and the plastic storage bin with her corsets. When she pulled the bin down from the top shelf, the dust coating the lid made her sneeze. It had been months since she'd worn one, though she and Kyle went to a kink event nearly every week. It had just seemed like too much trouble, and Kyle hadn't cared one way or the other.

"That should've been a fucking clue," she muttered, and sneezed again.

Back in the bedroom, she crammed the dresses into the already full suitcases, then zipped them closed and wrestled them to the floor. She pulled the duvet off the bed, then the sheets, and added the pillow she'd broken in how she liked it to the pile before heading into the bathroom for her toiletries.

She needed a box for the kitchen, and found one in the office, full of Kyle's tax files. She dumped them without remorse onto his desk chair and packed it tight with utensils, measuring cups, and the egg timer in the shape of a cow—and she took the pink binder clip off the damn contract, too. She pulled a garbage bag from under the sink for the potholders and dishtowels, then added her bedding, towels, and every spare sheet from the hall linen closet.

The sonofabitch had been sleeping on a bare mattress when she'd moved in, and he could damn well do it again.

She gathered her laptop and tablet from the living room, her extra phone charger and the blanket her aunt had crocheted for her in college. The electronics went into the tote she used as a purse, the blanket into the garbage bag. Then she dragged everything to the front door and took a last tour of the apartment.

She made a list of all the things she'd need to come back for. The prints and photos on the walls, the table by the front door. Her stand mixer still sat on the kitchen counter, her dishes in the cabinets. There were pieces of sculpture and statuary she'd collected over the years scattered throughout the apartment that would need to be carefully wrapped and packed, as would her reproduction Tiffany lamp. Her grandmother's mirror hung above the entry table, and the chair and dresser that were the only pieces of furniture she'd kept when she'd moved in with Kyle.

She quelled the twinge of anxiety at the thought of leaving so many of her things behind and grabbed her keys. It took three trips and some creative arranging, but she managed to get everything into her ancient Camry. By the time she climbed the stairs for the last time, she was sweating, her tank top sticking to her back. She'd retrieved one of the hair ties she kept on the stick shift of her car, so her hair was off her neck. But sweat trickled between her breasts and down the backs of her legs, and the only thing keeping her moving was righteous rage.

Back in the apartment, she hefted her tote with a grunt, and started to take the front door key off her key ring. She wanted to leave it right in the middle of his damned contract where he couldn't possibly miss it, but she hesitated. She had to retrieve the rest of her things, and if she left her key behind now, she'd have to go through Kyle to do it.

"The hell I will," she muttered, and palming her keys, turned to go. Then she caught her reflection in the mirror over the entry table and winced. She was a mess. Half her honey-blonde hair had fallen out of its hastily constructed topknot to hang, limp and damp with sweat, to her shoulders. She'd sweated off her makeup except for a solid smudge of mascara under each eye — which, except for the faint flush of exertion on her cheeks, was the only color on her already pale face. Even her eyes looked dull.

Dull and beige. It was a good way to describe her relationship with Kyle. *And now, over.*

She hitched her bag higher on her shoulder, and her gaze landed on the chain encircling her neck. The everyday collar was only slightly longer than a choker, with a tiny key charm that nestled in the hollow of her throat. The necklace's standard clasp had been removed and replaced with silver rings that attached to the charm, turning a standard removeable chain into a permanent one. The only way to get it off was to break it.

She stared at it, remembering how she'd felt when Kyle had fastened it around her neck. She'd been so happy, so full of hope. Now, staring at the tiny key that had meant so much, all she felt was anger and sadness.

She dropped her bag to the floor and grabbed the necklace in both sweaty fists. The little silver rings gave way easily, pulling free with barely a twist, and the key fell with a musical clink to the floor at her feet.

She picked it and stared at it, small and insignificant in her palm, the broken chain dangling from her fingers. A year of her life in two broken pieces of silver, she thought, her throat tight, and wanted to rage and scream at the waste of it all.

Instead she walked to the table, dropped the charm and the necklace on the contract, then walked back to the mirror and pulled it off the wall. With the heavy tote on one arm and the mirror tucked under the other, she walked out.

* * * *

Olivia drove automatically, weaving through traffic without really noticing it as she considered her next step. Finding a new place to live was first on her agenda, and that meant a large cash outlay—first and last month's rent, security deposit, plus the cost of movers, though she might be able to avoid that last item if some of her friends were willing to help. A couple of guys with a pickup could probably handle the dozen or so boxes of her belongings, plus the few pieces of furniture she hadn't sold when she'd moved in with Kyle.

Shit, she was going to have to buy furniture.

Mentally kissing a good chunk of her savings goodbye, she continued to drive. The sun was bright in the sky, making her wish for the sunglasses in the bottom of her bag. Unfortunately, she'd loaded all her electronics in on top of them, and since she'd have to pull over in order to safely dig them out, she flipped the visor down and kept driving.

She pulled to a stop at a red light, thumbs tapping on the steering wheel as she mentally worked through her list. After finding an apartment, getting the rest of her stuff moved, and buying new furniture, there was only one thing left to do.

Find a new Dom.

"Dammit." The light changed, and she stomped on the gas. Under the anger and outrage, the strongest emotion she felt at the ending of her relationship was disappointment. She'd chosen Kyle because his kinks aligned closely with hers, and after a year together, she'd finally felt like they were ready to take the steps to fully explore them. But instead of settling happily into the kinky relationship of her dreams, she was homeless and Dom-less and back at square one.

"Dammit," she muttered again, and forced herself to ease off the gas. A speeding ticket would just put a cap on her day. She tried some of the yoga breathing her friend Sadie was so damn fond of, deep inhales and controlled exhales, and by the time she pulled to a stop on a quiet tree-lined street, she was more tired than angry.

She looked up at the house with a sense of relief. She always felt at home here, in the brick two-story that had been lovingly and painstakingly renovated. When Cade had bought the house a year ago, the brick had been crumbling, the porch sagging, and the interior firmly stuck in the last century. When he'd shown her the pictures and told her he intended to live there during the renovations—which he was going to do himself—she'd thought he was in over his head.

It had taken him several months to do all the work, but he'd repaired the brick and rebuilt the front porch, and he'd taken the interior from chopped-up rooms with stained floors and crumbling plaster to a bright, open space with restored woodwork and plenty of light.

The last time she'd been there he'd been trying to decide on tile for the downstairs powder room. He'd been torn between a modern glass subway tile and an old-fashioned penny tile that mimicked what might have been installed when the house had been built in the nineteen-twenties.

She wondered idly which one he'd chosen.

Any one of her girlfriends would have welcomed her with open arms and a sympathetic ear—well, any of them except Becca, who had plans—which was why she'd come here instead. She didn't want to talk about it, at least not yet, and it would be easier to avoid questions at Cade's.

Mostly because he wasn't there.

She glanced at the clock on her dashboard, noting that it was just past six. His phone would be off if his scene had already begun, but she knew he'd check his messages when he turned it back on, so she dug out her phone and tapped out a quick text.

I left Kyle. Hope it's ok if I crash in your guest room, she wrote, and, hoping that would be it, turned off the ignition and climbed out of the car.

She was popping the trunk when her phone dinged with an incoming text.

"Shit," she muttered, and dug it out of her pocket.

What happened?

It's complicated, she typed back, and hoped that would be enough.

A new message popped up within seconds. *Are you okay?*

She smiled. Of course he would ask that first, she thought with a sigh, and responded quickly so he wouldn't worry. *I'm fine. Pissed off, but unhurt.*

You still have your key? The alarm code?

Olivia sagged with relief. *Yeah.*

I'll be home late, or possibly tomorrow. Lock up behind you.

Tomorrow? "Go, Becca," she murmured with a little grin. It was impossible to keep secrets in the kink community, so even though Cade hadn't said a word, she knew his play date tonight was a threesome with Becca and her partner, Nick. It was Becca's fantasy to be with two Doms, and after months of discussion and planning, she'd finally given Nick the green light to make it come true.

She felt a little twinge of envy for her friend. *Thanks, Cade. I'll cook breakfast,* she told him.

I'll hold you to that, he responded, and added pancakes, bacon, and eggs emojis.

She responded with a thumbs-up, then tucked her phone away. She had a couple of trips to make with her stuff, then she could raid Cade's fridge for something cold to drink. There wouldn't be beer, but he always kept a couple of Cokes in the crisper drawer.

With the promise of an icy soda waiting for her, she pulled out the first suitcase.

Chapter Two

Cade sat in one of the chairs in the parlor of the hotel suite, doing his best to finish dressing quietly. He'd gathered his clothes while Nick and Rebecca were in the bath, and was reaching for his shoes when he heard his name.

He glanced up at Nick, freshly showered and wrapped in a hotel robe. "She okay?"

"Yeah, she's fine. Thirsty, so I came out for more water." Nick held up the bottle, then tucked it into the pocket of the hotel robe he'd donned. "What are you doing?"

Cade tugged on the shoe, his fingers flying over the laces. "You two should be alone."

"It's a two-bedroom suite," Nick pointed out. "I thought you were going to stay, have breakfast with us in the morning."

"I was planning on it," Cade said, head still bent to his task. "But now I think it's better if I head home."

Home, where Olivia was. He'd managed to shuffle thoughts of her aside for most of the evening—not hard, considering he'd spent it helping Nick fulfill his girlfriend's fantasy of being topped—and fucked—by two Doms. But now that the scene and the sex were over, he found himself eager to go.

"I'm sorry," Nick said.

"For what?" Genuinely perplexed at the question, Cade rose to his feet. "I had fun, y'all had fun, Rebecca got to see me naked."

He grinned, and for a second, he thought he'd pulled it off. But Nick had always been quick, and he'd always been blunt.

"Then why do you look like your cat died?"

Cade laughed and dragged a hand over his hair. He'd let it grow out over the last few months, and wasn't quite used to finding tousled waves instead of a buzz cut. "Trust you to say the quiet part out loud."

"If we did or said anything—" Nick began.

Cade held up a hand. "Neither of you did anything," he said, then let his hand drop. "I promise. I just...saw what I'm missing, is all."

He shrugged, an uncomfortable shift of his shoulders. "Not your fault."

"You want to talk about it?"

It was tempting. But Nick had Rebecca to tend to, and he had to get it straight in his own head before he could explain it to anyone. "I'll take a rain check. I better get home and see what's up with Olivia."

"Right." Nick followed him to the door. "If she needs anything..."

Cade turned at the door. "I'll let you know."

"Nick? Cade?"

A sleepy-eyed Rebecca walked out of the bedroom, dwarfed in her hotel robe. She rubbed her face, smearing the eyeliner that was all that remained of her makeup. She looked freshly scrubbed and charmingly debauched all at once. "What's wrong?"

"Nothing's wrong," Cade assured her as she drifted across the room. Nick extended a hand and she slipped hers into it, nestling into the curve of his body.

She leaned her head on Nick's chest, her dark hair stark against the bright white of his robe. She sent Cade a sleepy smile. "I thought you were staying."

Cade smiled back, slow and wicked, and hoped he could pull it off. "Looking for another round, darlin'?"

Her cheeks went adorably pink. "I think I'm going to need a while to recover from the last one," she admitted, and both men laughed. "But you don't have to go."

"I'd love to stay," he said, and it was only half a lie. "But Olivia texted me that she needs a place to crash tonight. I need to check on her."

Rebecca straightened with a frown. "What happened?"

"She left Kyle," Cade began.

"Is she all right? Did he do anything? Does she need anything? What happened?"

"Right now, all I know is she said she needs a place to stay tonight." Cade's gaze met Nick's over Rebecca's head in a moment of shared amusement. "I'll tell her to call you tomorrow, all right?"

"All right." Rebecca hesitated slightly, then stepped away from Nick, crossing the short distance to stand in front of Cade. She looked up at him, all big gray eyes and glowing skin. "Can I give you a hug?"

If there was a man who could hold out against that, it wasn't Cade. "Of course you can."

She went up on her toes, wrapping her arms around his shoulders as Cade bent his knees to meet her halfway. "Tell her how you feel," she whispered, and he jerked in surprise. Her arms tightened, keeping him close. "Tell her," she said again, and Cade closed his eyes.

Rebecca clung for a heartbeat more, staying on her toes to press a kiss to his cheek. Then she dropped to her heels and stepped back into the circle of Nick's arms.

"Drive safe," Nick said quietly, and Cade nodded.

"I will." The knob turned silently under his hand, the door swinging open to the dimly lit hallway beyond. He took a step forward, into that void.

"Cade."

He glanced back over his shoulder at Rebecca's call.

"Thank you," she said simply.

He nodded, not trusting himself to speak, then stepped into the darkened hall, the door closing behind him with a click.

He took the stairs down to the lobby, too restless to wait for the elevator, and dug his ticket out of his wallet for the valet. There was no one else waiting, so the car was brought around in a matter of minutes. He slipped the valet a generous tip for the speed, then tucked himself behind the wheel of the classic Stingray convertible.

He drove with the top down, the wind blowing through his hair. The scene and the sex had left him physically sated, but he kept thinking about Rebecca's whispered words. She hadn't been around long—less than a year—but she'd seen what he'd been hiding for almost two years, and called him on it. Even through his discomfort, he had to admire both her intuition and her guts.

But he didn't want to think about his feelings for Olivia, so he put them aside and let the quiet drive soothe him. He loved this car—the pickup was for practicality, but the Stingray was pure pleasure. With summer in full swing, he tried to get it out of the garage as much as possible.

When he'd bought his house, the first project he'd undertaken had been to build the garage. His mother had lobbied hard for the kitchen to be first, and his sisters had added their weight to the argument, but he'd held his ground. The garage meant he had parking space for both the truck and the Corvette, with a security system to keep both vehicles secure.

His mother had railed at him, then insisted he add the same system to the house. Which had always been his plan, but he'd argued with her anyway, just for the joy of watching her lose her temper. Mercedes Hollis considered herself a level-headed, practical woman, but she was the only one who thought so. His sisters took after their mother, and nothing amused him more than when he had all four Hollis women shouting at him. If he could get his mother so worked up she forgot her English and reverted to shouting at him in her native Portuguese, his day was made.

His father would pat his wife on the shoulder and urge her to calm down, which only increased both the vehemence and volume of the rant, and Cade and his dad would grin at each other over her head.

Which reminded him, it had been a while since he'd made it to Sunday dinner. He'd been out of town the last two weekends, and he figured if he missed another week, his mother would threaten to take his name off the family Christmas letter. He pulled through the alley behind his house, hitting the remote for the garage as he pulled up, and made a mental note to call her in the morning.

Maybe if he groveled sufficiently, and went to the butcher for the pig feet, she'd make feijoada.

He parked the car and set the garage alarm, then headed for the house. It was dark, the only light the one he'd left on over the kitchen sink. He let himself in, noting that the alarm was off. He reset it with a grim shake of his head for his negligent houseguest, then walked through the dimly lit kitchen and dining room into the living room.

There was a garbage bag — full, by the looks of it — at the end of his large sectional sofa. Two suitcases sat on one side, a plastic tote and one large cardboard box flanked the other. And sprawled on the couch, fast asleep, was Olivia.

She was curled under the blanket he kept stored in the ottoman, a huge quilt his oldest sister had made for him. One side was flannel, and the other was made up of the pockets from dozens of pairs of jeans. It was ugly as homemade sin, and the denim made it heavy — it was a running family joke that Claudia had invented weighted blankets by mistake.

He'd have gotten rid of it years ago, but his mother would kill him. So he stored it in the ottoman, easily accessible for when his mother visited or the heat went out in January.

Or, he amended mentally, *if Olivia came over and didn't have the code to adjust the thermostat.*

She was curled in the corner of the sectional, the quilt tucked under her chin as she slept. Her honey-blonde hair was in a messy pile on top of her head, leaving her face unframed. She looked innocent in sleep, with her round cheeks flushed pink and her thick eyelashes forming shadows on her soft skin. Her mouth, however, shattered any illusion of innocence.

It had been nearly two years since they'd played together, and still, he could recall every detail of how it had felt to look down and see that plush mouth wrapped around him, streaks of dark pink lipstick clinging to his skin, struggling to swallow him while her big hazel eyes filled with tears.

Her mouth was naked now, her lips soft and slightly parted. Her whole face was bare of cosmetics, her skin pale but for the faint flush on her cheeks. It made her seem younger than her thirty-three years, and added to the air of vulnerability that clung to her like smoke. And, as he was a man who found vulnerability almost irresistible, contributed to the sudden uncomfortable fit of his slacks.

Used to the fact that his dick had a mind of its own when Olivia was around, he ignored it and picked up the garbage bag. It was heavier than he'd expected, but soft, likely filled with bedding or towels. He adjusted his grip and peered into the open carboard box. It was full of kitchen stuff, neatly and tightly packed. Since he doubted she'd need a set of measuring cups or an instant read thermometer tonight, he nudged it aside and picked up the plastic tote under it.

It was light, so he tucked it under his arm, and with the garbage bag slung over his shoulder, walked quietly to the stairs.

The second floor was dark, and his cat had a tendency to sprawl across the top of the steps or dart between his feet when he walked, so he moved cautiously until he reached the guest bedroom. He opened the door, then set the tote and garbage bag on the floor before flipping on the light and looking around with a critical eye.

He tried to keep the room guest-ready, since his mother had a habit of volunteering his house to out-of-town visitors, so the bed was already made. He noted that his cleaning lady had taken care of the layer of dust that had coated the small desk the last time he'd poked his head in, and the plant on the little table by the south facing window was thriving.

Lucy clearly deserved a raise.

He made a mental note to take care of it in the morning, and, leaving the light on and the door open, ducked into the hall bath. Clean towels were stacked on the open shelf under the sink, and the subway tile he'd laid himself gleamed. There were a couple of bottles in the shower, the shampoo and conditioner his sister Tatiana favored, plus a small bottle of body wash that had been part of a gift basket he'd gotten for Christmas last year.

Satisfied that the rooms were ready for her, he trooped back down the stairs for the rest of Olivia's stuff.

When everything but the box of kitchen supplies had been delivered to the guest room, he stood once again at the end of the couch. She was still asleep, but she'd shoved the heavy quilt down to her waist. The black tank top she wore was nothing special, a simple ribbed cotton that should've looked utilitarian and practical. But it was snug on her breasts and rucked up at the waist, showcasing luscious tits and the sweet curve of her belly. The dip of her belly button was a faint shadow just above her waistband, and predictably, his slacks once again grew uncomfortable. A plaintive meow made him jerk, startled, and he looked down at the fluffy white cat winding around his ankles. She looked up at him and meowed again, butting her head against his shin and shedding on his pants.

"Hey, Phoebe," he murmured softly, and since his clothes were already destined for the dry cleaner, bent to pick her up. He rubbed his fingertips on the top of her head, just behind her ears, and smiled when she began to purr. "Where have you been, hmmm? And why do you stink?"

"I gave her a can of tuna."

He glanced up to see Olivia sitting up, blinking groggily, a pillow crease on her cheek. Her hair was falling out of its topknot, and she reached up to tug the rest of it free. Her arm flexed, the quarter-sleeve tattoo a flash of color in the darkness.

"So I smell," he said mildly, and tried to ignore what that subtle flex of muscle did to his heart rate. "She has an automatic feeder, you know. Plenty of kibble."

"I know." Olivia yawned, covering her mouth with the back of her hand, then shoved the blanket aside and swung her feet to the floor. "But she looked so pitiful."

Cade looked away from smooth, pale legs to find the cat eyeing him with smug blue eyes. "The pitiful bit, huh?"

"I know it's an act." Olivia stood to stretch. He kept his eyes on the cat, but his peripheral vision was excellent. "But she's really good at it."

He lifted his head and smiled at her. "Why do you think I keep tuna in the cabinet?"

She smiled back, the crease in her cheek deepening like a temporary dimple, but her eyes were heavy and troubled, reminding him that there was a reason she was camped out on his sofa on a Friday night.

"Do you want to talk about it?" he asked, and was watching her closely enough to catch the flinch.

"Not yet." She turned back to the couch and began to fold the blanket, her lush mouth turned down in a frown.

Cade let the cat leap out of his arms and stepped forward. "Here, give me that end. You take the other."

"I love this blanket," she said. "It's so cozy."

He pulled his two ends together. "It's a beast. I'd give it away, but my mother would kill me."

She glanced at him, eyes curious. "I thought your sister Claudia made it."

"She wouldn't care," he said, giving the blanket a shake. It was like shaking a block of cement. "Mom's the sentimental one. She still has the ashtray I made in eighth-grade woodshop, and she's never smoked a day in her life."

Olivia passed over her end of the blanket. "You made an ashtray out of wood?"

"I was in eighth grade," he explained, pleased to see the smile light her eyes. "My grasp of the laws of thermodynamics was incomplete."

"Wood burns, Cade." She grabbed the folded end of the blanket, eyes dancing. "Who doesn't know that by the eighth grade?"

"In my defense, it was supposed to be a bowl." He lifted the lid on the ottoman, then took the folded blanket from her and shoved it inside. "But I got a little aggressive with the chisel, and took a chunk out of the rim. I didn't want to start over, so I just took out three more chunks, sanded them smooth, and called it an ashtray. My mom displays it with the good dishes."

"That's sweet."

He rolled his eyes and turned to her, his hands tucked safely in his pockets. "It's diabolical," he said, and changed the subject. "Have you eaten?"

"Oh." She laid a hand on her stomach, still bared by the rucked-up tank. "Yeah, I had something...before."

She flinched again, and his hands curled into fists in his pockets. "If you don't want to talk about it, it's fine," he began, making the effort to keep his voice calm. "But I need to know if he's going to come after you."

She snorted, the soft look in her eyes going hard. "Not likely."

Interesting reaction. "You don't think he will?"

"Me leaving was his idea," she offered drily.

He had more questions, but he bit them back. She wasn't ready, and he wouldn't push. Not yet. "All right. Do we have to get anything else from the apartment?"

She lifted both hands to her hair in a gesture of frustration, the sleek muscles in her arms flexing under soft skin, then dropped them to her sides with a sigh. "Not tonight. I packed up everything essential."

"I took them upstairs," he said when she frowned at the space where her belongings had been. "The guest room is all set up for you."

"Thanks, Cade."

"Anytime, fofa."

She smiled a little at the nickname, one he'd given her soon after they'd met. He'd told her it meant "cutie" in Portuguese, which was mostly the truth.

A plaintive meow made them both look down at Phoebe, once again rubbing herself against his leg. "I'm never getting the cat hair out of these pants."

"They're nice pants," she said, and her lips took on an impish curve.

He tilted his head, curious. "What's that smile for?"

"I just think it's cute you dressed up for a threesome."

He shook his head, amused and unsurprised. "Is there anything y'all don't talk about?"

"Not really." She raised an expectant eyebrow. "So, how'd it go?"

He tucked his tongue in his cheek. "It went well."

She snorted. "It went well? That's all you're going to say?"

"If Rebecca wants to share the details, she can. I don't kiss and tell."

"Spoilsport," she accused mildly.

"Fair warning—she knows you're here. She'll probably have as many questions for you as you'll have for her."

She grimaced. "They all will. I have to figure out what to tell them."

"The truth usually works best."

"I know," she said, her shoulders hunching a little. "But I have to get a handle on it first."

"They'll wait until you're ready," he told her. "So will I."

"Thanks, Cade."

"Anytime," he said, forcing the words past the tightness in his throat. She looked so small and sad. "Want to watch a movie?"

"No, thanks. I think I'll go to bed."

"All right." He shifted aside to let her pass. It was pure coincidence that he happened to take a deep breath just when she drew close, filling his lungs with her scent. Sweat and the faintly citrus scent of her shampoo, plus a whiff of the tuna she'd given the cat.

Not a seductive combination, but he was seduced all the same.

"Are you going to stay up?" she asked, one foot on the bottom stair, her hand on the newel post.

He knew wouldn't sleep, not with her down the hall. "For a little while."

"Okay. I'll see you in the morning, then."

"Good night," he said, and tortured himself by watching her ass climb his stairs.

"Cade?"

He jerked his gaze to her face, the back of his neck heating. "Yeah?"

"Thanks again. For letting me stay. And for, you know, not asking questions."

"You're always welcome here," he told her. "As for the questions, I will eventually ask."

"I know." Her smile was tight. "But I appreciate the stay of execution."

It was an interesting choice of words, but he let it go. "Sleep well, fofa."

"Night," she replied softly, and disappeared up the stairs.

He waited until he heard the bedroom door shut, then went through his nightly routine. Checking doors and windows, the alarm, turning off the kitchen light. With the security light on the garage shining in through the kitchen windows, he opened the door to the basement and flipped on the lights. The fluorescents flickered on—he needed to find time to replace those with something less horrible—illuminating the corner of the unfinished basement he'd set up as a home gym.

He stripped down to his underwear and picked up a set of dumbbells, ready to do arm curls until his dick went down or his arms fell off…whichever came first.

* * * *

Olivia went downstairs in the morning in her favorite sundress. It was cornflower blue, the skirt perfect for twirling, and it had pockets. She wore it whenever she needed cheering up, and it almost never failed to lift her spirits. Unfortunately, it wasn't quite doing the trick this morning.

She'd heard Cade go downstairs half an hour ago, the wooden stairs in the old house creaking and groaning under his feet. He'd done extensive renovations to make the hundred-year-old dwelling fit for modern living, but the stairs creaked, and the walls weren't quite plumb. Cade said that was how he liked it.

Olivia liked it too. She just wished she could employ a bit more stealth on a morning like this. She clung to the faint hope that he was in the basement working out, or had maybe run to the store, and she'd have a little more time to settle before the inevitable questions began.

But of course, the minute she cleared the stairs and turned into the living room, he materialized out of the dining room like a wraith in jeans. And nothing else.

She blinked twice, but the vision didn't change. Jeans and no shirt, his bare feet poking out from under the frayed hems.

"Good morning."

"Morning," she parroted back automatically. She felt like her mouth was moving without conscious direction from her brain, which was still frozen at the sight of Cade wearing nothing but jeans.

Which was weird, because it wasn't like she hadn't seen him shirtless before. Hell, she'd seen him naked before. So why was the sight of his bare chest making her short circuit?

"Sleep okay?"

"Yes, fine."

Not that it wasn't an impressive chest. He mostly managed construction projects now instead of working on them, but the years he'd spent swinging a hammer were evident. Thick muscle was covered by golden-brown skin, the smooth landscape of it interrupted only by a sexy smattering of hair over his breastbone. It continued down, nearly disappearing over his abdomen, only to pick back up on the south side of his belly button, trailing down to disappear into the waistband of his jeans.

Unbuttoned. His jeans were zipped but unbuttoned, and riding low enough for her to glimpse the deep vee of muscle just under his hipbones and, dear *God*, that was a hell of a view first thing in the morning. Who needed coffee when Cade's abs could make her feel like this?

She jerked her gaze to his face and worked up a smile, hoping that the heat flooding her body wasn't visible in her face. She'd never been a blusher, but the way her luck was running, this would be the day she'd start. "I slept great," she said, and kept smiling even when he looked at her curiously.

"I believe you," he said, humor lighting his eyes.

"Well," she said briskly, and kept her eyes from dropping to his crotch again through sheer force of will. "I'll get breakfast started."

"Already on it. How do you feel about bacon?"

She blinked. "I thought I was cooking this morning."

"I wanted to let you sleep," he said, and turned to walk into the kitchen.

She wanted to be relieved that she'd longer be tempted to stare at his dick, but the truth was, the back view was just as enticing as the front. Muscles shifted and rippled under silky skin, well defined and mouthwatering. There was a scar on his left shoulder blade from some long-ago accident, white against the warm brown of his skin, and his jeans were low enough to show off the dimples at the base of his spine.

Shit. She didn't know he had those. Back dimples were her kryptonite.

Thrown off kilter by the sudden onset of lust, she followed him into the kitchen and tried to find something else to look at.

Of all the changes he'd made to the house, the most obvious ones were here. He'd gutted the kitchen, taking it down to the studs and rebuilding it from scratch, knocking down walls to create one large open room that spanned the back of the house. The kitchen was on one side, and he'd created a lounge area with a gas fireplace and cozy chairs on the other.

Soft gray cabinets took up the entire left wall, rising to the twelve-foot ceiling. Space had been carved out for the sub-zero refrigerator and the six-burner range in a deep royal blue that she knew he'd waited three months for.

She'd never considered the attractiveness of kitchen appliances before, but that stove was undeniably sexy.

The run of lower cabinets continued along the back wall, with the sink under the wide window, and ended at the French doors to the back deck. The massive island housed more storage and about an acre of counterspace in gleaming white. There were four barstools on the opposite side, upholstered in a blue velvet that perfectly matched the color of the stove.

She took a seat on one of the barstools and tried not to stare at his back dimples. "The kitchen is my favorite room in your house."

He picked up a fork and poked at the bacon sizzling in a pan. "Mine, too. And with the custom hood installed, it's finally finished."

"Oh!" She looked above his head to the hood vent, a gleaming copper that matched the knobs on the range. "I didn't even notice."

He tore off a handful of paper towels to drain the bacon, shooting her a look over his shoulder. "Observant this morning, aren't we?"

"Give me a break. I haven't had coffee yet." *Also, I'm very distracted and inconveniently aroused at the sight of your half-naked body.*

He jerked a chin at the coffee pot tucked into the corner. "Help yourself."

Grateful for something to do, she slid off the stool and pulled a thick white mug down from the open shelving next to the window. "You want?"

"Yeah, thanks."

She poured two cups, adding a cube of sugar to his and three to hers from the little dish next to the coffeepot. "Do you have any half and half?"

"I've got cream and two percent milk."

"Cream works," she decided, and very carefully walked past him to get to the refrigerator.

She doctored her cup so the dark brew turned a creamy beige, then set his on the counter next to the stove. "One sugar, right?"

"Thanks." He flashed her a smile that set her pulse racing, and she took her coffee back to the counter, hoping the six or so feet between them would allow her hormones to calm the fuck down.

Maybe she was ovulating, she mused, sipping her coffee. Wait, that couldn't be it, because her birth control prevented ovulation. Shit, maybe her birth control was failing.

She pulled her phone out of the pocket of her dress to search *"signs that birth control pills aren't working"*.

"Here you go," he said, setting a plate in front of her piled with bacon, scrambled eggs, and half an English muffin with a pat of butter melting in its center.

"Wow." She laid her phone face down in her lap as he came around the counter to take the stool next to hers. The food smelled amazing, and on cue, her stomach rumbled. "I just realized I'm starving."

"So, eat." He handed her a fork. "And when you're done, you can tell me what happened with Kyle."

Chapter Three

Cade watched Olivia over the rim of his coffee mug. All that was left of her breakfast was a smear of egg on the plate, and her coffee cup was almost empty. "You're stalling."

Her hazel eyes flashed, more gold than green now, and her mouth twisted in annoyance. "And you're pushing."

"I don't need specifics." He knew once she started talking, the details would come pouring out. "Just give me the basics."

"The basics," she repeated. Her foot was bouncing on the rung of the stool, making her knee jiggle, and she was tapping her fingernails on the counter so fast it sounded like a woodpecker. "The basics are that we broke up. Happy now?"

"Olivia," he said, a subtle note of warning in his voice. He did it deliberately, then had to fight back a smile when her scowl deepened.

"Don't think I don't know what you're doing," she warned him. "Hauling out the Dom voice to get me to talk."

He said nothing, merely sipped his coffee and watched her fidget, almost a neon sign advertising her discomfort. Olivia was normally a physically quiet woman, with very few wasted or uneconomical movements. Unless she was upset, or agitated—then she couldn't sit still to save her life. It was only a matter of time until she broke.

"He gave me an ultimatum, all right?"

Interesting. He'd imagined a fight, or a scene gone bad. "What kind of ultimatum?"

She shrugged, a sharp jerk of her shoulders, and slid her gaze away from his. "The kind I couldn't live with. So, that was that."

"That must have been some ultimatum."

She shrugged again, still not looking at him.

"Olivia." He waited until her eyes jerked back to his. "I just want to help."

"I know." She sighed, slumping on the stool as though all the starch had gone out of her spine. "I know you are. It's just...well, it's embarrassing."

He frowned. "Would you rather talk to Rebecca, or Amanda?"

"No."

She looked so forlorn he wanted to scoop her into his lap and cuddle her. "They're not going to judge you, fofa."

"I'm judging me," she muttered, dropping her gaze to the floor.

"You shouldn't."

"I'm just so mad that I wasted the last year hoping for..."

"Hoping for what?" he prompted. "Olivia. Talk to me."

For a moment he didn't think she'd answer. Then she blurted out, "I spent all that time with Kyle, working up to doing consensual non-consent play, and just when I thought we were close, he throws a Master/slave contract in my face and says if I don't sign it, we're through."

"He did *what?*"

"And he wouldn't even *talk* to me about it." Her hands fisted in her lap, squeezing her phone so hard he could hear the rubber case grind against the plastic. "He just said sign it or pack your shit, and left to go to the baseball game with his friends."

"Wait a minute, wait a minute." He held up a hand. "You guys have been living together for, what, six months? And you haven't done *any* CNC play?"

She huffed out an irritated breath. "Of course, we've done some. Like somnophilia—you know, when I'm asleep, and he fucks—"

"I know what somnophilia is."

"Right. Sorry." She shifted on the stool. "Anyway, we've done that, and scenes where I struggle and he holds me down, or I say no and he ignores it."

"But?" Cade prompted when she fell silent.

"But we never got to the heavier role-play I wanted. And now we never will, and I have to start over completely with someone else, and it just makes me so *mad*." Her face had gone from sad to stormy, her body rigid with outrage. "Like, sugar in his gas tank mad."

"That's pretty mad," he allowed. "Don't do that, by the way."

"I won't. But I have to go back over there to get the rest of my stuff, and I'm afraid if I see him, I'm going to set something on fire. Like his pubic hair."

He fought to keep the smile off his face. "Don't do that, either. Do you still have your key?"

"Yes."

"Can you make me a list of everything in the apartment that's yours?"

"I made one already. Why?"

"Because you're going to give me the key, and I'll go get your stuff today."

She blinked. "Today? No. I mean, I don't have a place to stay yet, and there are a couple of heavy things—"

"It's not a problem. I'll call one of the guys for help. Jack, since you don't want any of the girls in your face just yet."

"Cade, it's really nice of you to offer, but—"

"How much do you have?"

She paused to think, fingertips drumming on the counter. "A dozen boxes worth of small stuff, probably, and three larger pieces. But it can all wait."

"A bed? Couch?"

She shook her head. "I sold those when I moved in with Kyle. There's just a dresser, a small console table, and my reading chair."

"Where's your list?"

"In my purse, but it's in shorthand."

He rose from his stool and circled the island. He opened a drawer, took out a pad of paper and a pen, and slid them across the countertop. "Write it down in whole words, and I'll go get it. Sounds like I can fit everything in the truck, but I'll have Jack bring his, too, just in case."

She picked up the pen, toying with it as she studied him. "I need to find an apartment first, Cade. It doesn't make sense to move everything twice."

"It makes less sense to leave it at Kyle's. I've got plenty of space in the basement, so storage isn't a problem. And you'll feel better with your things here."

She tapped the pen on the pad of paper and chewed on her lower lip the way she did when she was uncertain. He did his best to ignore it, but he was grateful for the island between them that hid his inevitable reaction.

"You're not going to take no for an answer, are you?"

"Consider this a consensual non-consent scene," he told her, and she snorted.

"Fine," she conceded, a small smile lifting the corners of her mouth. "But I reserve the right to safeword at any time."

"Naturally." He nodded at the pad of paper. "Write your list. I'm going to get dressed, then we'll figure out if we need help."

"Okay."

He set his coffee cup in the sink, pleased when he heard the scratch of pen on paper behind him. He glanced back to see her bent over the counter, her hair swinging forward to brush the countertop. She listed her belongings in neat, flowing script, her brow wrinkled in concentration.

Unable to resist, he rounded the counter and pressed a kiss to the crown of her head. "It's going to be okay, fofa."

She looked up. "Thanks, Cade."

"You're welcome," he said, and forced himself to go upstairs before he gave in to the urge to make things complicated.

* * * *

Cade climbed out of his truck in front of Olivia's former apartment and lifted a hand at the man leaning on the building. "Jack. Thanks for coming."

"No problem." Jack stepped forward, dressed in worn jeans and a gray T-shirt that bared the ink on his right arm. His hair, brown with lighter streaks of gold, was longer than Cade remembered, tied back in a low tail. A thick beard shadowed his jaw, and aviator sunglasses shielded his eyes. "It's been a while."

"It's construction season," Cade offered by way of explanation, and Jack nodded in understanding.

"So, what are we looking at here?"

Cade shoved his sunglasses to the top of his head. "The short story is, Olivia and Kyle broke up, so we're here to get the rest of her stuff."

Jack nodded. "And the long one?"

"Is not mine to tell."

"Fair enough." Jack slipped off his glasses and hooked them in the collar of his shirt, his dark eyes narrowed against the sunlight. "Is Kyle here?"

Cade shook his head. "Don't know. I called him, but he didn't pick up. I didn't leave a message."

"You expecting a fight?"

"I don't know what to expect."

"Well, let's find out." Jack turned to his truck, parked in front of Cade's, and hauled a flat stack of boxes, a thick ream of oatmeal-colored packing paper, and two rolls of packing tape out of the bed. "After you."

Kyle didn't answer the door, so Cade pulled Olivia's key out of his pocket and used it.

"Kyle," he called out. "It's Cade and Jack. You here?"

They waited for a moment, and when no one replied, Jack stepped inside. "Doesn't look like anyone's home."

"I'm going to check it out, just to make sure," Cade told him, and headed down the hall.

A swift search revealed that the apartment was indeed empty. "He's not here," Cade began, walking back into the open living and dining area. He frowned when he saw Jack standing at the small dining room table. "What's that?"

Jack rapped a knuckle on the table. "I think it's the long story."

Cade moved closer, recognizing what had been Olivia's everyday collar lying on top of a thick stack of papers. He skimmed the top page, his mouth twisting in a grimace. "Yeah, that's it."

"Quite a statement." Jack lifted up one end of the broken necklace. "Olivia doesn't strike me as the type to make this type of gesture lightly."

Cade met his friend's steady gaze. "She was a tad upset."

"I'll bet." Jack straightened. "So, what are we packing?"

Cade dug into his pocket for the lists Olivia had made. "She wrote it out by room. Kitchen, living, bedroom. Where do you want to start?"

Jack's mouth quirked under his beard. "I do love an organized woman. I'll take the kitchen."

Cade handed over the list. "There are only a couple of things in the bedroom, so I'll do the living room first."

Thanks to Olivia's detailed directions, it took them less than an hour to get everything packed up, and even with the larger pieces of furniture — the 'reading chair' was a six-foot tufted velvet chaise—they got everything into the two pickups with room to spare.

When they got back to Cade's, they moved the boxes in first. "Just stack them in the dining room," Cade told Jack. "She can decide later where she wants them."

Jack set down the box he was holding with a grunt. "Where is she?"

Cade frowned. "I don't know." He glanced around the kitchen, then spotted the note propped up against the coffeemaker. "Errands, apparently."

Jack followed him back outside. "Where are we putting the furniture?"

Cade hauled another box out of the truck as he considered. The logical place was the basement—it was out of the way, and they'd only need to get it down one set of stairs. But the basement wasn't finished, and if the plan he was formulating worked out, she'd have more access to her things if they were in the third-floor bonus space.

"Third floor," he said, and handed Jack the box.

Jack held his gaze for a long moment, then shrugged and turned for the house. "Your call."

Grateful for the lack of questions, Cade grabbed the next box and followed him in. "You want a cold drink?"

"Let's get everything in first. Then I want whatever you have that's cold enough to have ice crystals."

"You got it."

When the boxes were all stacked along the dining room wall, they started on the furniture. The console table was the lightest and easiest to move, so they did that first.

"This is a nice space," Jack observed as they placed it under the window. "You planning to turn it into a bedroom?"

"Nah." Cade paused to wipe the sweat from his brow. "It was half done when I bought the place, so I finished it off, but there's no closet and no bathroom, so it's just a bonus room."

"Might make a nice playroom," Jack mused. "Plenty of space for a bed, some equipment... The high ceilings would be good for suspension."

"I thought about it," Cade admitted, and headed back downstairs, "but do you know how often my mother stops by unexpectedly?"

Jack let out a short laugh. "She doesn't respect your privacy?"

"Hell, no." Cade grinned. "She won't go digging into closets or drawers, but an entire room she's not allowed to see?"

"Not gonna fly, huh?"

"Not in a million years."

By the time they muscled the dresser off the truck and up the two flights of stairs, followed by the chair, Cade wanted to swim in a vat of ice water. He settled for a Coke, and passed one to Jack as well. "Thanks for the hand."

"Anytime," Jack said, clinking his bottle against Cade's. "But the next time you have to move that chair, we're getting more help."

Cade drained half the bottle in one swallow, and sighed. "Damn, I'm tired."

Jack eyed him with amusement. "Nick and Rebecca wear you out last night?"

"Is there no such thing as a secret in this crowd?"

Jack let out a bark of laughter. "Did you expect there would be?"

Cade thought about it. "Actually, no."

"So? How'd it go?"

Cade, shrugged. If Nick and Rebecca didn't mind people knowing, he didn't. "It was good. Fun."

"Uh-huh. And Olivia?"

Cade frowned. "Olivia wasn't there."

"No, Olivia is here. In your house. And unless I miss my guess, you're planning for her to stay a while."

Cade shifted to put his empty bottle in the recycling bin under the sink. "She needs a place to stay. I've got an extra room."

"And you're in love with her."

He looked up into Jack's knowing gaze, the words hanging in the air between them like a cloud. "I've been in love with her for two years," he said calmly. "It doesn't mean I can't be her friend."

"She wasn't single before," Jack pointed out.

"What's your point, Jack?"

Jack lifted one eyebrow, as though the answer to that should be obvious. "How long do you think you'll be able keep things platonic if she's living here?"

"What makes you think I want to keep things platonic?"

Jack blinked in surprise, then narrowed his eyes. "You're making your move."

"For better or for worse."

Jack was silent for a moment, his dark eyes searching. Then he shrugged and polished off his Coke. "I hope it works out."

It was Cade's turn to be surprised. "That's it?"

"What else is there?" Jack walked to the sink to put his bottle in the bin, then straightened. "You're a big boy, and she's a big girl. Neither of you need me to play Daddy."

"Really don't," Cade muttered.

Jack pulled his sunglasses from the neck of his T-shirt and slipped them on. "But if you need to talk, you've got my number."

Surprised and touched, Cade followed his friend to the back door. "Thanks, Jack."

Jack tapped two fingers to his forehead in a casual salute. "Anytime."

Cade closed the door behind him, locking it automatically, then headed for the stairs. He needed a shower, and he needed to call his mother about Sunday dinner. Then he needed to figure out exactly how to ask Olivia to move in with him.

* * * *

The house was empty when Olivia got back from the grocery store, but it was obvious Cade had been back. Packing boxes lined one wall of the dining room, numbered and labeled. She recognized Cade's distinctive scrawl, and assumed the boxes marked with neat printing were Jack's handiwork.

She ran her fingertips over the words *kitchen stuff, Box #7 of 16* with a frown. By the looks of the boxes, and the vast difference in the two men's handwriting, Cade had packed up the living room and the bedroom, while Jack had spent most of his time in the kitchen. It felt silly to be relieved by that, but for some reason she was grateful that her more personal belongings had been packed by Cade.

She wondered briefly why the boxes were in the dining room instead of the basement, then shrugged. He probably wanted to give her the opportunity to go through them before they got stored, she thought, and continued into the kitchen. She put away the groceries with brisk efficiency, then tucked the reusable bags away and pulled out an ice-cold Coke.

She used the bottle opener Cade kept on the side of the fridge, then tossed the cap in the recycling and crossed the room to the lounge area. She sank into one of the leather chairs flanking the fireplace, appreciating the way the seat cradled her butt. She slipped off her shoes, wiggled her toes with relief, and propped her bare feet on the low table in front of her.

She sipped her Coke, and since no one was around to see it, settled in for a long brood. She had text messages from Sadie and Rebecca this morning, wanting to make sure she was all right. They'd each offered to meet her for coffee or a drink to talk, but she'd declined. She didn't feel like hashing it out with her friends yet, though talking with Cade that morning hadn't been as difficult as she'd anticipated. His unwavering support had been comforting.

Her thoughts scattered when a soft weight landed in her lap, and she jolted, spilling a bit of Coke onto her leg. Her soft oath turned into a sharp one when little needles stabbed into her legs, and she looked down at Phoebe with a laugh.

"Well, hello." She set her Coke on the table and picked up the cat, who immediately began to purr. "I'm sorry, but I've been told not to give you any more tuna."

Phoebe just closed her striking blue eyes and tilted her head, and Olivia obligingly scratched behind her hears.

"Is that better?" she asked, smiling when she got a rumbling purr in response. "I don't blame you. I could use a massage myself. Maybe I should call Sadie and see if she can fit me in this week."

The cat flipped herself over for a tummy rub, and Olivia obliged. Phoebe's belly was soft and warm, and stroking her was oddly hypnotic. She found herself drifting, Phoebe's purrs the only sound in the quiet room, and all the emotions she'd been ignoring since last night came rushing to the forefront.

There were a lot of feelings to sort through, but the two most prominent were anger and disappointment.

"I'm so pissed," she murmured, still stroking the cat. "And hurt. How the hell could he think that presenting me with that ultimatum was okay?"

Phoebe let out a plaintive meow and wriggled in Olivia's lap.

"Though now that I think about it, maybe that was the point," Olivia continued. "Maybe he wanted me to break up with him, and that was a guaranteed way to make it happen."

She huffed out a breath, anger pulling ahead of disappointment in the Olivia's Uncomfortable Emotions Race. "I'm not kink shaming, you understand. I just don't want a Master/slave relationship."

She looked down at the cat, who was staring at her with what Olivia decided to interpret as understanding. "Which he knew, by the way. We had that talk at the very beginning, and he didn't want one either."

Phoebe meowed, and Olivia realized she'd stopped petting her. "Sorry," she said, and began to stroke again. "So if he knew I didn't want a Master/slave relationship, and he didn't want one, then him presenting me with that contract was either a test—of what, I have no idea—or a way for him to get me to break up with him. Which I did."

She dropped her head back to rest on the chair. "Son of a bitch."

She sat there, stroking the cat and staring at the ceiling. Almost a year of her life, wasted. And now she had to start all over again.

The weight of it felt crushing. It had taken her so long to come to terms with her kink, years of work in therapy to see it as a potential joy rather than a crippling liability. Rape fantasies weren't rare, but they were often misunderstood, even in BDSM circles, and worrying that wanting those kinds of scenes would make her an outcast in the only community in which she'd felt she belonged had kept her silent and yearning for too long.

Even after she'd found a way to accept those needs, it had taken her a while to find the courage to share them with play partners. She'd forced herself to be honest about it, because if she couldn't articulate her needs, she could hardly expect anyone to meet them. Being a Dom doesn't make someone a mind reader, and healthy relationships — especially BDSM relationships, no matter how temporary or transitory — required good communication.

She hadn't done CNC play with any of her casual partners. At least, not explicitly. There were always elements — being held down, saying 'no' or 'stop' over and over again. Plenty of Doms were comfortable with that level of CNC — safewords were used for a reason, after all — but for the heavier stuff, the role-playing that she craved, she'd wanted a deeper connection.

So she'd sought out a relationship with a Dom who could give her what she wanted, and tried to build the kind of trust that would be necessary to do it safely.

And he'd manipulated her into dumping him.

The surge of anger made her grit her teeth, and when Cade walked through the back door, she was entertaining a small fantasy where she took all of Kyle's vintage records — including the rare pressings that he kept sealed — and set them on fire, using that damn contract as kindling.

Cade looked down at her, one eyebrow raised in question as he shut the door at his back. "That's a scary smile. What are you thinking about?"

"Nothing," she said, and blinked back to reality. "Just a harmless little fantasy. Where have you been?"

He held up a canvas shopping bag. "Butcher."

She stayed in her chair, the cat purring like a motorboat in her lap, watching as he began unloading packages wrapped in white paper. "I see steaks, and ribs, but what's that?"

"This?" He lifted the lumpy package. "Pig's feet, for my mom."

"Um. Why does your mom need pig's feet?"

"Because they're a key ingredient in her black bean soup, and if I buy them for her, she'll be much more likely to make it for Sunday dinner."

"You're bribing your mom with pig's feet?"

He tucked the packages into the fridge, then turned with a grin. "Works better than flowers."

"Someday I have to meet your mother," she decided.

He tucked the grocery bag in the pantry, then crossed the room to sit in the chair across from her, propping his feet on the table next to hers. "Did you see your boxes?"

She nodded. "Thanks for getting my stuff."

"We got all the things on your lists, but you should go through them, make sure we didn't miss anything."

"If it wasn't on the list, it wasn't mine." She hesitated, chewing her lip. "Did Kyle give you any grief over it?"

"He wasn't there."

That surprised her. "He wasn't?"

Cade shook his head. "I called him to let him know we were coming, but he didn't pick up, either."

She frowned. "Had the bed been slept in?"

"It was stripped, which is how I assume you left it."

"It is."

"I'm sure he's fine," he began, and she let out a harsh laugh.

"Oh, I'm sure he's fine too, hiding out at his friend's house. The fucking coward."

Surprise flared in Cade's eyes—she rarely swore, and only when she was really upset—then his gaze narrowed. "Why do you think he's hiding?"

"Because I think that Master/slave contract was bullshit."

Cade's expression turned thoughtful. "You think he was trying to get you to break up with him?"

She nodded, grateful she didn't have to explain. "He told me he wasn't cut out for that kind of thing."

"People change," Cade ventured.

"He didn't," she said decisively. "At least, not like that. Our D/s was always really light. Not a lot of rules, and most of them revolved around sex."

"That's not unusual. Most people have a sexual element to their D/s."

"Yeah, but…" She shook her head. "It always felt like an afterthought, you know? Like something he did just to check a box."

He frowned. "Did that bother you?"

"Somewhat," she allowed. "I mean, I don't want so much D/s that it takes over my life, but the rules should matter. Otherwise, what's the point?"

He hummed in agreement. "Did you ever say anything?"

"No." She sighed. "I didn't want to rock the boat."

"Olivia."

"I know, I know." She grimaced at his chiding tone. "I should've said something. I just wanted the CNC so badly, and I didn't want to spook him."

He just stared at her, incredulous, and she sighed again. "Don't give me that look."

"You deserve it," he said, so sternly she winced again. "Relationships are a two-way street, even kinky ones. *Especially* kinky ones."

"And Doms aren't mind readers," she recited. "I know."

"Then act like it," he said, and he sounded so pissed she blinked in surprise.

"Whoa. Where did that come from?"

"From watching you spend a year with someone who was never going to give you what you want," he shot back.

"Well, I didn't know that!"

"Because you weren't paying attention." He pulled his feet from the table and sat up, somehow managing to loom over her from six feet away. "You were so focused on the end goal, you missed all the warning signs."

"Wait a minute."

"It's not your turn to talk yet," he said, and she shut her mouth with a snap.

"Compatibility matters, Olivia, and you and Kyle weren't compatible."

"We got along fine," she began, then bit her lip when he narrowed his eyes. "Still not my turn to talk?"

"No. 'Get along fine' works for a pickup scene, but it's not nearly enough for the kind of play you want to do. CNC is tricky, and it's scary, and you need so much than 'get along fine' to do it well."

What did he think she'd been trying to do with Kyle for the last year, for heaven's sake? Building trust had been the whole point of moving in together. "I thought we were compatible."

"Why?"

"What do you mean, why?"

"I mean, what possible reason would you have to think you were compatible? Aside from he's a Dom, you're a submissive, and he told you he was willing to explore consensual non-consent?"

She opened her mouth, then shut it again. "Fooey."

A glimmer of amusement edged into his unforgiving gaze. "Fooey?"

"That's what I say when I realize I've been an idiot, okay?" She let her head drop back to stare at the ceiling with suddenly watery eyes. "Fooey."

"Oh, shit. Are you crying?"

"No." She squeezed her eyes shut so he wouldn't notice she was lying, which only squeezed the not-tears out faster.

He let out a choked sound, like a muffled laugh, and the chair scraped against the floor when he stood.

She kept her eyes shut and tried to ignore the sounds of him moving closer. She was expecting the touch on her cheek, but still, she jolted a little when his thumb brushed against the wet trail at her temple. "What's this, then?"

"I'm allergic to cats?"

"You are not allergic to cats," he said, so close she could feel his breath on her skin. "You spend hours petting Phoebe every time you come over, and you've never so much as sneezed."

"They're sudden-onset allergies," she claimed, her eyes still closed, and faked a sneeze.

"Fofa," he said softly, and the nickname ripped a sob out of her chest.

"I'm fine," she sobbed, hugging Phoebe so hard the cat began to squirm, clearly uncomfortable with this level of emotional neediness. "I just need a Benadryl."

"You don't need a Benadryl." He pried her hands open so the cat could jump to safety. Then he was lifting her up as easily as he would Phoebe and sitting down with her on his lap. "You're sad."

A second sob escaped, and she buried her face in his neck. It was warm and solid and smelled faintly of peppermint, and it was so unexpectedly comforting she sobbed harder. "I'm not sad."

"No?" He swept his hand up her back and down again in a soothing caress. "What are you, then?"

"I'm mad," she said, the words muffled against his skin. "I spent a year with the wrong guy, and now I have to start all over again."

He laughed, his breath a soft puff against her hair.

"It's not funny," she protested, and wiped her dripping nose on his shirt in retaliation.

"I'm not laughing at you," he assured her. "I'm relieved."

She lifted her head, blinking away the tears that blurred her vision. "Why are you relieved?"

"Two reasons." He wiped the tears from her face with a gentle hand. "First, it's a lot easier to deal with unmet expectations than a broken heart."

"True," she muttered grudgingly. "What's the second reason?"

"Anger is productive. We can work with anger."

She blinked. "Seriously?"

"Once you figure out why you're mad — which you have, so well done — then you can figure out what to do differently next time."

"There won't be a next time." She let her head thump back down on to his shoulder. "I'm never going to get the CNC scenes of my dreams."

He pressed a kiss to her hair, his body shaking lightly under hers with what she assumed was more laughter. "Yes, you will."

"No, I won't," she said on a wail. "I've been in the kink scene for six years in multiple cities, and in that entire time I've only found two people who were open to consensual non-consent play. Well, four, actually, but two of them were women, so that didn't work out."

"Straight people problems," he said soberly, but she heard the snicker underneath.

"Said the smug bisexual," she mumbled, and wiped her nose on his shirt again.

"Stop using my shirt as a handkerchief," he told her, and punctuated the order with a light slap on her rump.

"Oh, don't spank me," she wailed. "I'm sad and horny and that's just mean."

He laughed so hard the whole chair was shaking, and in spite of the lingering sense of despair, she lifted her head to smile at him. "Are you finished?"

He grinned and dropped a kiss on her nose. "Who was the other one?"

"Other one what?" she asked absently. Her nose tingled where his lips had brushed her skin, and wasn't that strange?

"You said you met four people who were into consensual non-consent. Two were women, and I assume one of them was Kyle. Who was the other one?"

"Oh. You."

He raised an eyebrow. "We never talked about that."

"I know."

"We did what, three scenes together?"

"Something like that," she said with the casual nonchalance of a woman trying to pretend she didn't remember every second of those three scenes in vivid, technicolor detail.

"I didn't know you were interested in consensual non-consent. Not until after you'd started seeing Kyle."

"I know."

"Why?"

She shrugged, sticking with casual nonchalance. "It just never came up, I guess."

"But you knew it was one of my kinks."

"No, I didn't."

"Yes, you did. You just said, you've met four people who were into CNC—"

"I know what I said."

His eyes narrowed warningly. "Olivia."

She sighed. "Fine. I was going to tell you, but it was after you'd already quit, and I didn't want you to feel pressured."

He shook his head, his stern expression giving way to bemusement. "You've lost me. After I quit what?"

She kept her gaze fixed on his beard. It lay flat against his jaw, the whiskers silky smooth instead of rough, and dark, with none of the toffee-colored highlights he had in his hair to soften it. The edges of his mustache were neat and trimmed, but he let the rest go, so it crept up his checks and down his neck. It made him look a little wild, as though his charm and polish were a thin veneer that could fall away at any moment to reveal the wolf beneath.

And now she *really* was horny.

"Olivia."

She blinked, her eyes darting guiltily to his. "What?"

"After I quit what?"

"CNC play, of course," she said, perplexed.

He was staring at her as though she had a mushroom growing out of her nose. "I never quit CNC play."

She frowned. "Yes, you did."

"No, I didn't."

She shook her head. "But you did. Amanda told me."

"Amanda?" Now he looked even more confused. "When?"

"I don't know." She tried to think back. "I'd worked up the nerve to talk to you about it, but you were out of town on a job, and I was a little blue. Amanda asked what was wrong, and I told her that I'd wanted to talk to you about doing a CNC scene, and she told me not to because you'd decided not to do them anymore."

"Why would she…" He trailed off, his look of confusion giving way to one of realization. His head dropped back against the chair. "Oh, damn."

"What?"

"I never said I wasn't going to do CNC scenes anymore."

She blinked. "You didn't?"

"No."

"Wait, wait, wait." She sat up straight, bracing her hands against his chest. "Amanda *lied* to me?"

He shook his head. "I don't think so. She just didn't have all the information."

"I don't understand."

He looked grim. "Do you remember Tim and Andrew?"

She frowned. "They moved to Indianapolis last year, right?"

"Yeah. They had a friend who was in town for a visit, a submissive who'd been wanting a CNC scene. They introduced us."

He sighed, and he sounded so forlorn and sad that her belly twisted. But she kept silent, and he continued.

"I liked him, and we did a scene together at a party. You weren't there, I don't think. But it went well, so when he asked for something darker before he left town, I didn't see any reason not to agree. We negotiated, but only generally, because he didn't want a lot of detail to interfere with his headspace. He was experienced enough, and the set-up was fairly straightforward. I didn't anticipate any problems."

"But something happened," she prompted gently when he fell silent.

"He'd rented a room for the night at one of the airport hotels. Just a businessman passing through. I was supposed to break in while he was showering and overpower him. He'd given the extra key to Tim, and he passed it to me. I let myself in, caught him when he was finishing up in the bath. It started out fine, but after a few minutes...I can't really explain it, but the vibe changed.

"I almost kept going," he admitted. "He had a safeword, and a gesture, and hadn't used either. But it felt off, and I didn't know him well enough to read him with any confidence. So I called it, which may have been the smartest thing I've ever done."

"He wasn't role-playing," she guessed.

"Terrified out of his skin," he said bluntly. "I called Tim and Andrew—they knew it was happening that night—and they came right over. Turns out, he was a lot less experienced with CNC than he'd implied."

"Oh, no."

"Yeah." His smile looked more like a grimace. "We met for lunch a couple of days later, just before he left town, to talk it out. We parted on good terms, and he didn't blame me for things going sideways. But I'm never not going to feel horrible about that night."

The haunted look in his eyes was breaking her heart. "It sounds awful."

His smile was sardonic. "Awful is an understatement. Anyway, I decided if I didn't want to be in that situation again—and I very much do not—I'd need to reevaluate how I do CNC. No more casual scenes."

"So when Amanda told me you weren't doing CNC anymore…"

"She didn't quite have the full story."

She stared at him. "Oh, my God."

He reached up to gently tweak her nose. "I would have said yes."

"Oh my God," she wailed, and let her head fall back to his shoulder with a thump. "I can't believe this."

"That'll teach you to listen to gossip," he said, then twitched when she dug her fingers into his ribs. "Hey, quit it."

"I'm allowed to retaliate when you tease me," she pouted, and did it again, then had to grab onto his shoulders when he twitched so hard she nearly fell off his lap.

She stared up at him, delight blooming. "You're ticklish."

"Don't even start," he warned, then twitched again when she dug her fingers into his side. "Dammit."

"You're *really* ticklish," she said gleefully, and began dancing her fingertips up and down his ribs. He cursed under his breath in Portuguese, then it was her turn to squeak when he grabbed her hands and yanked them behind her back. "Hey!"

He laughed, holding her wrists against her spine so her elbows stuck out like bony wings. "You mess with the bull, you get the horns."

"You're a bull?" she managed, and rotated her wrists, trying to break his hold. He merely tightened his grip, holding her easily in place, and the lust that had been simmering in her blood all morning hit boiling point.

The urge to laugh faded, taking a back seat to the heat roaring through her. She tried to jerk her hands free again, testing him, and in response he pulled her wrists away from her body and down, straightening her elbows and forcing her to lean back. She fought to keep her head up, neck straining with the effort. She was off balance and completely at his mercy, his grip the only thing keeping her from ending up in a heap on the floor, and *holy shit*.

Sensation flooded her body. Her breasts felt heavy against the bodice of the sundress, her nipples suddenly so sensitive that the soft fabric felt like burlap. A familiar, heavy heat seeped into her pelvis, her core tightening and her panties growing damp.

She was more turned on after fifteen seconds of wrestling and restraint with Cade than she had been in any scene with Kyle in the last six months, and every nerve in her body was screaming for more.

He was looking down at her with that familiar smile, the playful triumph in his gaze joined by something else, something dark and dangerous that made her pulse pound under his restraining fingers.

"Um. Cade?"

He leaned down, putting his face so close to hers their noses brushed. "Yes, fofa?"

His face filled her vision, his light peppermint scent teasing her nose. She could kiss him, she realized. If she just angled her head slightly and strained forward a fraction of an inch, her lips would touch his.

And she almost did it. But he was still watching her with that odd light in his eyes, and she felt confused and turned around and wonderfully out of her depth. Forcing herself to ignore her baser instincts—the ones screaming at her to go for it—she cleared her throat. "This is starting to turn me on."

There was a brief flare of surprise in his eyes, then his smile turned sharp. Her breath caught in her throat and her pulse pounded harder. "Well," he murmured, and dipped his head so his nose brushed against the curve of her jaw. "That's interesting."

"It is?" she managed in a squeak, shivering in his hold as he dragged his jaw down her neck. His whiskers were faintly abrasive against her tender skin, waking up the nerves and making them sing.

"*I'm* certainly interested," he purred, his lips barely brushing her throat.

Her eyes felt heavy, so she let them drift shut. "Oh. Good."

"Like that, do you?" His lips moved to her ear, his breath hot against her skin.

She'd have sworn her limbs had gone boneless. "Yes."

"And you?" His teeth skimmed her earlobe, clacking gently against the small gold stud she wore. "Are you interested?"

She felt like she could melt into a puddle, right there in his lap. "In what?"

His low chuckle vibrated in her ear. "If you have to ask, I must be doing this wrong."

"Oh." She angled her head, arching her neck to bare it to his lips. "That."

"That," he agreed, and ran his tongue from her jaw to her collarbone.

"I've always been interested in that," she confessed, and he went still under her.

"Always?" he asked, lifting his head, and she forced her eyes open to look into his face.

"Always," she repeated, fighting the urge to squirm. His brown eyes, so soft and lazily aroused only moments ago, had narrowed sharply. She felt like a bug on a board, exposed and vulnerable.

God, it was so hot.

"You've been keeping secrets," he accused, anticipation and menace deepening his voice, and she shivered again.

"Everyone keeps secrets."

"True enough." He put his mouth to her ear again. "I want yours."

"Okay," she said breathlessly, more than agreeable, and his answering laugh made her shiver again.

"But first things first." He straightened, bringing her with him, and his grip on her wrists gentled. "We should talk."

She blinked, confused. "Talk?"

"Before this goes any further." He lifted one eyebrow in question. "Don't you think?"

"Right. Sure. Talking is smart."

"I couldn't agree more," he said, and nudged her off his lap to stand next to his chair.

She wanted to crawl right back in. "When should we do that?"

He rose to his feet, so close she could see the damp hollow of his throat, and the pulse that fluttered there. "How about tomorrow afternoon?"

"What's wrong with now?" she blurted out, subtlety beyond her now.

"Well, I need to get the pig's feet to my mom, then I have a meeting."

"On a Saturday?"

"Not a work meeting," he said, his mouth quirking with amusement. "An AA meeting."

She should've guessed that. "Oh."

"And for another, I want you to think about what you want before we start negotiating."

"I know what I want," she said, and would've been annoyed at the implication that she didn't, except that he put his hands on her bare arms, warm and solid, and the resulting rush of heat made her forget all about being annoyed.

"So do I," he said, arrogant and a little smug, and she thought she might find room to be annoyed after all. "But I still want you to think about it."

Exasperated and aroused and very definitely annoyed, she scowled up into his handsome, smiling face. "Why?"

"Because what I want is to destroy you." His eyes glittered at her, all semblance of charm and seduction gone, replaced by nefarious intent and dark, depraved lust. "I want to tear you to pieces, then put you back together again. Mind, body, soul. And you have to decide if you're going to let me."

She stood, stunned and speechless, as he pressed a chaste kiss to her cheek, released her arms and stepped around her.

"A bunch of us usually meet for dinner after the meeting," he said, and she turned to watch him open the fridge, take out the butcher-paper-wrapped package, then stride to the back door. "I'll probably be back late. Tomorrow I'll be at my mom's for most of the day, and I should be back around four. Can you be ready to talk by then?"

She felt like she was half a step behind and struggling to catch up. "Yes."

"Do you need anything while I'm out?"

She shook her head, thrown by the benign domesticity of the question. *He just said he wants to destroy me, and now he's asking for a grocery list?* "No."

"All right, then." The smile he sent was friendly, until she looked at his eyes. "See you tomorrow, fofa."

"Bye," she said faintly, and watched him walk out the door.

She had no idea how long she'd been standing there, staring at the space he'd just vacated and wondering what the heck just happened, when her phone buzzed. She fished it out of the pocket of her dress and blinked to bring the screen into focus.

It was a text from Amanda.

Heard about Kyle. If you need to talk, you know where to find me.

Olivia started to type back a quick *thanks but no thanks*, then she hesitated, thumbs poised over the screen. She didn't need to talk about Kyle, but she could definitely use some advice about Cade.

Are you free for coffee now? she typed back, then picked up her Coke. It had gone flat, so she dumped it down the sink. Her phone dinged as she was putting the bottle in the recycling bin.

Meeting Rebecca and Sadie at Black Bean Cafe in an hour, the message read. *You're welcome to join us.*

Olivia frowned at the screen. Normally, she'd prefer to have a conversation like this in a less public venue. But the Black Bean Café had high booths that provided at least a bit of privacy, and the music was always just loud enough to mask the conversations around them. Add in the noise of a busy café — the rattle of dishes, the clang of silverware, the never-ending shouts of the baristas calling out orders — the odds of someone overhearing were slim to none.

"Yes," she muttered, and tapped out *Perfect, meet you there*. She sent the text, then slipped the phone back into her pocket and hurried upstairs to grab her purse.

Chapter Four

She walked into the café and shrugged on her hoodie, grateful she'd remembered to bring it. The place was packed, full of people taking advantage of the gorgeous summer Saturday, and they had the a/c turned up to arctic blast. She spotted Amanda in a booth on the far side, Sadie and Rebecca with her, and after acknowledging them with a wave, went to the counter to order.

The line moved quickly, the baristas working with choreographed efficiently behind the counter, and within a few minutes she had her iced vanilla coffee in hand and was sliding into the booth next to Amanda.

"Hey," she said, smiling at her friends. "What are we talking about?"

"Well, we *were* talking about Rebecca's threesome," Sadie offered, her ginger hair wobbling a little in its messy topknot. She gestured with her green smoothie. "But that's old news. What the fuck happened with Kyle?"

"Jesus, Sadie." Amanda wrapped a shielding arm around Olivia's shoulders. "At least let her say hello, first."

"She said hello," Sadie pointed out.

Rebecca, sitting next to Sadie across the table, rolled her eyes. Her dark hair was pulled into a sleek tail, her gray eyes soft with sympathy. "Ignore her."

"It's okay," Olivia said with a laugh. "Do you want the long story, the short story, or the other story?"

"Other story?" Amanda frowned, her eyes soft with concern behind the lenses of her glasses. "Did something else happen?"

"Not with Kyle," Olivia said, and lifted her drink for a sip. "But it's kind of related."

"Well, that sounds juicy as fuck, but let's deal with Kyle first." Sadie leaned over the table, her voice dropping so everyone had to lean in to hear her. "All we know is that you broke up with him, then ended up staying at Cade's last night."

Olivia nodded. "True and true."

"The question is, why?" Sadie raised one curved eyebrow. "You've put up with his bullshit for a year, so what finally pushed you over the edge?"

"Sadie," Rebecca hissed.

"What? It's true."

Olivia looked around at her friend's faces. "Am I the only one who didn't see it?"

"Well..." Rebecca hedged.

"It can be hard to see what's wrong from inside a relationship..." Amanda began.

"Yes," Sadie said baldly.

Olivia took a moment for that information to sink in. "Well, shit."

"We didn't know if anything was wrong," Amanda rushed to say, shooting Sadie a quelling look from across the table. "It's just...well, we could tell you weren't happy."

"I wasn't," Olivia said slowly. "I guess it just took something big for me to realize it."

"Which was…" Sadie prompted.

In for a penny. "He gave me an ultimatum."

"What kind of an ultimatum?"

"A Master/slave contract."

For a moment, all three women stared at her, identical expressions of shock on their faces. Sadie was, predictably, the first to recover.

"Hold the fuck up." She lifted a hand. "Had the two of you discussed entering into a Master/slave relationship?"

"No."

"Had you ever indicated that such a relationship was something you might consider?"

Surprised to be enjoying herself, Olivia sipped her iced coffee. "No."

"Had *he* ever said he wanted that kind of relationship?" Amanda asked.

"Not until he handed me the contract last night, and told me to either sign it or get out."

"Well, fuck him." Sadie leaned back, her look of surprise morphing into a grim glare. "I hope you set his shit on fire on your way out."

Rebecca and Amanda wore similar looks, giving Olivia a warm feeling in the pit of her stomach. She didn't know why she'd been dreading this—all this righteous anger on her behalf was just what she needed. "Nope. I just packed up what I could, left my broken collar on his ridiculous contract, and left."

"Wow." Rebecca leaned forward to lay a hand on Olivia's. "And I thought I had a busy night."

"Yours was probably a lot more fun," Olivia allowed, and patted her hand.

"Yeah, yeah. You can get the details on that from her later." Sadie waved Rebecca back with an impatient hand. "I want to hear the rest."

"Wait." Amanda aimed a finger at Sadie, then turned to Olivia. "Do you need to get the rest of your things from the apartment?"

Olivia shook her head. "I wrote out a list this morning, and Cade went to pick everything up."

"Alone?"

"Jack went with him," Olivia told Rebecca. "And there wasn't much. I sold or gave away most of my big stuff when I moved in with Kyle."

"Which brings me to the big question," Sadie interrupted. "Are you living with Cade now?"

"No. I stayed there last night," Olivia explained, "but I planned to start looking for another place today. Although…"

"Although?" Sadie perked up. "Although what?"

"Although," Olivia continued slowly, "that was before."

"Before what?"

"Before Cade said he wanted to destroy me, then put me back together again."

"Sing hallelujah," Amanda muttered at the same time Rebecca said, "It's about time," and Sadie said, loudest of all, "I hope you said yes."

"You think I should say yes?" Olivia asked, just to hear Sadie's answer.

"I mean, hello. The man is sex on a stick. Not that I've ever seen his stick, but he fills out a pair of leathers just fine. Unless that's a sock?"

Rebecca cleared her throat, blushing furiously. "It's not a sock."

"No, it's not." Olivia had very fond memories of Cade's not-a-sock.

"That's right, I forgot you played with him before." Sadie angled her head, her eyes bright with curiosity. "What, a year and a half ago?"

"Give or take, yeah. Before Kyle."

"Excuse me." Rebecca raised her hand. "I'm sorry, I know I'm the newbie around here, but I just have to ask. No offense meant to Kyle, but how did you go from Cade to him?"

"That's what I want to know," Sadie put in. "With all offense meant to Kyle."

"Kyle's attractive," Rebecca said, jabbing her elbow into Sadie's side. "But you and Cade are so much more compatible. Especially considering the CNC thing."

"Well, that's part of why." Olivia turned to Amanda. "Remember when you told me that Cade had decided not to do CNC scenes anymore?"

"Oh, right." Amanda grimaced. "I'd forgotten about that."

Sadie frowned. "What are we talking about?"

Amanda lowered her voice. "Cade had a scene go sideways on him, and I guess it was pretty bad. James told me after that, Cade decided not to do consensual non-consent play anymore."

"When was this?"

"Right as I was about to ask him if he'd consider doing CNC with me," Olivia put in.

"Oh, damn." Rebecca winced. "That sucks."

"Especially since it's not true."

"What?"

"James got it wrong," Olivia repeated, and turned to face Amanda. "He did decide not to do consensual non-consent with casual partners, or for pickup scenes. But he never wanted to quit completely. He just wanted to be more careful."

Amanda's eyes went round with realization. "You mean, this whole time…"

"Yeah."

Amanda closed her eyes on a curse, and Olivia reached over to pat her hand. "It's not your fault. I'm the one who didn't talk to him."

"Yeah, but I'm *why* you didn't talk to him." Amanda sighed. "I'm really sorry."

"You were trying to help," Olivia soothed.

"Some help," Amanda muttered.

"Never mind all of that," Sadie interrupted with impatient wave of her hand. "There's a question on the table."

"Which is?" Rebecca prompted when Sadie fell silent.

"Are you, or are you not, going to let Cade destroy you?"

"Oh, *that* question," Rebecca said, and turned to eye Olivia expectantly.

"Hell, yes," Olivia said.

"Oh, boy." Sadie wiggled in delight. "Tell us everything, and don't spare the details."

"There's nothing to tell yet," Olivia began, and had to stifle a laugh when Sadie's face fell.

"Nothing? He didn't do *anything*?"

"He said we needed to talk first, and there wasn't time because he had to take a pig's foot to his mom before his meeting."

Sadie blinked. "I don't know how to process that."

"My God, she's been struck speechless," Amanda said, and let out a rolling laugh. "I never thought I'd see the day."

"He had a meeting on a Saturday?" Rebecca asked as Sadie flipped her middle finger at Amanda.

"It was an AA meeting," Olivia told her.

"Oh, right."

"So when is this talk supposed to take place?" Sadie wanted to know.

"Tomorrow afternoon. He wants me to think about what I want, and be ready to talk about it then."

"I think that's reasonable," Amanda allowed.

"I think it's smart," Rebecca put in.

"I think it's fucking diabolical," Sadie declared.

"Yes!" Olivia cried, and some of the sexual frustration she'd felt watching Cade walk out of the door came rushing back. "He got me all wound up, then he just...walked out."

"Bastard," Sadie muttered.

"It's still smart," Amanda argued. "He wants to make sure you've thought it through, that you're considering all the implications."

"I don't know if I even know what all the implications are." Olivia sighed. "I just know I spent a year and a half trying to think of him as just a friend, and now all I can think about is jumping his bones."

Sadie grinned. "Get it, girl."

"Wait a second." Rebecca leaned forward. "You've had feelings for him all this time?"

"Feelings?" Olivia frowned. "You mean, besides the let's-get-naked kind? I don't know."

"You don't know?" Amanda asked.

"I was trying to make my relationship work," Olivia explained. "I couldn't do that if I was lusting after another man. I guess I just put the possibility of more out of my mind."

"I get that," Rebecca allowed. "I did the same thing with Nick until I just couldn't take it anymore."

Olivia chewed her lip, indecision drowning out the excitement she'd felt only moments ago. "Maybe we shouldn't do anything."

"Why the hell not?" Sadie wanted to know.

"What if I do have feelings for him?" Dread sat like a ball of lead in her stomach. "What then?"

"The line is, 'and they lived happily ever after'," Sadie said.

"Not if he doesn't feel the same," Olivia began, but Sadie was shaking her head.

"Trust me, he does."

"How do you know?"

"Because he told me so."

Olivia's jaw dropped. "What?"

"Well, he didn't tell me directly," Sadie amended. "But I overheard him tell Jack, so, really, same thing."

Olivia felt like she'd entered an alternate universe. "When? What did he say?"

"It was last fall, at the monthly warehouse party. November, I think? I was hiding in that storage room behind the restrooms, trying to avoid that fire play guy."

"Kevin," Amanda remembered. "Yeah, he was creepy."

"Right?" Sadie grimaced. "He wanted to burn my pubic off."

"Ugh," Rebecca said. "And also, ow."

"Hello?" Olivia waved a hand. "Can we focus, here?"

"Sorry, sorry. Cade and Jack were in the men's room, and there must be a vent in there that connects the two rooms, because you can hear everything. It's like having a hidden microphone next to the urinals."

Rebecca wrinkled her nose. "Gross."

"Mostly, but between the pissing and the handwashing, I heard Cade say that he was trying to respect your relationship with Kyle, but that if you weren't involved, he'd be on you like...like..." She flapped a hand. "Quick, I need a metaphor."

"Simile," Rebecca said.

"What?"

"Saying something is like something else is a simile, not a metaphor," Rebecca explained.

Sadie stared at her. "Are you kidding me right now?"

"He'd be on you like something that would be on something else aggressively and fast," Amanda put in.

"That." Sadie nodded and turned back to Olivia. "So I think it's safe to say he has feelings for you."

"Oh." Olivia eased back against the booth, her drink forgotten in front of her, and tried to digest this new information.

"I think you broke her," Rebecca told Sadie.

"I'm not broken," Olivia said absently. "I'm processing."

"Hopefully about jumping that stick," Sadie said, then turned to Rebecca. "It was good, right?"

"You are out of control," Amanda admonished.

"What? She should have all the information available so she can make an informed decision."

"She's fucked him, too," Rebecca reminded her.

"Oh, right." Sadie eyed Olivia with interest. "I forgot."

"It was very good," Olivia said before Sadie could ask.

"There you go, then," Sadie said, and sat back with a smug smile.

"You okay, sweetie?" Amanda asked quietly.

"I'm just grappling with the fact that I could've been with Cade all this time."

"Yeah, that's a kick in the pants," Sadie agreed.

Olivia sat quietly, and the others fell silent, too. She was aware of Sadie sliding out of the booth, and after a hushed conversation with Amanda, Rebecca following, but they didn't speak to her as they left. That was fine with Olivia. She had enough to think about.

She toyed with her drink, sliding the plastic cup around on the table as she tried to think things through logically. Her friendship with Cade was important to her, and if someone had asked her yesterday, she would have said it was too important to risk for a scene, or sex. But that was before Kyle had set their relationship on fire, destroying it beyond any hope of repair, and it was before Cade had made it clear that he wanted more. The way he'd restrained her in his kitchen had been almost unbearably arousing, and it was only a pale, watery version of the scenes that she longed for. The idea of what he could do to her if he really let himself off the leash left her stunned and all but shaking with want.

She stared at the ice melting in her cup. Cade wanted her, and she wanted him, and the only question now was what was she going to do about it.

The clank of dishes startled her out of her thoughts, and she looked up to see that Sadie and Rebecca had returned and were passing out plates, napkins, and forks.

"What's all that?" she asked, grateful for the distraction.

"We needed sustenance," Rebecca said cheerfully. "And we thought you might need some, too."

"Okay," Olivia replied, frowning at the table, which, other than the recently distributed plates and their drinks, was empty.

"Here we are," someone said, and Olivia glanced up as a server placed an entire carrot cake and four glasses of milk on the table. She laid a knife next to the cake plate with a smile. "Enjoy."

"Oh, we will," Amanda said with a laugh, and picked up the knife.

"So?" Sadie asked, accepting the slab of cake Amanda slid over to her. "What're you going to do?"

"Jesus, Sadie." Rebecca handed Sadie a fork. "Eat your cake and give her a minute."

"Sorry." Sadie took the fork and stabbed her cake. "I don't mean to push."

"Yes, you do," Olivia said, and Sadie glanced up in surprise as Amanda laughed.

"Okay, I do. But only because I think you and Cade could be really great together."

"So do I," Amanda said, sliding a wedge of cake in front of Olivia.

"Ditto," Rebecca chimed in. "But what we think isn't important."

"I'm forced to agree," Sadie mumbled around a mouthful of carrot cake. "Holy crap, this is good."

"What's important," Rebecca went on, "is what *you* think."

Olivia picked up her fork and carved off a bite of cake. "I think I want Cade," she said, then shoved her fork in her mouth to keep from taking the words back.

"Yes!" Sadie cried, spraying cake crumbs across the table.

"Ew." Rebecca grimaced and reached for a napkin.

"I second that, both the *yes* and the *ew*," Amanda said as Rebecca mopped the table and Sadie mopped her face.

"I'm scared," Olivia admitted, and swallowed her cake. "Damn, that is good."

Rebecca set the soiled napkins aside. "Switching from friends to lovers is a big deal."

"You did this with Nick." Olivia chewed thoughtfully. Rebecca had been her boyfriend Nick's assistant before they'd become lovers. "Were you nervous?"

"Oh, yeah. He'd been my boss for three years, and as frustrating as that dynamic was, it was safe."

"But he wasn't your boss when you got together," Sadie pointed out. "By that point, you pretty much had nothing to lose."

"True," Rebecca conceded. "I'd already hit my breaking point, so it was probably a little easier for me to set fire to my bridges."

"This metaphor is confusing," Sadie complained, then smirked. "Or is it a simile?"

"My choices were more cut and dried," Rebecca went on, flipping Sadie the bird and ignoring the resulting snickers. "I'd already quit my job, and we didn't share a social circle. If things didn't work out, I could make a clean break. I wouldn't run into him at parties, wouldn't see him at work. I had a scorched-earth option that's not available to you."

"I know. That's what scares me." Olivia drew a deep breath. "But…"

"But?" Sadie prompted.

"But I feel like we could be good together, too," Olivia said slowly. "Like, dream-come-true, happily-ever-after good. And not trying scares me a lot more than having to see him at a party if it doesn't work out."

Sadie let out a cheer, and Amanda murmured, "Atta girl," and gave her an encouraging squeeze.

Sadie beamed and lifted her glass of milk. "To Olivia, a brave bitch."

Olivia laughed as Rebecca and Amanda echoed the cheer. "Y'all are the best. I don't know how to thank you."

"You don't have to," Amanda said, giving Olivia in a one-armed hug.

"But if you want to, I wouldn't mind hearing the details," Sadie put in, waggling her eyebrows in an exaggerated leer.

Olivia laughed. "Deal."

* * * *

Olivia sat at the kitchen counter the next afternoon, one eye on the clock. It was a few minutes before four, and she was so on edge she was about to jump out of her skin.

She'd come home from her coffee shop support group on Saturday afternoon to a quiet house. True to his word, Cade had stayed out late, and she'd used the time to finish unpacking her clothes. She'd considered starting on the boxes that still sat in the dining room, but thought better of it. She didn't know if she was going to be staying, and she didn't want to make assumptions.

With nothing else to do, she'd explored the house—giving his bedroom a wide berth—and discovered her furniture on the third floor. She thought it was a good sign that he'd put it up there, rather than the basement like they'd talked about, and had gone to bed with her favorite vibrator, hoping to take the edge off.

By the time she'd rolled out of bed on Sunday morning, he was already gone, a note on the kitchen counter explaining that his mother had convinced him to join the family for Mass. He still expected to be home around four, and was looking forward to their talk.

With a whole day of waiting stretching in front of her, she'd taken a long bath, done all her laundry, re-read a favorite book, put together a lasagna from scratch, cleaned the kitchen, and was now looking at apartment listings on her laptop. Or trying to—she kept watching the clock.

She forced herself to refocus on the screen in front of her and scroll through the listings. She wanted to stay in the neighborhood, as it was close to work and all her friends, but what was available was either not enough space, over her budget, or of questionable quality.

She clicked on a listing for a one-bedroom with den and scrolled through the pictures. The bedroom was small but adequate, the kitchen narrow but workable. But the shower looked like someone had been using it as a growth lab for the kind of mold that devoured entire cities, and the toilet—

"Wait a minute." She clicked through all the pictures again, looking carefully, but there was no toilet. Either they'd left it out because out it didn't look good—a daunting prospect considering the shower had been photographed in high definition—or the apartment had no toilet.

"Next," she muttered, and got up to get a glass of water just as the back door opened.

Cade stepped inside. "Hi."

"Hi." Olivia forced herself to keep going, pulling a glass from the cabinet and walking to the freezer for ice. "How was dinner at your mom's?"

"Good." He lifted his hand to show her the insulated bag that he carried. "I've got leftovers."

"The black bean soup?" she guessed, filling her glass at the filtered spout inside the refrigerator.

"Yeah." He set the bag on the counter, then tucked his hands in the pockets of his cargo shorts. "Smells like you've got something else cooking, though."

"Lasagna." She walked back to the counter and sat down, rubbing her damp palms on the skirt of her sundress. "I didn't know if you had anything planned, so…"

"It smells good." He picked up the bag and moved to the fridge, smiling at her with such easy charm she relaxed. "What're you looking at?".

"Apartments." She refocused on the screen with a grimace. "This one doesn't seem to have a toilet."

"I'd take it off the list, then."

"No kidding."

He stored his leftovers in the fridge and pulled out a Coke, then circled the counter to sit beside her.

"You don't have to look for a place right away." He popped the top on the Coke. "You're welcome to stay here, even if you decide not to take me up on my offer."

"That wouldn't be awkward?"

She kept her eyes on the laptop screen, but she could hear the shrug in his voice. "We've been not sleeping together for years. Why would it be awkward now?"

It would be awkward for me, she thought, and blurted out, "I thought about what I wanted."

He set his Coke on the counter. "Did you?"

"Yes." She closed the laptop and turned to face him, her hands clenched together in her lap. He was perched on a stool, his legs sprawled out in front of him as though he hadn't a care in the world. But his eyes were sharp, his attention squarely on her.

"And what did you decide?"

Here we go. She drew a deep breath, then blew it out slowly. "I want you to rape me."

Chapter Five

Cade had been prepared for Olivia to answer his question a lot of different ways, but he hadn't quite imagined that. He felt as though all the blood had drained out of his head and into his cock, leaving him disoriented and glad to be sitting. When he finally found his voice, it came out in a wheeze. "Jesus Christ, Olivia."

She winced. "I probably should've said that differently, huh?"

He thumped his chest to get his lungs working again. "It's fine. Probably just a minor heart attack, nothing to worry about."

"Sorry," she said, chewing on her lip in a way that was not helping the blood get back to his brain. "What I meant was, I'd like to explore consensual non-consent play with you."

"Yeah, I got that." He reached for his Coke and took a long drink, hoping it would cool the sudden fire in his blood. "Is that how you usually approach negotiations?"

"I'm a little rusty. It's been a while since I played with anyone new."

"For the record, it's better to work up to it. Start out with some small talk, maybe a joke."

"Okay. Knock-knock."

His lips gave an involuntary twitch. "Who's there?"

"Someone."

"Someone, who?"

"Someone who wants to fuck you."

It was a terrible joke, but he smiled anyway. "Just fuck?"

"No." A hint of color bloomed on her cheeks, but her eyes were clear and steady. "I want it all."

"Consensual non-consent," he said, wanting to make sure there was no misunderstanding.

"Yes."

"I'm not rescinding my rule about casual play," he warned, watching her expression carefully.

"I don't expect you to." She sat up straighter on the stool, her hands folded neatly in her lap. She looked like a student preparing for a lecture. "But I need to know exactly what that means."

Appreciating her directness, he nodded. "It means if we're going to go there—if I'm going to take you there—then we can't just be play partners. For this kind of play, the level of trust that's required, I need a committed relationship."

Her eyes went wide, surprise clear in the gold-flecked hazel, and her mouth parted on a soundless *oh*.

"That means we're romantically and sexually exclusive," he continued. "Neither of us dates other people, neither of us plays with other people. It's all or nothing, fofa."

"All or nothing," she echoed.

He nodded, his heart in his throat. "If that's not something you can agree to, then I'm sorry, but we can't do this."

He wanted to get his hands on her more than he wanted his next breath, but on this point, he had to stand firm. Aside from the practical reasons — practicing consensual non-consent required a level of trust and communication that was hard to do with casual arrangements — he'd loved her for too long to do this by half measures.

He was finally getting his chance, and he wasn't holding back.

"For how long?" she asked, eyes still wide.

The word *forever* leapt to his tongue, and he swallowed it back. She wasn't ready to hear that, and frankly, he wasn't ready to say it. "For as long as we both want."

"Do you…would I live here?"

"I'd prefer it," he said calmly while his heartbeat thudded in his ears. "But that's up to you. If you'd be more comfortable in your own place, that's okay, too."

"My stuff is in your bonus space instead of in the basement."

The mild accusation in her tone made him want to smile. "I wanted you to have access to it while you were here. And I already told you that you could stay as long as you wanted."

"As your roommate?"

"It's an option," he said, his heart dropping at the thought of her being so close, and yet so far away.

"But if we decide to play together, we wouldn't be roommates, would we?"

He held her gaze, noted the caution there with approval. He'd have been concerned if she wasn't wary. "No, we wouldn't. Roommates have boundaries that wouldn't be feasible for a relationship that includes CNC."

"But you're not saying no boundaries, right?"

He couldn't hold back a chuckle. "No. That wouldn't be healthy, either."

"Whew." She sagged against the counter, a wide smile curving her lips. "I was about to run for the door."

"Good," he said approvingly. "You should run from anyone who thinks you shouldn't have any boundaries."

"Including you?" she teased.

"Including me."

"Noted," she said, still smiling. "So, what now?"

It was a good question. He eyed her for a moment, considering. She was a physical therapist, and he knew she often worked weekends or odd hours when assigned to the hospital rotation. "What's your work schedule like this week?"

"I'm in the clinic this month, so standard office hours. Monday through Friday, eight to five."

"No weekends?"

"No. Why?"

"I'm in the office for meetings tomorrow," he mused, ignoring the question. "Then I fly out to a job site in Oklahoma City. I get back on Friday morning."

"You'll be gone all week?"

The dismay in her expression made him smile. "I propose we take the week to negotiate."

Hannah Murray

"How are we supposed to do that if I'm here and you're in Oklahoma?"

"Email," he told her. "I've got a questionnaire I'll send you."

"I already have a yes/no/maybe list," she began.

He shook his head. "This is a list of questions specific to CNC. I want to know about the scenes you've done already, and the ones you want to do. I want to know how you want to play those scenes, how you want them to make you feel. There are a lot of different ways to do this, and I want us on the same page."

"Oh. Okay."

"We'll talk about other things, too. I'm going to want some level of D/s for our time together, so think about what kind of boundaries you want to set for that. I'll do the same."

"You want to talk all of this out via email?" She frowned. "Couldn't we just hash it out over dinner or something?"

He shook his head. "I want you to really think about the questions and take your time answering them. If it takes all week to do that, fine. If it takes two weeks to do that, that's also fine."

"It will not take two weeks," she assured him, an edge in her voice that made him grin.

"On Friday, when I get back, we'll go out for dinner and talk it through. Wherever we are in the negotiation process."

She chewed her lip for a moment, then nodded. "Okay, I can do that."

"Good. In the meantime, no orgasms."

Her jaw dropped. "What?"

"No orgasms," he repeated, amused to see dismay and outrage leap into her eyes. "Is there a problem?"

"Yes!"

"What is it?"

Her mouth worked, but no sound came out. Finally, she said, "I'm not going to fuck someone else, if that's what you're worried about."

"I'm not," he said calmly.

"Then…why?"

The genuine confusion on her face was cute, and it told him that this very basic, very common D/s rule had not been part of her relationship with Kyle. "Because," he replied simply.

Her shock was rapidly fading, replaced with a narrow-eyed stare and a charming flush of color on her cheeks. "Oh," she breathed. "You *are* mean."

He leaned forward, shoving his way into her personal space, and waited to see what she'd do. She jolted, but her eyes narrowed even further, delighting him. "Darling girl," he purred, putting as much menace into the soft words as he could manage. "You have no idea."

She swallowed hard. At this distance he could see her eyes, the gold flecks bright against the melded green and brown. Her pulse pounded under the soft curve of her jaw, in the hollow of her throat. Her breath came just a little bit faster than normal, fear and lust making her pant.

"But," he drawled softly, "if you want one for the road, so to speak, you can have it."

Wariness crept into her gaze. She was a fast learner. "What's the catch?"

"The catch," he mused, and scanned her body openly. He took his time, letting her feel the weight and the heat of his gaze, before lifting his eyes to her face once more. "The catch is that you have to do it here, and now. Or not at all."

"You mean—" She broke off, her voice thin and tight. She swallowed, then tried again. "You want me to masturbate in front of you?"

He smiled into her eyes, pleased that the word *masturbate* hadn't given her any trouble. She wasn't shy or prudish, but the dynamic between them had changed, and she was nervous.

Which he liked just fine.

"That's what I want," he said, and eased back to relax on his stool, one arm resting casually on the counter. "Lose the dress."

She stared at him for so long he thought she was going to say no. "Is this a test?" she finally asked.

"In a way," he acknowledged calmly. "But it's not one you can fail. If you don't take your dress off and make yourself come for me now, the only consequence is that you don't get to come. If you do, then you get one last orgasm to hold you over. It's always up to you, fofa."

She blinked at the use of the nickname. He hadn't meant to use it—it had slipped free out of habit—and some of the tension seemed to flow out of her.

He made a note to be careful not to use it when they played. Something like that—a nickname, or habitual term of endearment—could dull the edges of an otherwise harsh and fearful scene. Which wasn't necessarily a bad thing, unless harsh and fearful was the point.

She lifted her hands to the buttons that ran down the front of her dress. He'd assumed they were decorative, but she began to undo them one by one, her fingers trembling slightly. The small sign of nerves had him going rock hard, and he had to quell the urge to shift in his chair to ease the pressure.

He stayed still, his pose relaxed, as she unbuttoned the dress all the way to the hem, and inch by inch her body was revealed to him. He'd seen her naked before, of course, when they'd played together two years ago, and several times since at club events or parties. So he wasn't surprised by the soft, plump breasts with their puffy pale brown nipples. The small strawberry birthmark on the inner curve of her left breast was exactly where he remembered it, and her belly had the same sweet curve. The jut of her hipbones, the round thighs—none of it was new. But seeing it laid bare at his direction, for his eyes, was indescribably, almost unbearably arousing.

"Very nice," he said, his voice low and approving. She sat still, the dress spread out on either side of her, a soft frame for the body beneath it. She sat unmoving as he looked, and an observer might think that she was unaffected by both her nudity and his lazy perusal.

But he knew where to look for those small signs of arousal, and to him they were bright as neon signs. Her pulse fluttered in her throat, her nipples darkened and drew into tight little buds. Her thighs shifted subtly, an instinctive and futile attempt to put friction and pressure where she needed it.

She wore panties, a simple pair of white cotton hipster briefs that he imagined she'd chosen because they wouldn't be visible under the dress. She never wore thongs or G-strings, preferring to go without underwear altogether rather than subject herself to what she'd once described as *"a fabric enema"*, and he found himself smiling at the memory.

The briefs suited her, and something about seeing innocent white cotton covering what he knew was a bare pussy appealed to the pervert in him.

And the damp spot on the cloth was like the bullseye on a target.

"Put your hand inside your panties and your fingers in your cunt," he ordered.

She slid her fingers under the cotton, her breath hitching as her fingers made contact with the tender flesh beneath. He watched closely, tracking her movements as she slid her fingers—two or three, he couldn't quite tell—into her pussy.

She gave a full-body shudder that made him smile, and he lifted his gaze to hers. "Are you wet?"

She nodded, the movement jerky and uncoordinated. Her eyes had grown heavy and her plush lips were parted, damp and glistening. She was breathing faster, her breasts shimmying gently with the rise and fall of her chest.

"Show me."

She pulled her hand from her panties, the quiet slap of the elastic waistband hitting her stomach echoing softly. She held out her hand, her trembling fingers glistening with her arousal.

"Good girl. Back in your panties now, but don't put them in your cunt."

She delved her hand into her panties again, wetter now, the damp spot spreading. He could see the outline of her fingers through the cotton, and the damp flesh beneath. "How do you masturbate?"

She licked her lips. "How do you mean?"

"Do you put your fingers in your cunt and fuck yourself with them? Do you rub your clit? Do you use a vibrator, a dildo?"

Her breathing had picked up speed again. "If I have time, I use a dildo or a vibrator to…to fuck myself, and rub my clit with my fingers."

"And if you don't have time?"

"Then I just rub my clit."

"Spread your legs and show me."

She scooted forward on the stool, one hand braced on the counter for balance, and planted her feet wide on the rungs. He could clearly see her pussy now, the panties all but transparent, clinging wetly to her plump outer labia as her fingers began to move.

Cade forced himself to stay in his seat. He wanted to pull her off the stool, spread her out on the kitchen floor and fuck her until they both came screaming, but he didn't. That wasn't part of the plan, so he stayed in his seat, watching her work herself closer and closer to orgasm, and reminded himself that this was just the beginning.

Images of all the things he wanted to do with her flitted through his mind as he watched her stroke her pussy behind the thin barrier of her panties. Every fantasy he had, every dark, forbidden desire, bore her name. Her face was the one he wanted to push into the mattress until she could barely breathe, her body the one he wanted in his hands. He wanted her tears, her cries of anguish and despair. He wanted her pleas for mercy, given with the certain knowledge that none would be forthcoming. He wanted to destroy her, lovingly put her back together, then destroy her again.

He wanted it all.

Her breathing had changed, each exhale a small whimper. She was close now, her eyes so heavy they were nearly closed, her teeth sunk into her lower lip as though to stifle the sounds she couldn't help making.

"Are you going to come, Olivia?"

"Yes." She was holding the edge of the counter so tightly that her knuckles were white. "I'm so close."

Her thighs were trembling, and she started to close them. She tended to close her legs when she came, something she'd explained to him when he'd tied her legs open the first time they'd played together. But forcing them to stay open made her come harder, and he wanted her to come hard.

"Keep your fucking legs open," he snapped. She jolted, her eyes flying wide and her legs freezing halfway closed. "Open them, Olivia. And don't stop working your clit."

Panting, she obeyed, moving her legs so far apart the tendons on her inner thighs stood out. Her hand picked up speed, her whimpers turning to moans as she raced to the finish.

She went still for one sharp, razor-thin moment, tension visible in the taut muscles of her thighs, in the arch of her neck, then the orgasm overtook her. She let out a surprisingly soft cry and convulsed, her belly rippling and thighs shaking.

He watched her ride it out, part of his mind cataloguing the details for later. The way her whole chest flushed when she came, her nipples tight and reddish brown. The way her teeth bit into her lower lip and her legs jerked as though controlled by invisible marionette strings.

He filed away every nuance of her expression, every tremble of her body. And when she subsided, sheened with sweat and breathing hard, he stood.

"I hope you enjoyed that," he said mildly, and stepped between her spread thighs. He ignored her instinctive startle and drew the edges of her bodice together. He began to refasten the dress, fumbling only a little with the tiny buttons.

"I did," she admitted with a hint of defiance.

"Good," he said, and he meant it. He wanted her to enjoy everything they did together, even when it made her cry. Maybe especially when it made her cry. "Because it's the last one you get this week."

"I was hoping you'd forget about that," she said, and he looked up into her sleepy eyes.

"No, you weren't."

"No, I wasn't," she echoed, and her lips curved into a soft smile. "Any other rules for this week?"

"I want you to check in with me every day at least twice," he decided, smoothing her skirt over her knees.

She frowned. "Why?"

"I want to know about your day," he told her, and grasped her hands to pull her to her feet. "If something happens that impacts you, I want to hear about it. Good, bad, or otherwise."

"Okay," she said agreeably, but there was a little line between her eyebrows that told him she was thinking.

"This is part of my D/s requirements," he went on calmly. "Even if it was possible for me to be with you every second of the day, I doubt you would want that."

She cleared her throat and took a sudden interest in the ceiling, making him grin.

"But I need to know how you're feeling, what your mood is, how the things that happen during your day affect you." He tapped her chin firmly, and she brought her gaze back to his. "I don't want to plan an abduction scene on a day when you don't feel well, or you've unexpectedly gotten your period, or something shitty happened at work."

Realization dawned in her pretty eyes. "Oh."

"And since asking those questions out of the blue would tip you off to my dastardly plans, we're just going to make that information you share with me every day. Understood?"

"Understood. Just two texts a day?"

"That's just for this week, because I'm out of town, and to get you into the habit. But you can text me anything, at any time. If it's significant for you, it's significant for me."

"I don't want to blow up your phone while you're working," she began.

"I know how to turn the ringer off," he informed her, and squeezed her hands. "Let's do it this way. If it's something that affects your mood or your plans, text me. Anything else can wait until we talk."

She nodded. "I can do that."

"Good." He pressed a kiss to her forehead. "What time will the lasagna be ready?"

The change of topic made her blink, and she glanced over at the stove, and the timer that was counting down. "Seventeen minutes. But it'll keep."

"I need to run out for about an hour and a half," he told her. "Can you hold dinner until I get back?"

"Sure. Do you want me to take care of that before you go?"

"Take care of what?"

"That," she said, pointing at his crotch and the erection trying to forge a path through his shorts.

"I'm fine," he said, and bit his cheek to keep from smiling at her look of disbelief. "I'm savoring the anticipation."

"They're your balls," she muttered with a shrug. "If you want them blue, who am I to argue?"

"Don't worry," he chuckled. "You'll get plenty of chances to take care of my balls. I'll see you in a couple of hours."

He dropped another kiss on her forehead and left before he could cave and demand a blow job. In his truck, he took a moment to pull out his phone. He sent his sponsor a quick text asking him to meet for breakfast the next day, then started the truck and pulled out of the garage. He'd hit his usual Sunday afternoon meeting, and talk with Max tomorrow morning. He didn't believe that starting a relationship with Olivia was a threat to his sobriety, but it paid to be vigilant. After all, significant life changes could wreak havoc in unexpected ways.

He was rather looking forward to the havoc.

Chapter Six

Cade pushed his empty plate to the side and picked up his coffee. "You're quiet."

Across from him, Max pursed his lips. "I'm thinking."

Cade glanced pointedly at his watch. "Can you think a little faster? I've got a flight in six hours."

"Asshole," Max said, but there was no heat behind it, and his brown eyes were dancing. He leaned back in the booth, the lights of the diner bouncing off his bald Black head. He was a big man, built like a boxer, with a sweet smile, a sharp brain, and a sly sense of humor. "All right. You've known this woman for a while, right?"

"A couple of years."

"And you've been in love with her for how long?"

Cade set down his coffee. "A couple of years."

"That's a long time to carry a torch for someone."

Cade forced himself to relax. He knew from experience that Max couldn't be rushed. "She was with someone else until recently."

"Right. She ditched this guy two days ago, and now she's living with you."

"Three days," Cade corrected, irritation flaring to life. "It's not like that."

Max spread his hands wide. "I'm just laying out the facts, brother."

Cade made an effort to unclench his jaw. "It's not like that."

"Okay, it's not like that." Max crossed his arms across his chest, biceps bulging. "She know you're an alcoholic?"

"She knows." She'd asked him once, after a game night when she was helping clean up, why there was no alcohol allowed, and he'd found himself spilling the whole story. She'd listened quietly with kind eyes, and he often thought that was when he'd started falling for her.

"And she respects your commitment to staying sober?"

"I've never asked her outright, but I'd say yes."

"Ask her outright," Max advised, and picked up his coffee. "Now, onto the rape fantasy. You're sure she's into that?"

I want you to rape me, Cade remembered, and nodded. "I'm sure."

"And those boundaries you put in place to keep yourself safe? Are those changing?"

"No," Cade said firmly.

"Good."

Cade waited a moment, but Max just sipped his coffee. "Is that it?"

"Are you asking me as your friend, or your sponsor?"

Cade steeled himself. He'd asked Max to be his sponsor because he was kink-friendly, and because he knew the older man wasn't the type to sugarcoat. He always spoke truth, and sometimes truth could be brutal. "Both."

"Okay. As your sponsor, I advise you to keep going to meetings. Don't start skipping just because you've got pussy waiting at home," Max said, and Cade choked on his coffee.

Max passed him a napkin and kept talking. "I'll remind you that any new relationship can create stress on your sobriety. Kink-based relationships, with those high emotional stakes, can be even more taxing. Add in the consensual non-consent and it's...well. I don't have to tell you how that can go sideways."

Cade finished wiping his face and dropped the napkin on his empty plate. "No, you don't."

"Okay, then."

Cade waited a beat. "And as my friend?"

"As your friend?" Max set his coffee cup down, his face creasing in a wide grin. "I think you're a lucky son of a bitch."

"Thanks," Cade said with a short laugh, and rubbed a hand down his face. "I feel like I won the kink lottery."

"No shit," Max snickered, then sobered. "I really hope it works out, Cade."

So do I, Cade thought, and picked up his coffee once again. *So do I.*

* * * *

Over the next four days, Cade went to meetings, visited job sites, went to more meetings, and did his best to make sure by the time he got back to his hotel room, he had just enough energy to check his emails, read Olivia's goodnight text, and fall into bed.

Unfortunately, his emails usually included one from her, with another round of answers to the questions he'd sent her before he left town on Monday, so reading them was far from restful. And her goodnight texts just conjured up images of her lying in bed, and there was no way he was sleeping with that picture in his mind.

He did so many pushups in that hotel room he was surprised he didn't leave handprints in the rug.

He could've jerked off, and probably should have, just to relieve some of the God-awful tension. But every time he started to, something held him back. He didn't want his fist—he wanted *her*.

So he did pushups in his hotel room, and ran on the treadmill in the small fitness center, and did pullups in the bathroom doorway. He took cold showers that were woefully ineffective, and took every opportunity to swing a hammer at the job site. He went to meetings and he checked in with Max—who thought he should just jerk off already—and every day, he talked to Olivia.

They had a couple of phone conversations, but most of their communication happened over email and text. She was sending him the answers to his questions a handful at a time, and it was clear she was putting considerable thought into them. He checked his messages each night with a sense of giddy anticipation, and afterward usually did pushups until his arms were numb, then took a cold shower. He'd asked her to describe her ideal scenes, and her emails were like a customized porn loop in his mind.

By the time Friday morning rolled around, she'd answered every question he'd sent her, and they were so clearly on the same page he was tempted to forego the discussion he'd intended to have with her over dinner and jump right into the scene he'd scripted. But he reminded himself that going over everything in person, where he could see her face and hear her voice, was a necessary step. Olivia was too important to risk a misunderstanding.

No, he'd stick to the plan. They'd have dinner, talk things through. And if they were as in sync as he thought they were, he could set his plans in motion with no reservations. Though what he'd come up with for their first CNC scene together wasn't as physically violent or emotionally heavy as some of the scenarios she'd described to him, it wasn't a beginner scene, either. She'd had those, and he didn't see the need to replicate them. This would be the first test of trust and compatibility, and he had his fingers crossed that it would be just the beginning.

* * * *

Olivia had lunch with Sadie on Friday afternoon. She'd thought it might be a nice distraction, but it wasn't working. "I feel like I have a fever."

Sadie dipped a fat French fry in the puddle of ketchup on her plate. "You don't have a fever."

"I know I don't *have* a fever. I said I *feel* like I do." Olivia picked up her burger, then put it back down again. "I can't eat this."

"You should." Sadie gestured with another fry. "Cade gets home tonight, right? You might need your strength."

"Thank you, Sadie, that's very helpful." Olivia pressed a hand to her stomach. "Maybe I have a stomach bug."

"You don't have a fever and you don't have a stomach bug. You're just horny."

"Well, no fucking shit."

Sadie froze, a French fry halfway to her mouth, her eyes like saucers. "Wow."

"What?"

"I don't think I've ever heard you swear before."

"Yeah, well." Olivia plunked her elbows on the table and buried her face in her hands. "I'm a little worked up."

"Clearly. Maybe you should take the rest of the day off work. My three o'clock canceled, so I can bring my table over and give you a massage if you want."

"I wish I could." Olivia dropped her hands and leaned back. "I've got patients all afternoon."

"Well, you've got to do something to calm down. Go rub one out in the ladies' room or something."

"I can't do that either," Olivia said, miserably aroused.

"Why not?"

"Because I promised Cade I wouldn't."

Sadie shook her head sadly. "You're never going to make it through dinner."

"I know." She wanted to rest her head on the table, but she didn't want to get cheeseburger grease in her hair. "Do you think this is part of his plan?"

"What, to drive you wild with lust, make you wait until you're ready to explode, then take you out in public and force you to talk about all the filthy things you want him to do to you?" Sadie paused to sip her soda. "Honey, he's a Dom. Of course it's part of the plan."

"I'll be dead by the time he picks me up."

"He's going to pick you up at his own house?"

"He said he wanted it to feel like a first date."

"Aw." Sadie propped her chin on her fist. "That's sweet. I knew he had a thing for you."

"I have a thing for him, too," Olivia confessed, fiddling with the napkin in her lap. "I just didn't think I could do anything about it."

"So you, what? Just forgot about it?"

"I'm very good at compartmentalizing things."

"Fuck, I guess so. Well." Sadie lifted her glass in a toast. "Here's to letting Cade out of his compartment, and here's hoping you survive it."

* * * *

At five minutes to seven, Olivia was lying on her reading chair in the third-floor bonus space, practicing her deep breathing. After lunch, she'd gone back to work, letting her full schedule of back-to-back patients distract her. But then she'd gotten back to Cade's house, and fed Cade's cat, and taken a shower in Cade's shower—okay, the guest shower, but still—and now she was trying not to have a heart attack while she waited for the doorbell to ring.

She'd sent him a text when she got off work to ask him what she should wear—she had no idea if he'd planned a fancy or a casual evening—and the only thing he'd texted back was *wear what you normally would on a first date*.

But did that mean a first vanilla-date, or a first kinky-date? She'd started to ask, then thought better of it. She didn't want to end up sitting in a fancy restaurant in fetish wear, and she didn't know yet if he was the kind of Dom who'd enjoy fucking with her that way. So she'd put her phone away, pulled out her classic little black dress and paired it with a pair of red heels that matched her lipstick.

She'd just finished styling her hair in soft, shimmering waves that would hopefully entice him to get his hands in it when her phone dinged. The message from Cade had simply read *one last thing – no panties.*

Well, shit. The black dress wasn't lined, so now she had to change. Leaving the black one in a heap on the guest bed, she'd pulled out a one-shoulder sheath in bold fuchsia silk. It had a narrow skirt with a hem that hit just below the knee, and a black sash at the waist. It was elegant, more suited to a cocktail party than dinner, but it was the only thing she had that was fully lined. Which was going to come in handy for another reason, because she'd torn the clasp off her strapless bra the last time she'd worn it and hadn't replaced it yet, which meant she was free-boobin' tonight.

It was way too obvious that she was braless beneath the soft silk, even with the lining, but a short black cardigan covered her nipples and had the added benefit of taking some of the fancy out of the dress. It also covered her tattoo, which she didn't love, but keeping her nipples covered was more important. She'd swapped out the red shoes for black strappy heels, the red lipstick for pink, then lay down on the chaise and tried to remember how to breathe.

It helped to distract herself with the changes she'd made in the last week to the third floor. Cade had told her she could do anything she liked with the space, and she'd taken him at his word. She'd arranged her books and knickknacks on the built-in shelves that lined one wall, and hung her mirror by the door. She liked the console table under the window, so she'd left it there, adding her Tiffany lamp and angling the chaise next to it, so she had both natural light and the lamp for reading.

She'd hung a couple of her favorite prints, covered the bare wood floors with a trio of rugs, and draped her crocheted blanket over the chaise. The result was a warm, cozy space that made her feel relaxed and at home. After a few moments of deep breathing and staring at the Matisse print on the wall, she felt markedly calmer.

Until the doorbell rang.

She scrambled to her feet, her heart in her throat, and scooped up her small evening purse. Her heels were just high enough that she need to take the stairs slowly or risk a broken neck, and she clung to the railing all the way down. She didn't want the most exciting night of her life to end in the ER.

Might end up there anyway, she thought, and stopped at the bottom of the stairs for one last deep breath. Then she stepped forward, reaching for the door, and tripped over the cat, who was apparently just as eager as she was to welcome Cade home.

Her sharp cry echoed in the entryway, and she fell hard against the front door, rattling it in its frame.

"Olivia?" Cade called out, and she heard his key turn the lock. "Are you all right?"

"I'm fine," she managed, and pushed herself away from the door just as it swung open. Her hair, so carefully coiffed only minutes earlier, hung in her face, and there was a lipstick stain on the wall beside the door. *Great.*

He stepped inside, concern clear in his dark eyes. "What happened?"

"Phoebe missed you," she said dryly, and tried not to drool.

He was wearing a suit, dark slacks and a jacket over a snowy white shirt. His already bronzed skin was a shade or two darker, making her wonder if he'd been working outside this week. He lifted a hand to her face, the crisp white cuffs of his shirt sliding back to reveal his watch, and why was that so goddamn sexy?

"Did you hurt yourself?" he asked, his fingers warm on her cheek, and she shook off the sudden wave of lust to answer him.

"Just my pride," she admitted. "And possibly your drywall."

He looked at the wall, chuckling at the bright smear of pink before turning back. "I've been wondering if I should add a pop of color to the entry."

He was staring at her mouth, and she fought the urge to dash for the nearest mirror. "Is it smeared too badly?"

"Just enough," he murmured, and the feral lust in his dark eyes made her breath stutter in her throat. "It's just smudged a little. Do you need a minute to fix it?"

"I can do it in the car."

"Well, then." He held out his arm.

The old-fashioned and courtly gesture made her heart sigh a little, even as the look in his eye made it pound. She slid her hand in the crook of his elbow, then started when a plaintive meow sounded at her feet.

She down at the cat, now winding her way between Cade's ankles. "Sorry, Phoebe," he said, and gently nudged her aside. "This date is humans only."

Phoebe let out an offended yowl and turned to walk slowly away, her tail high in the air, the feline equivalent of a lifted middle finger. Cade watched her go, amused, then turned back to Olivia. "Shall we?" he asked, and escorted her out through the door.

* * * *

Olivia knew Sadie and the others would want to hear the details of the date, so she tried to pay attention to where they went and what they ate and the things they talked about. But she was very much afraid the only answers she'd be able to give to those questions were "a restaurant", "food", and "stuff", because all her attention was on Cade.

Part of it was lust. A whole week of anticipation — and no way to give herself any relief — meant she was primed. And he wasn't helping by looking so marvelously edible. If she were the kind of woman who enjoyed taking the reins in a sexual encounter, she'd have already slipped him her panties and a note that read "meet me in the bathroom". Except she wasn't that kind of woman, and she wasn't wearing panties, so all she could do was sit there and hope that when she stood, the back of her dress would not be sporting a wet spot.

Once the waiter had brought their drinks and taken their orders — for food, she assumed, she honestly couldn't remember even looking at a menu — Cade lifted his sparkling water with lime for a sip, watching her over the rim so carefully she wondered if she'd smeared her lipstick again.

"I have a couple of questions," he said once he'd put the drink down again.

"Oh?" she said and tried to pay attention to the sounds coming out of his mouth rather than the mouth itself.

"We got most of the details hashed out via email this week," he went on, calm and cool on the other side of the table while she tried not to burst into flames. "But I want to go over a few things."

"All right."

"Is your safeword still the same?"

She blinked, surprised to realize that hadn't come up this week. And that he remembered it after two years. "I've gotten used to using the stoplight system because it's so common, but, yeah. You remember my safeword?"

He grinned, his teeth a flash of white in the dimly lit restaurant. "You're the only person I know who uses 'safeword' as a safeword."

"More people should," she said with a shrug. "It's clear, unambiguous, and instantly recognizable."

"You're not wrong. Which one do you want to use for CNC scenes?"

She frowned. "Do I need to choose?"

"Some people like to have a CNC scene safeword so they can use their regular one as part of the scene. Like if they use the stoplight system, but want that to be ignored in a CNC situation."

"Oh, that makes sense." She thought for a moment. "How about we keep 'safeword' as the actual 'stop everything right now' safeword. Then I can use the stoplight system as part of the scene if I want?"

"Good enough. How's your ability to suspend disbelief?"

She picked up her water for a fortifying sip. "What do you mean?"

"We've talked about a lot of pretty heavy scenarios," he said, his voice low. "How deep are you likely to get?"

She took another sip of her water, then put it down and folded her hands in her lap. "I've never done any intricate role-play before—not like what we've been talking about—but even with the lighter stuff, I tend to go all in."

"What about coming out of that headspace? How difficult is that for you?"

"It can be hard," she admitted. "Once the scene is done, I need time to get sort of re-grounded back in reality. Aftercare helps a lot. So does a nap, if I can squeeze it in."

That got her a gentle smile. "I'll make a note to work in plenty of nap time. Last question, then we can enjoy our meals. Do you want me to tell you when I'm transitioning into a scene?"

She frowned. "Like, what? 'Hey, I'm kidnapping you tomorrow, be ready'? That's not going to work."

"No, it won't. But what if I want to pretend I'm taking you home after a first date?"

"Oh. Oh!" Her eyes went wide as realization dawned. "Um. In that case, you should probably tell me, especially if you want me to react in a certain way. Otherwise, I might muck it up."

"Noted," he said, and even in the dim light, she could see his eyes were dancing.

"I'm not making this weird, am I?" she asked, her fingers twisting together in her lap.

"You're making it fun," he told her, and he was so openly pleased she sighed with relief.

"Oh, good." She sat back in her chair as the waiter approached, then blinked at the dish he set in front of her. "Did I order a shrimp cocktail?"

Cade laughed again and raised his glass as the waiter set a plate of seared scallops in front of him. "Here's to fun."

Chapter Seven

Cade pulled up to the curb in front of his house, Olivia in the passenger seat, her face lit by the glow of the streetlamp. She'd relaxed during dinner, the tension she'd been holding at the beginning of the evening dissipating with good food and good conversation. She even looked a bit sleepy now, though it was barely ten o'clock.

"Thank you for dinner," she said, a smile curving her pretty mouth.

"Thanks for finally going out with me," he said, following the first-date script he'd laid out in his head.

"I'm glad I did," she said, ducking her head shyly. "I had a good time."

He kept his expression open, his smile easy. "The evening's not over yet."

She blinked, a slow flutter of eyelashes that couldn't quite hide the confusion in her eyes. "It's not?"

"I have to walk you to your door," he teased gently, and was delighted with her answering giggle.

"Of course," she said, and reached for her door handle.

"Hey." He put some snap in his voice and watched her eyes go wide. "I'll get that. Don't you move, all right?"

Her hand slid away from the door to join the other in her lap. "All right."

He stepped out of the car, taking his time rounding the hood. He'd debated whether to take the 'Vette or the truck tonight, and was glad he'd taken the sports car. The truck had its advantages — like having to help her up into the high seat — but the smaller interior of the Stingray translated to a physical intimacy that the truck couldn't provide. They'd sat nearly shoulder to shoulder, and every time he'd shifted gears, his knuckles had grazed her bare leg. She'd broken out in goosebumps every time he'd made contact.

He leaned down to open her door, pleased to see that her earlier sleepiness had faded, and she watched him now with wide and careful eyes. He held out a hand, waiting patiently for her to take it. When she finally did, her fingers trembled against his palm.

He pulled her to her feet gently, resisting with ease the urge to yank her against him. There would be time for that, for the roughness and violence they both craved. But tonight, they'd do it a different way.

He closed the car door behind her and tucked her hand in the crook of his arm, shortening his stride to match hers as she picked her way up the sidewalk in those needle-thin heels. He appreciated what they did for her legs, and that they brought her closer to his own five foot ten inches, but he got the impression she didn't wear them often.

She stumbled a little, and he tightened his grip to steady her. "All right?"

"Fine," she said, a little breathless, and looked up at him with sheepish eyes. "I don't wear heels very much, but I wanted to look nice tonight."

He didn't know if that was the truth or her playing the part, but it was perfect. "You look beautiful."

"Thanks." They stepped up onto the front porch, and she let go of his arm to dig in the little bag she'd brought. She fished out her key and fitted it into the lock, turning to smile at him. "Thank you for seeing me to my door."

"You're welcome," he said, and pasted on his most charming smile. "I had a great time tonight."

"Me too." She nudged the door open a crack. "I almost wish it didn't have to end."

"It doesn't have to," he said smoothly. "How about a night cap?"

"I don't keep liquor in the house," she said apologetically.

"I'll settle for a cup of coffee," he told her.

"I have to be up early for work," she hedged, and a hint of wariness appeared in her eyes.

"One cup of coffee," he cajoled, all but oozing charm now. "Then I'll leave you to your beauty sleep."

She chewed her lip, drawing attention to that plush mouth. Her lipstick was gone now, wicked away by dinner and drink, but her lips were just as enticing naked as they were painted.

"Okay," she finally said, and held up a finger. "One cup of coffee."

He held out his hands, all amiable innocence. "You have my word."

Her smile trembled at the corners, as though she couldn't quite stretch it far enough, then she said, "Come on in," and stepped through the front door.

He followed.

Olivia walked through the entry way into the living room, her nerves dancing. She laid her handbag on the table at the end of the sofa and continued through the dining room to the kitchen. She knew Cade was following—she could hear his footsteps on the wood floors—but more, she could *feel* him behind her. She imagined him stalking after her, like a lion after a gazelle, and had to suppress a shiver of excitement. Part of her wanted to just tell him to skip the game and fuck her now, but she didn't.

She wanted the game as much as he did. Maybe more.

She forced herself to walk to the coffee maker, to pull the bag of grounds out of the cabinet and measure them out, then fill the pot at the sink. She was so focused on the task that when she heard him say, "Nice place," she nearly dropped the pot.

"Thanks." She managed to pour the water in the coffee maker without spilling, then slid the pot into place and hit the button before turning to face him. He was closer than she'd realized, in front of her rather than on the other side of the counter, and she let out a little laugh to cover her nerves. "What are you doing?"

"Just watching you," he said, and the look on his face made her breath catch in her throat. His smile had gone sharp at the edges, the veneer of charm thinner. There was malice lurking in the dark brown depths of his eyes, and a sick kind of glee, and it was shockingly real.

They were on the roller coaster now, the car chugging its way slowly to the top, the heady mix of excitement and terror making her belly flip as she waited for the inevitable fall.

She wasn't sure what to do. If anything like this had happened to her for real—and she'd had her share of dates turn creepy—she knew exactly what her next move would be. But kneeing him in the balls might be taking the role-play a little too far.

There was plenty of room between the island and the counter for two people to stand comfortably, but he was crowding her, and with the countertop behind her she couldn't back up. She could move to her right, toward the stove, and calculated there was a decent chance she could slip past him—she might even be able to make the dining room before he caught her.

Or she could move to her left, where the counter made a ninety-degree turn under the window. He was already half blocking the path there, so her chances of escape dropped considerably if she took that route.

The choice was clear.

"The coffee will be ready in just a minute," she said, and stepped to the left.

He followed, stepping forward at the same time, leaving barely a foot of space between them. "You got anything sweet to go with it?"

She stared up at him, her heart in her throat. "You want dessert?"

He shrugged. "I've got a sweet tooth."

"You had tiramisu at the restaurant."

"Didn't really satisfy me," he said, and edged closer. There were mere inches between them now. "But you know what would?"

She reached back, bracing herself on the counter. The pose forced her breasts forward, and, though he didn't look down, his smile turned smugly sharp.

She had to swallow before she could speak. "What?"

"A kiss." He lifted a hand to her face, his eyes narrowing when she flinched. His fingers skimmed down her cheek to her lips, his touch so light she could barely feel it. "Been wanting to taste this pretty mouth for months, now."

She forced another laugh and reached up to push his hand away. "Cade, come on."

"Come on, what?" He caught her hand, squeezing her fingers when she tried to pull away. Not enough to hurt, not really, but the threat was there. "It's just a kiss, Olivia. Just one little kiss. What can it hurt?"

Her heart was pounding. She tried to pull her hand free, but he tightened his grip, and she winced as the ring she wore on her middle finger dug into her skin. "You're hurting me," she whispered, her voice hitching, and he smiled.

"I don't want to hurt you," he assured her, moving forward to force her against the counter, the cool edge of stone digging into her spine. "And I won't. If you're nice to me."

Fantasy and reality were starting to blur, the knowledge she'd been clinging to since she'd stepped out of the car — that that this was Cade, and this was the game — faded into the misty recesses of her mind, pushed there by his smooth voice and devil's smile. In its place was fear, bright and sharp and delicious.

"I don't want to kiss you," she managed through dry lips.

"Aw. That hurts my feelings, Olivia." He lifted his free hand to brush the hair away from her face. It settled on her neck, heavier than it should be as he smiled gently with venom filled eyes. "You don't want to hurt my feelings, do you?"

Fear slithered through her like smoke, thick and insidious. "No."

"One kiss." His voice was cajoling, a caress wrapped in barbed wire. "I won't even stay for a cup of coffee."

She hesitated, searching his face for something, anything that reminded her of her friend. But there was only this slick stranger, faintly menacing, squeezing her fingers with one hand and holding her neck with the other, waiting for either her capitulation or her defiance.

Either way, he would have his kiss.

"Okay," she said, and swallowed the lump in her throat. "One kiss."

"There, see?" he crooned softly, and the sly satisfaction in his tone made her shiver. "That wasn't so hard."

He let go of her hand to slide his arm around her waist, pulling her firmly forward so she was plastered against him from breast to knee. He slid his other hand to the back of her head, his fingertips digging hard into her scalp. She pulled away slightly, just to see what would happen if she resisted, and his hand tightened immediately.

"Now, now, none of that," he chided softly, so close his breath danced over her skin. His eyes had narrowed and darkened, like a shadowy cartoon villain. "I thought you were going to be nice to me."

She forced herself to relax in his hold, going as limp as possible, but the moment she stopped holding herself so rigidly, the trembles started.

"That's better." He smiled his devil's smile, slow and sinister. "Open your mouth."

The command startled her, but she let her lips fall apart, and he made a little sound of annoyance.

"Wider. Like you're about to get a fat cock between those slutty porn-star lips."

Shock had her jerking back, but there was nowhere to go. He laughed, low and mocking. "What, nobody ever told you that before?"

"No," she said, and stepped to the side. But he followed, pinning her into the corner with the weight of his body, one hand still wrapped in her hair. "I'm not a slut."

"With that mouth, baby, you're the queen of the sluts." He pulled his arm from around her waist— superfluous now that she was well and truly pinned— and grabbed her chin. "Then there's the way you're dressed. Bright pink dress, fuck me heels."

She shook her head, wincing when the hand in her hair tightened and his fingertips dug into her chin. "I just wanted to look nice."

"And you do," he assured her. "Very nice. Now open your fucking mouth."

He jammed his thumb between her lips, hooking it behind her bottom teeth, and pulled, forcing her jaw open. She felt obscene, standing there with her mouth open, his erection digging into her belly and her own arousal dripping down her thighs. "That's it," he said with a chuckle, and she flinched even as her pussy gushed. "Hold still, now."

He lowered his head and licked into her mouth.

It was the most obscene kiss of her life. His thumb kept her mouth open as he swirled his tongue between her lips, skimming her teeth, the insides of her cheeks.

He lapped at her like a puppy, almost playfully, but there was nothing innocent about it.

She kept her tongue still and her body pliant, not fighting him but not participating either, and after a moment he lifted his head to smirk at her.

"You got your kiss," she began, but he was still holding her mouth open, and the words were garbled and unintelligible.

His smirk deepened, but he released his hold on her chin. "Sorry, what was that?"

She flexed her jaw carefully, wincing at the ache. "You got your kiss," she repeated, and lifted her chin in a show of bravado. "You can go now."

"You think that was a kiss?" He shook his head, tsking softly. He tightened his hand in her hair, jerking her head back so hard and fast that she cried out. "It doesn't count if you don't kiss me back."

"You didn't say that," she said, her vision blurring as tears stung her eyes. Her scalp was burning, and fear swamped her mind. "You just said you wanted a kiss."

"And you haven't given me one yet." He used his grip on her hair to jerk her head forward so they were once again face to face, his other hand coming up to circle her throat. "Come on, baby. Show me what that mouth can do."

She was braced for violence, so the gentleness with which he pressed his lips to hers was almost a shock. She met his questing tongue with her own, tentative at first, then more boldly. He tasted like the tiramisu he'd had at the restaurant, and under it like Cade, familiar and welcome.

But her scalp still stung from his grip on her hair, and his hand was heavy on her throat. So she pulled her mouth away, twisting her face to the side, and panted, "There, you got your kiss. Now get the hell out of here."

He chuckled low in her ear. "That's not really what you want, is it?"

She trembled against him, fear rising again as she strained against his grip. "Yes. I want you to leave."

"Hmm." He skimmed his lips over the delicate shell of her ear, then down the side of her neck. "I don't think you do."

"I do," she insisted, the words sharp with fear. She shoved against the solid wall of his chest, panic rising when he didn't budge by so much as an inch.

"Yeah?" He lifted his head, the taunting gleam in his eye matching the smirk on his lips. "You gonna tell me your nipples are hard because it's cold?"

The realization that he could feel them through their clothes had shame curling through her. She hunched her shoulders forward, trying to push back far enough to keep her breasts from touching his chest, but his hand only tightened on her throat, holding her still.

"And I guess your pussy is only wet because you're sweating."

"It's not wet," she protested automatically.

"Oh, no?" He grinned, feral and sharp. "Let's see."

She twisted against him, struggling for real now, putting all her weight into it. But he controlled her with ease, grabbing her hands in one of his and using his weight to pin her to the counter, shoved his other hand up her dress.

His laugh was darkly triumphant, and had her cringing in shame again. "You're fucking soaked," he crowed, his fingers sliding through the wetness on her thigh. She clamped her legs together, trying to keep him from going any higher, but he jammed a knee between hers, prying her thighs apart, then his hand was on her bare pussy.

"No fucking panties?" he growled as fear and shame and lust swirled inside her. He cupped her pussy hard, grinding his palm against her, and even with her labia shielding her clit, the burst of sensation made her jerk.

"No panties," he repeated, releasing her hands and yanking at the neckline of her dress. A seam ripped, the sound mingling with her ragged breathing. Her bodice slithered to her waist as his fingers found her bare breast. "And no bra. Tell me again you're not a slut?"

"I'm not," she protested weakly.

"My hand is dripping wet," he pointed out, grinding it against her pussy. "And your nipples are so hard I bet they could cut glass."

She pushed against him, one tear slipping down her cheek. "Please. Don't."

"You don't mean that." His lips skimmed her cheek, almost gentle as he rubbed the tear away. "This wet fucking pussy doesn't mean that."

He squeezed her breast, his fingers tugging and rolling her nipple. "These hard nipples don't mean that."

"I want you to go," she managed, a second tear following the first, a sob in her throat. She looked up into his eyes, filled with determination and lust and smug triumph. The combination filled her with fear and despair and a dark, shameful lust.

"Aw, baby," he crooned softly, mockingly. "I just want to make you feel good. Don't you want to feel good?"

She twisted against him, choking back a cry when his fingers tightened warningly on her nipple. "Please, just go."

"Don't you want to make me feel good?" he continued, ignoring her plea. He moved his hand, shoving the dress up to her waist before she could react. She moved to cover herself, but he caught her hands easily and maneuvered them behind her back.

"Look at you," he said, and she glanced down.

Her dress was rucked to her waist, her bare pussy and slick thighs clearly visible. She still wore the cardigan, but it had slid down one shoulder, and her breasts were bared, the torn bodice hanging to her waist.

He tucked her wrists into one hand and brought the other up to cup her breast. He squeezed, pushing the nipple high, chuckling when it tightened even further.

"Please stop," she whispered, and his eyes slid to hers. "I don't want this."

"I don't believe you," he whispered back, and leaned down to lick her nipple.

She shrank back, fighting the flood of sensation. His mouth was hot on her breast, his teeth sharp. "No. No."

"I think you want to get fucked," he said against her skin, the words hitting like slaps. "I think you need a hard cock in that needy little cunt so bad you can barely think."

"Stop. Please stop."

"I think if I stuck my cock in you right now, you'd go off like the fucking fourth of July." He ground his pelvis against her, his thick cock hitting her clit just right, and she couldn't prevent the sharp cry.

He lifted his head to grin at her, smug and mean. "The fucking fourth of July," he repeated, and let go of her breast.

She began to struggle again when he dragged at his belt, worked his pants open and shoved his underwear down. His cock sprang free, hard and impossibly thick. He fisted it, squeezing hard, and a drop of thick fluid pearled at the tip.

"Yeah, you want this," he said, ignoring her increasingly panicked struggles. He shoved his other leg between her knees so she straddled him, her toes barely touching the ground, and slapped the head of his cock against her clit.

It was heavy and hot, and the little droplets of pre-come that splashed on the bare skin of her mound felt like hot wax.

"No, no, no." The lack of a condom sent her panic sky high, and she kicked out, trying to catch him with the high heels she still wore. His hand came up, a flash in the corner of her eye a split second before it made contact with her face.

The sharp pain had tears springing instantly to her eyes, and she cried out, unable to hold the sound back. She jerked her head around, her cheek throbbing as she stared at him.

"I don't want to hurt you," he said, and he sounded so sincere she could almost believe him. He lowered his hand to his cock, gripping it tight, and brought it between her trembling thighs. "I just want to make you feel good."

"Don't," she moaned weakly, her face hot from the slap and the tears that were now streaming unchecked. The broad head of his cock was wedged against her, pushing against the delicate opening. She was wet, but he was big, and she struggled in his hold. She thought for a moment that he wouldn't be able to do it, but then he shoved her leg high and angled his hips, and she screamed when he drove deep.

She arched back, trying to get away, but she couldn't. Between the hard counter and skewered on his cock, there was nowhere to go.

"Fuck, yeah," he muttered. He pulled back slightly then pushed forward again, wedging himself deeper. "Feels good, doesn't it?"

"No," she gasped. She hung in his arms, pinned against the counter and held up only by the weight of his body. She was stretched wide, the delicate entrance of her body burning as she struggled to accommodate him, and tears flowed down her cheeks. "It hurts."

"Liar." He pulled almost all the way out before shoving back in this time. "I can feel your cunt grabbing my cock, sucking me in. You fucking love this."

She shook her head frantically, her hands curling into useless fists behind her. "No, no."

He laughed, harsh and mean, and slammed into her. He let go of her hands to grab her ass, digging in hard to hold her still for his pounding. She brought her hands forward to push against his chest, but he was immovable. The countertop was digging into her back, each thrust jamming her into it. "Please, Cade. You're hurting me!"

Sweat dripped off his nose to splash onto her bare breast. "I think you like a little pain."

"No." She shook her head frantically, shrinking back when he bent his head. His teeth closed on her nipple, gently at first, then hard enough to make her scream.

His laugh vibrated against her breast, and he bit her again, pulling on her nipple hard before letting it bounce free. "Damn, your cunt got tight when I did that. Do it again, baby."

She moaned in distress when he bent his head to her other breast, and by the time he lifted his head again, she was sobbing with pain and despair. "Please, stop. Please."

"I can't stop now, baby," he panted, grunting as he rutted into her. "You want to come, don't you?"

"No," she groaned, the very thought of an orgasm making her stomach twist with nausea.

"Sure you do," he countered. He shifted his grip to free one hand, bringing it to the top of her mound. She twisted to get away, but he merely followed, his thumb hitting her clit with devastating accuracy, and to her dismay, he began to rub.

Her cunt clenched, rippling around his invading length. "Fuck, yeah," he muttered, rubbing harder. "I knew you'd love it. You wanna come, sweetie?"

"No, no, no," she panted, curling her nails into his chest. She fought the tension building in her belly. "I don't want this."

"Yeah, you do." He was driving hard now, fucking into her with bruising strength, his thumb hard and unyielding on her clit. "Come on, honey, do it. Squeeze my dick."

She fought it, but he was relentless, using his strength and skill against her, and she met the oncoming orgasm with a wail of despair.

"There it fucking is," he growled, hammering into her even harder, his thumb working her clit ruthlessly. The waves of sensation hit her like lightning, bright and sharp, her cunt pulsing on his invading length as she shook and shuddered in his arms.

It went on and on, physical pleasure mixing with emotional despair, until she felt battered and raw. When the sensations finally ebbed, she let her head fall back, unable to hold it up. She felt broken, bouncing between him and the hard countertop as he continued to pump between her limp thighs.

"Stop," she whispered, the word barely audible over his wild grunts. But he heard her, and fisted a hand in her hair to drag her head up. She peered at him through blurry eyes, the sneer on his face making her shudder with renewed fear.

"Stop?" he mocked, jamming himself into her hard enough to make her gasp. "I can't stop now. I got this cunt broken in, just the way I like it. Wet, and about to get wetter."

Her eyes went wide at the implication. "You can't come inside me."

"Can't I?" He raised one eyebrow, hips flying.

She shook her head frantically, desperately, barely wincing as his grip tugged at her scalp. "I'm not on birth control. You can't."

"That sounds like a you problem," he said, laughing when she began to struggle again. He pinned her arms, his grip bruising, and to her dismay she felt the stirrings of another orgasm.

He felt it, too. "Turns you on, doesn't it?" he panted. "Your lips say you don't want my come, but your greedy cunt says different."

"No, dammit," she cried, her pussy clenching even tighter on his cock. She didn't understand it, didn't *want* it, but it was happening anyway.

"Hope you got some Plan B, baby," he panted in her ear, his shoulders hunching as his hips sped up. "'Cause I'm gonna fill you up."

He bit her neck, hard, and laughed when her cunt clamped down again. He lifted his head to sneer at her. "You gonna come again, sugar?"

She shook her head frantically, tangled hair flying, and desperately hoped she wasn't lying. "No."

"I think you are. I think that greedy pussy wants my come."

"Stop it," she moaned. She needed him to shut up and finish already, before her body betrayed her. She squeezed her eyes tight, trying to block him out. But his words were somehow louder, the tension in her pelvis heavier without her sight.

"I can feel it," he whispered, and bit her again. "I feel you tightening up. Yeah, you're going to come again, and so am I. I'm going to pump that greedy pussy full, and you're going to suck it all up, not waste a single drop—"

She lost the rest of his words in the violent roaring in her ears, and came again. He shouted, and his cock grew bigger and harder, then the heat hit. He was coming inside her, and it felt so fucking good she sunk her teeth into his shoulder and held on as he pumped and cursed and shouted. When he slumped against her, his face buried in her neck and his heart thudding against her breast, she had everything she'd ever wanted.

Chapter Eight

Cade wrapped his arms around Olivia and breathed her in. She was dead weight against him, and he thought for a moment she might have passed out. But she was rubbing her forehead against his shoulder, like a kitten looking for pets, and her fingers were playing in his hair.

He'd planned a dramatic ending to the scene, where he pulled out and left her standing there with come dripping down her thighs. But he was afraid if he tried, his legs would give out, and he didn't think he could let her go, anyway. "You with me, fofa?"

"I'm here," she mumbled. "You okay?"

"I thought that was my line."

"Okay, go ahead."

He smiled against her damp skin. "You okay?"

"I'm happy." She turned her head so her cheek lay against his shoulder, her nose in his neck. "You?"

"Good, except for a logistical issue."

"Hmm. What's that?"

"My pants are around my ankles," he explained. "If I try to walk, I'll fall."

"That sounds like a you problem," she said sleepily, and he laughed.

"You'll fall, too," he pointed out, nuzzling her temple. Her skin was warm and salty, and he couldn't resist flicking his tongue out for a taste.

"Oh, right." She snuggled into him with a little sigh. "What do we do?"

"I'm going to lift you onto the counter so I can pull my pants up."

"Ew." She lifted her head, her nose adorably wrinkled. "I'm going to leak come all over your countertops."

He dropped a kiss on her nose and wrapped his hands around her hips. "I'll wipe them down with bleach later. Ready?"

She yawned. "Ready."

"One, two, three." He lifted her off him, both of them sighing as they separated, and set her on the counter. "All right?"

"Sure." She waved a hand at him. "Pull your pants up, will you? This is a respectable establishment."

He yanked his pants up and fastened them, shaking his head at her. "I forgot how goofy you get after a scene."

"I don't get goofy," she protested, and yawned again. "I'm just relaxed."

"Oh, is that what it is?" He reached for her feet, unbuckling first one shoe, then the other, letting them fall to the floor. "Does that mean you're not relaxed the rest of the time?"

"Pretty much."

"Hmm." He straightened, pleased when she draped her arms around his neck. "We might have to do something about that."

"You can try, but it probably won't work," she told him, her expression sober. "I'm a very tense person."

He smiled into her sleepy, serious eyes. "Do you think so?"

"Yep," she said, and laid her head on his shoulder. "What now?"

"Aftercare," he said, and scooped her off the counter and into his arms.

"My dress needs aftercare," she informed him as he carried her out of the kitchen. "You ripped it. And it probably has jizz stains on it now."

"It definitely has jizz stains on it," he said, taking the stairs slowly so as not to jostle her. "I'll pay for the dry-cleaning."

"And the repairs?"

"And the repairs," he agreed, amused at the orders she was flinging his way. Apparently being 'relaxed' meant she forgot who was the Dom.

"Good," she mumbled, and lifted her head from his chest to peer around curiously. "We're in your room."

"I know." He continued past the bed into the adjoining bath. "And now we're in my bathroom."

"Wow. That's a big tub."

He set her on her feet, holding her steady as she swayed. When he was certain she wasn't going to fall, he turned to the tub and opened the taps. When the water was running hot, he flipped the switch to close the drain. She was still standing in the middle of the room, making no move to get undressed, so he reached for the sash still knotted at her waist. "You haven't been in here yet?"

"Of course not. It's your room."

He set the sash on the edge of the sink, shaking his head. "You're the only person I know who could have an entire house to herself for a week and not go exploring," he told her, and reached for the cardigan.

"I did plenty of exploring," she protested, her eyes drifting closed. "I know the contents of your kitchen cabinets by heart at this point."

"Yeah?" He eased the cardigan off and set it on top of the sash, then reached for the hem of her dress. "What canned vegetable do I have the most of?"

"Black beans," she said immediately, and opened her eyes. "Although technically, that's a legume. I think."

"Legumes are vegetables. Lift your arms."

"There's an entire cupboard full of canned black beans. Why do you have so many?" she asked, raising her arms obediently so he could whisk the dress over her head. He set it on the sink with the rest of her clothes, then nudged her toward the tub.

"Because I love them, but I don't have the patience to make them from scratch," he said, and helped her step into the rapidly filling tub. "Don't tell my mother."

She sank into the water with a hiss of discomfort, and he frowned. "Too hot?"

"A little," she said. He reached out to adjust the taps, then began shedding his own clothes.

She crossed her arms on the wide lip of the bath and laid her head on them, watching him strip. "Why can't I tell your mother you eat black beans?"

"You can tell her I eat them," he said, enjoying the way her eyes widened as he strode toward her naked. "You just can't tell her I eat them out of a can. Scootch forward a bit."

She shifted obediently, and he slid in behind her. He spread his legs wide, cradling her between them, and tugged her back. "How's that?"

"Comfy," she said, relaxing against him with a sigh.

The water level was nearing the overflow drain, so he reached out to nudge it off with one foot, then eased back against the tub. "How do you feel otherwise?"

"Good," she said, her cheek rubbing against his chest as she twisted her head to look up at him.

"No bad moments?"

She smiled shyly. "Just the ones I wanted."

He chuckled. "All right, then. Do you want to talk about it now, or later?"

"Can we wait until later?" she asked, peering up at him through damp lashes. He didn't know if they were wet from the water, or the tears she'd shed earlier. "I kind of just want to chill right now."

"Sure, fofa." He pressed a kiss to her forehead. "As long as you're feeling okay."

"I feel great," she said, then wrinkled her nose. "And a little sticky."

He grinned and picked up a loofah and a bottle of body wash. "Well, that I can take care of."

He poured a generous dollop of body wash onto the sponge and worked up a lather, the soap's peppermint scent filling the air.

"That's why you sometimes smell like peppermint."

He tapped the sponge on her nose, leaving a dollop of bubbles behind, before stroking the sponge over her chest. "Like it?"

She pursed her lips and blew, sending the suds dancing into the air. "It's refreshing."

"In some places more than others," he told her, and waggled his brows when she looked at him with surprise.

"Really?"

"You'll see," he assured her.

"That's not ominous at all," she quipped, but she turned and settled back against him. "Cade?"

"Hmm?"

"Thank you."

His hand stilled for a moment, then resumed making lazy circles over her breasts with the loofah. "For what?"

"For making my dreams come true."

"We're just getting started," he assured her.

"I can't wait."

Neither could he.

* * * *

Olivia woke the next morning with a song in her heart and a smile on her face. The other side of the king-sized bed was empty, the sheets cool, so she assumed Cade had been up for a while. She was surprised she hadn't woken when he'd left the bed, as she tended to sleep light. But considering what she'd spent her evening doing, it was hardly a surprise that she'd slept through his departure.

She rolled out of bed and reached her arms to the sky, enjoying the stretch and pop of her muscles, then made the bed. The bath last night had taken care of most of her soreness, and the rest would probably dissipate once she got moving. Though by the feel of it, she definitely had a bruise on her lower back from being fucked into the countertop.

She stepped into the bath to look in the mirror, the dark smudge at the top curve of her ass confirming her suspicious. She'd never been one of those submissives who prided themselves on marks, but she was inordinately pleased to see the bruise, like a temporary memento of her first CNC scene with Cade.

She stared at it for a moment, a dreamy smile on her lips, then turned away from the mirror with a sigh. She hurried through her morning routine, though it gave her a little jolt to see her electric toothbrush on the counter next to Cade's. He'd been annoyed that she'd stayed in the guest room while he was gone, and after their bath, had ordered her to fetch her toothbrush and put it where it belonged.

If they were going to be together, he'd told her, his brows drown together in a grumpy frown, they were going to *be together.*

Then he'd declared that her first task today, after breakfast, was to officially move into his bedroom. The things she'd moved to the third floor could stay there, of course, but anything she'd normally keep in her bedroom — clothes, books, toiletries — was to be moved into the main bedroom without delay, or she could face the consequences.

She'd been half tempted to ask just what those consequences were, but she'd held her tongue and offered a meek *"Yes, Sir,"* that had made him laugh.

"Brat," he'd admonished gently, and tweaked her nose. *"No half measures, remember?"*

"Yes, Sir," she'd replied in the same subservient tone, then burst into giggles when he'd scooped her up and dropped her into bed.

She'd thought he'd make love to her again at that point, but instead he'd cuddled her close in the dark, and it had been almost as good as sex.

Though she wouldn't mind more sex soon, she thought, and grinned at her reflection.

She brushed her teeth quickly, then wove her hair into a loose braid. She started to go to the guest room for her robe, then on impulse picked up the dress shirt he'd worn last night. It clearly needed to be cleaned— the tails were wrinkled from being tucked into his slacks, and there were smears of pink lipstick on the front. But it still smelled like him, like sweat and peppermint soap, so she slipped it on and headed downstairs.

She stopped in the living room to fish her phone out of her evening bag, checking her messages on the way to the kitchen. Sadie had texted four times that morning, she noted with amusement, starting with *So? How'd it go?* at seven-thirty, and ending with *WOMAN IF YOU DON'T TEXT ME BACK AND LET ME KNOW YOUR'E OKAY, SO HELP ME GOD...* just a few minutes ago.

Not wanting to find out what 'so help me God' actually meant, and a little startled by the all caps, she fired off a quick *I'm fine, sorry, slept late*, then set her phone on the counter.

She could hear muffled thumps coming from the open basement door, and knowing Cade had a small gym set up down there, assumed he was working out. She saw no evidence he'd already eaten—though he was even neater than she was, so it was entirely possible he'd fixed something and washed up after himself. But she erred on the side of caution and began gathering the ingredients for pancakes for two.

His cupboards were well stocked and ruthlessly organized — even the cabinet dedicated to canned black beans — so it was easy to find all the ingredients she needed. There was no buttermilk in the fridge, but he had milk and apple cider vinegar, so she made do.

She was just slipping the butter into the microwave to melt when her phone dinged again. *Glad you're fine,* the message read, *but HOW WAS IT?*

Amused, she typed back, *I'll tell you later, got my hands full making breakfast at the moment,* and reached for the measuring cups. She hadn't even scooped out the first cup of flour when her phone rang.

Laughing, she answered the call and put it on speaker. "Hi, Sadie. What's up?"

"What's up, she says, as if I haven't been sitting on pins and needles all night. *How. Was. It?*"

Olivia dumped flour into a bowl and fought back a snicker. "I told you, it was fine."

Sadie sighed so loud it echoed in the kitchen. "Oh my God, you're the *worst.*"

"Sorry," Olivia said with a laugh. "I want to tell you all about it, I swear. But I'm in the middle of making pancakes."

"So? Multi-task, bitch."

Olivia laughed so hard she had to put down the baking soda for fear of spilling it all over the floor. "You're terrible."

"This is well established," Sadie said dismissively. "What is not well established is exactly how terrible Cade is. So dish."

"He's awful," Olivia said, pouring the butter and the curdled milk into the bowl. "Wretched. Rotten to the core."

"That good, huh?"

"So good," Olivia said with a sigh, and began to whisk. "Sadie, it was just so…so…"

"Wow," Sadie said when Olivia trailed off. "Left you speechless, huh? This is the point where normally I'd ask for the play-by-play, but I'm not sure I want to know."

Olivia paused in her whisking to frown at the phone. "Does consensual non-consent bother you?"

"Theoretically, no. But it's not one of my kinks, and honestly, I'm not sure if I want the nitty gritty."

"Then why are you asking?"

"Because you're my friend and this is a big deal for you, and I want you to know that I support you."

Olivia resumed whisking with a smile. "That's so sweet."

"Yeah, I'm a spoonful of sugar," Sadie said drily. "Okay, let's get to the important thing. What does Cade look like naked?"

Olivia bit back a snicker and set her whisk in the sink. "I thought you didn't want the nitty gritty?"

"That's just the CNC stuff. For the record, I *always* want the hot-naked-man stuff."

Olivia pulled a clean dish towel out of the drawer next to the stove and laid it over her bowl, then turned to set it at the back of the counter next to the coffee pot. The pot was empty—more evidence that Cade hadn't eaten yet—but she'd make a fresh one, and the heat it gave off would help the pancake batter proof. "You've seen Cade naked before, haven't you?"

"I haven't, actually. He doesn't strip down in the dungeon a lot. Believe me, I'd have noticed if he had."

"I guess that's true," Olivia mused, and carried the coffee pot to the sink.

"So? How hot is he?"

Olivia left the pot filling in the sink and pulled out the bag of coffee grounds as she thought about Cade naked. Muscled torso, tree trunk legs, and in between...

"Pretty hot," Olivia said, and carefully measured out grounds. "He's got a lot of muscles from working construction."

"I can see that," Sadie replied, clearly exasperated. "What about the muscle I can't see?"

Olivia cleared her throat and turned off the water. "I assume you're talking about his penis?"

"No, I want to hear about his sartorious."

Olivia bit the inside of her cheek to keep from laughing. "Well, it runs the length of the thigh to the inside of the knee, and is the longest muscle in the human body—"

"Oh my God!" Sadie yelled, exasperated, and Olivia lost her battle with laughter.

"Never make muscles jokes with a physical therapist," Olivia said between giggles.

"You are such a pain," Sadie grumbled, but Olivia could hear the amusement in her voice. "Maybe I'll just ask Rebecca."

"Okay," Olivia said, still laughing, and poured the water into the coffee pot. "Ask Rebecca."

"This is not how you're supposed to play this game," Sadie complained, and Olivia laughed again. "All right, fine. Just answer one question."

"What's that?"

"Are you happy?"

Olivia slid the pot in place and flipped the switch. "Yes." She didn't know how long it would last or where they'd end up, but right now, making pancakes and coffee to share with the man who'd pretended to rape her last night, she was all but swimming in bliss. "Yes, I'm happy."

"Well, then I'm happy for you. Even if you need How To Discuss Your Sex Life With Your Girlfriends lessons."

"Can I sign up for that at the community college?"

"No, but you can practice at SWWW next week?"

Olivia chuckled. SWWW stood for Submissive Wine and Whine Wednesday, Sadie's version of a submissive support group. "That sounds great. Thanks for checking on me, Sadie."

"That's what friends do. See you next Wednesday."

"Bye," Olivia said.

She picked up the phone to end the call, then someone said, "Morning, beautiful," at the same time something brushed against the back of her neck, and she screamed and threw her phone in the air.

Cade could hear Olivia talking on the phone when he came up the basement stairs. She sounded cheerful, skillfully dodging Sadie's attempts to worm the details of last night's scene out of her, and laughing at her friend's frustration. He liked the sound of her laughter almost as much as he liked her tears.

He topped the stairs, wiping the sweat off his face with the towel he'd slung around his neck. He started to call out, then he noticed what she was wearing and the words died on his tongue.

She'd put on the dress shirt he'd worn the night before. The wrinkled hem hung to mid-thigh, the curve of her ass pressing against the soft cotton as she stretched forward to pour water into the coffee pot. There was a covered bowl on the back of the counter, and ingredients scattered over the island, so he assumed she was making breakfast. He hadn't added meal prep or any other domestic chores to her list of daily tasks, because she had a job outside of being his submissive and because he was a grown man who knew how to take care of himself. But he might make a rule that if she was going to cook, she had to do it in one of his shirts.

He'd woken up tangled in her hair, his nose buried in the back of her neck, and the urge to fuck her then and there had been almost impossible to ignore. He knew that somnophilia was something she enjoyed — being taken advantage of while she was asleep, and therefore vulnerable, was a particular turn-on for her. It flipped his switches as well, and he would definitely be availing himself of her while she was sleeping in the future.

But last night's scene had been a heavy one — though physically lighter than many of the fantasies they'd discussed — and while she'd seemed fine, he wanted to give both of them time to settle before jumping into another scene. So he'd forced himself out of bed, and got his blood moving with a quick workout instead of a quick fuck.

But now her back was turned, and the borrowed shirt was climbing up the backs of her thighs while she fiddled with the coffee maker. His cock, having subsided during his workout, rose insistently in his shorts.

He ignored it, and the urge to come up behind her and push her to the floor, and crossed the kitchen. She'd braided her hair, baring her neck, so he bent to press his lips to her soft skin. "Morning, beautiful," he said just before his lips made contact.

Then he jerked back, quick reflexes saving him from a broken nose when her head snapped back. Her shrill scream was still ringing in the air when he caught her cell phone just before it landed in the sink.

She spun around, her eyes wide and wild. "What the fuck?"

"Okay, no coffee for you," he decided, and held out her phone. "You dropped this."

She ignored it, one hand braced on the counter behind her, the other pressed to her chest. Her eyes were like saucers, her pulse pounding in her throat. "You scared the crap out of me."

"So I see." He laid her phone on the island and leaned in to brush a kiss over her lips. Since they were still parted with shock, he slipped his tongue inside for a quick taste before pulling back. "Let's try this again. Morning, beautiful."

"Morning," she sighed, a sheepish smile curving her mouth. "Sorry."

The quick taste hadn't been enough, so he leaned in for another. "Are you always this jumpy in the morning?"

"Not usually," she breathed, rising on her toes to press her lips more firmly to his. "Mmm. You're sweaty."

"And you're wearing my shirt." He lifted a hand to toy with the button holding it together over her breasts. "Did I say you could wear my shirt?"

"No." She shivered against him. "Want it back?"

He started to say yes—they could go over last night after sex—then a low, rumbling gurgle filled the air.

He pulled back to look at her, one eyebrow raised. "Was that your stomach?"

Her cheeks didn't turn pink, but if 'blush' was an expression, she was wearing it. "I'm hungry."

"I guess so," he replied, and resigned to having blue balls at least through breakfast, dropped one last kiss on her mouth. "What're you making?"

"I was planning on pancakes," she said when he stepped back. "But I can make do with a bowl of cereal."

Amused at her hopeful tone, and at the way her gaze lingered on his bare, sweaty torso, he moved back to the other side of the island and chose a stool. "Eager little victim, aren't you?"

She aimed a pointed glance at the front of his shorts, which were clinging to his eager dick like plastic wrap. "If I'm eager, what are you?"

"In charge," he said. "Fuel now, fuck later."

"Fine." She pulled out a skillet and set it on the burner with a bit more force than was strictly necessary. "How did you sleep?"

"Like a rock," he replied, bemused that she'd managed to get the question out before he did. "You?"

"I slept great." She smiled at him—well, at his chest, she was still staring—and began to gather the ingredients scattered across the counter. "Your bed is really comfortable."

"It's not too firm for you?" He liked a hard mattress, and a lot of his bed partners found it great for fucking, not so great for sleeping. The bed in the guest room was much softer, with a plush pillow top, so he'd expected her to have some trouble with his firmer one.

She shook her head, tucking spices back into the cabinet. "When I went to buy my bed, I told the salesperson to give me the hardest mattress they had. They kept trying to talk me out of it."

"Sounds familiar." He sat quietly while she put away the rest of the ingredients and wiped down the counters. When she'd rinsed out the sponge and laid it on the edge of the sink, he said, "Are you ready to talk about last night?"

"Sure, if you don't mind me cooking while we talk."

He normally would want her full attention for a discussion like this, but he was getting hungry, too. "You've been fantasizing about rape play for a long time."

She picked up the bowl at the back of the counter and took the dishtowel off. "Years," she admitted.

"Did the reality beat your fantasy?"

"To hell and gone," she said with a laugh.

"The date-rape scenario worked for you, then?"

"Oh, yeah." She switched on the flame under the skillet and reached for the butter dish. "I'd never considered a scenario like that."

"No?"

She shook her head. "All my fantasies have been more physical, more violent, I guess. This was more…"

"Coercive?" he supplied.

She nodded and dropped a pat of butter in the skillet to sizzle. "I was braced for violence, so the sneak attack caught me by surprise."

"Good. Did you get what you needed from the aftercare?"

"Yeah." She rotated the skillet to swirl the butter around. "I like that you called me 'fofa' when it was over. That was nice. Grounding, you know?"

"I liked it, too." An understatement, he thought. "Was it realistic enough for you?"

"Oh, yeah. I wondered if I'd be able to get really into it, because we know each other so well. But it was like flipping a switch on reality. It just clicked off."

He nodded. "It'll probably get harder for you to suspend your disbelief as we go on together."

"Probably."

"But I have ideas about that," he continued, and waggled his eyebrows to make her laugh.

"I'm sure you do." She wet her fingers at the sink, then flicked the water into the skillet to see if it was hot enough. "Would you set the table? Or the counter, I guess."

"Sure." He rose from the stool to gather plates and silverware. "Syrup?"

"Yes, please."

He got it out of the fridge. "What do you want to drink?"

"I'm good with coffee."

He got two mugs down and filled them with the fragrant brew. "Is there anything about last night you'd change?"

She ladled batter into the skillet. "I don't think so. Well…"

"What?" he asked when she fell silent.

"I wouldn't have worn that pink dress if I'd known it was going to end up ripped and stained." She shot him the same look his mother gave him when he was five and used her good guest towels to wipe mud off the dog.

He just grinned. "You knew I wasn't going to wear a condom."

"Hmm." She tapped the spatula on the side of the pan. "And the rip?"

"Authenticity," he said, his tongue tucked firmly in his cheek. "You think if a guy doesn't care about getting your consent to fuck you, he'll give a shit about your clothes?"

She rolled her eyes and flipped the pancakes. "How many of these will you eat?"

"How many you got?"

"Next time I'll double the recipe," she decided. She turned the first three golden-brown cakes onto a plate and passed it to him. "Here, get started on those."

He didn't need to be asked twice. He'd finished the first batch by the time the rest were done, and she slipped another three on his plate before taking two for herself and settling on the stool beside him.

"These are good," he told her. "Family recipe?"

"Internet," she told him, drowning her short stack in syrup. "I don't have any family recipes."

That made him pause. "You don't?"

She shook her head. "No family, really."

He laid his fork down. He'd known she didn't have any siblings, but she'd never told him this. "Where are your parents?"

"They died when I was seventeen," she told him, sorrow darkening her eyes.

"I'm sorry," he said quietly, and laid a hand over hers. His family was loud and interfering and annoying, but he couldn't imagine his life without them.

"Thanks." She smiled faintly, her eyes still clouded. "It was a house fire. They were able to save some stuff in the garage—a dresser my dad was refinishing, a mirror that belonged to my grandma, stuff like that— but everything else was lost."

"You were able to get out?" he asked quietly.

She shook her head. "I was with a friend from school, touring colleges with her family. My parents were supposed to take me, but my dad had to work. They were asleep when the fire started. The medical examiner said he didn't think they even woke up."

"Ah, fofa." The look in her eyes was breaking his heart. He rose from his stool, pulling her up with him, and folded her into his arms. "I'm so sorry."

Her body was stiff against his, then she gave a hard shudder and relaxed into him, her arms creeping around his waist and holding on. "I was going to say it's okay," she mumbled into his bare chest, "but it sucks."

He laid his cheek against her hair. "Why haven't I ever heard this story?"

"I don't really talk about it." Her shoulders lifted and fell. "It's too hard."

"I understand."

"You have a big family, right?" she asked, tilting her head back to look at him.

"Big enough." He stroked his fingers over her cheek, wanting to soothe. "Mom, dad, three sisters."

A hint of amusement chased the lingering sadness from her eyes. "I remember. Are your sisters older or younger?"

"Claudia and Flavia are both older, and Tatchi is the baby."

"Tatchi?"

"Her name is Tatiana, but in Portuguese the t and the i together make a 'ch' sound. So instead of Tah-tee-ana, it's Tah-chee-ana," he explained. "Tatchi for short."

"Your mom's Brazilian, right?" Understanding dawned in her eyes when he nodded. "Is that why you can't tell her you eat black beans out of a can?"

"I wasn't kidding when I said it would break her heart," he said seriously. "Then she'd make me learn to make them from scratch, and I don't wanna."

"Lazy," she accused, and poked him in the ribs.

"Hey, hey, none of that," he warned, twitching away from her dancing fingers. "Tickling will get you beaten."

"Spoilsport," she accused but she was smiling. "Thanks for the hug."

"You're welcome." He dropped a soft kiss on her upturned mouth. "Anytime."

"Really?" She rose on her toes to kiss him again. "Anytime?"

"Anytime," he repeated. He threaded his fingers into her braid, tilting her head to deepen the contact. "Day or night."

"Who knew living here would come with such great perks?" she whispered against his mouth, and he chuckled.

"I'll show you perks," he said in the most sinister voice he could imagine, and she gave a shriek of mock fear just as the back door opened.

"Cade, Mom is riding my nerves like a Grand Canyon mule, so I'm crashing here tonight."

Olivia squeaked, Cade groaned, and his younger sister dropped a loaded duffel on the floor and grinned. "Am I interrupting something?"

"Speak of the fucking devil," Cade said, resigned, and held Olivia more firmly against him. She was squirming, trying to pull free, but there was no way he was letting her go, and not just because she was the only thing keeping his sister from seeing the erection trying to poke through his shorts.

"Language, menino," Tatiana chided, and the look of unholy glee on her face had his eyes narrowing.

"You're not staying here tonight," he told her firmly, already knowing it was a losing battle.

"I have to," she countered. "Mom invited Marcelo Silva over for dinner again."

"Oh, hell." He sighed, resigned. "Fine. One night. And I'll talk to Mom."

"Thank you," Tatchi said, then raised an eyebrow. "Aren't you going to introduce me to your friend?"

"No."

"Cade," Olivia said, and he looked down to find her trying not to smile at him.

"If I introduce you, she'll just try to talk to you, and believe me, that's not a good idea."

"Rude," Tatchi scoffed. "I'll have you know most people think I'm a delight."

"None of those people have had to live with you," he countered.

His baby sister crossed her arms over her chest and sent him a smug smile. "If you don't introduce me, I'm calling Claud and Via."

"Shit." Cade glared at her, then down at Olivia, who had her face buried in his neck to muffle the giggles. "Fine. Olivia, this is my younger sister Tatiana. Tatiana, this is Olivia. Try not to scare her off."

Olivia dug a finger into his ribs, and when he twitched, slipped neatly out of his arms. "It's nice to meet you," she said with a smile. "Would you like some pancakes?"

"It's nice to meet you too, and yes, I would." Tatchi crossed to the breakfast bar and sat on Cade's stool.

He shoved her off again. "Get out of my seat."

"Mature," she said mockingly, and stuck her tongue out at him as she slid onto the next stool.

"Mature," he drawled.

"Here you go," Olivia said, and laid a plate with the last two pancakes on it in front of his sister.

"Thank you, this looks great." Tatchi reached for the syrup. "So, how long have you known my brother?"

Olivia resumed her seat on Cade's other side and picked up her fork. "About a year and a half."

Syrup shot across the countertop as Tatchi whirled to stare at Cade. "You've been dating for a year and a half and didn't tell anyone?"

Cade grabbed the squeeze bottle out of her hands before she could get the floor all sticky. "No, we've known each other for a year and a half," he said, and set the syrup out of her reach. "We've been dating for a week."

"Oh." Tatchi swiped her finger thought the puddle of syrup on the counter and sucked it clean. "First sleepover, and you made her cook?"

"How do you know I didn't make it?"

"Because it involves more than three ingredients, and none of them are canned beans."

"Jesus Christ," Cade muttered, and went to the sink for a wet rag.

"Mom's going to be thrilled," Tatchi said silkily, and beamed innocently when Cade glared at her. "What? You don't think she'd be interested to know you're seeing someone?"

He glared at her and mopped the counter. "She'd be equally interested to know where you are right now, wouldn't she?"

Tatchi's eyes narrowed. "You wouldn't."

"Try me."

"Interesting," Olivia mused, and the siblings stopped glaring at each other to look at her. She gestured between them with her fork. "Is this what most sibling relationships are like?"

"Like what?" Cade asked.

"Mutually assured destruction."

"Pretty much," Tatchi said with a grin, and started eating again. "You must be an only child."

"Stop interrogating my girlfriend," Cade told his sister.

"Girlfriend, huh?" Tatchi pursed her lips and eyed her brother, looking so much like their mother he had to bite his tongue to hold back a grin.

Her eyes narrowed suspiciously. "What?"

"Nothing," he said blandly, and filed the observation away to use at some later date, when she was being really obnoxious.

"So, Olivia," Tatchi said, still watching her brother with narrowed eyes. "Tell me about yourself. What do you do? Where do you live? Why are you dating my jackass of a brother?"

"I'm a physical therapist," she began, her eyes flicking to Cade. He saw the question in them, and shrugged. They'd find out soon enough. "And at the moment, I live here."

Tatchi's eyes went wide and she choked on her pancakes, which Cade found pretty satisfying. When she'd stopped coughing, she wheezed, "You're *living here*?"

"Um. Yeah. I kind of lost my apartment last week, and Cade offered me his guest room."

"Right." Tatchi dropped her gaze pointedly at Olivia's legs, bare under Cade's shirt. "The guest room."

"That's where I started out," Olivia said with a smile. "Speaking of which, I should get my stuff out of there so you can settle in."

"She's nice, pretty, and considerate." Tatchi looked at Cade. "I still don't know why she's dating you."

"Oh, he has some redeeming qualities," Olivia said, her eyes sparkling at him over her coffee cup. He winked at her, grateful he was still on the other side of the island, because his shorts were doing fuck all to hide how much he wished his sister wasn't in the room.

Tatchi held up a hand. "Okay, ew. Can you not make swoony eyes at each other? I'm trying to eat."

"Get your own house," Cade suggested, and Olivia laughed.

"I'll get the guest room ready," Olivia said, her eyes dancing as she looked at Cade. "Okay if I take my coffee with me?"

"Of course, fofa."

"Thanks. It was nice meeting you, Tatchi. I'll see you later?"

"Sure." Tatchi sent her a beaming smile. "Thanks for the pancakes."

"You're welcome."

"I'll be up in a minute to give you a hand," Cade said.

She waved a hand. "Stay and talk with your sister. I've got it."

"I'll be up in a minute to give you a hand," he repeated pointedly. He watched her go, and when she was out of sight, turned back to his sister. "Don't start."

"Oh, I'm going to start," she replied with a grin, wiggling with glee. "I'm going to start *hard*. You called her fofa."

"Tatchi," he began warningly, but of course she ignored him.

"Fofa," she repeated. "A nickname normally reserved for a small child, or something fluffy and cute. Except in our family, where it means—"

"I know what it means," he cut her off.

"Uh-huh. Does *she* know what it means?"

"Not exactly," he hedged. "And don't tell her, either."

"Okay." She grinned and shoved pancakes in her mouth. "I'll just tell Mom."

"I'll never let you stay here again."

"Jeez. Touchy." She eyed him while she chewed. "Are you introducing her to the family soon? Because that might distract Mom from this whole Marcelo Silva business."

"No."

"Why not?"

"Because I'm trying to take things slow," he told her, and tossed the rag into the sink. "And you know Mom."

"She can be subtle," Tatchi said soberly, then snickered. "Oh my God, I couldn't even say that with a straight face."

Cade circled the counter, sat back down, and flicked her on the back of the head. "Brat."

"Jerk." She snatched his coffee cup in retaliation. "Can I at least be there when you tell Mom you're living with a woman you haven't introduced her to yet?"

"Can I be there when you tell her you keep resisting her attempts to set you up with Marcelo Silva because you're dating a botany major from New Jersey who grows his own weed?"

"Okay, fine, nobody tells Mom anything. On to more important questions — can I have a friend over tonight? I have a study group."

"Is that what we're calling it?"

"For the purposes of our parents, yes. And also, does you being sober mean I can't smoke weed in your house?"

"God, I hate you," he sighed, and got up to get himself another cup of coffee.

Chapter Nine

A week and a half later, Olivia found herself facing her curious friends in Sadie's living room for Whine and Wine Wednesday. As expected, she — and her relationship with Cade — were the center of attention.

"Now, when you say 'awesome'," Sadie asked, said from her perch on the couch with a glass of wine in one hand and a mini egg roll in the other, "are we talking about his penis?"

Rebecca sighed. "For God's sake, Sadie."

"What? Not all of us have sampled the goods," Sadie said, then turned back to Olivia expectantly. "Well?"

"Don't you want to wait for the others to get here?"

"Good idea," Rebecca said at the same time Sadie said, "Hell, no. They snooze, they lose. I want the dirt."

"Okay, well," Olivia began, then stopped at the knock on the door.

"Dammit," Sadie grumbled, and stomped to her front door. "Good, you're here. Wine over there, food over there. Help yourselves, but do it quietly, because

Olivia's about to tell us all about Cade's penis and I don't want to miss anything."

"I see nothing around here has changed," a low voice said drily.

"Hey, Sam," Olivia called out. "Hi, Amanda."

"There she is," Sam said, and crossed the room for a hug. "I hear you've had an eventful couple of weeks."

"Just a little," she said, and reached up to tap his dimpled chin. "What happened to the scruff?"

"Doesn't work with the PPE I have to wear at work," he explained, stepping aside so Amanda could hug Olivia in turn. He stroked his newly denuded chin and posed, one peaked eyebrow raised in question. "What do you think?"

She pursed her lips and pretended to think it over. "Sexy," she decided. "Kind of boyishly sinister."

"Boyishly sinister?" He laughed and shook his head. "And to think, I almost didn't come tonight."

"I'm glad you did." Olivia worked up a pout. "We don't see nearly enough of you anymore."

"I know. I love the ER, but twelve-hour night shifts have killed my social life."

"Not that I'm not thrilled you're here, Sam," Sadie interrupted. "But find a seat and shut up."

"She's a little scary," Olivia whispered.

"I'll protect you, darling," he said, and sent Sadie a sunny smile when she glared at them.

It took a few minutes, but soon they were all seated, beverages in hand, looking at Olivia expectantly. Amanda had wedged herself in between Rebecca and Sadie on the small sofa, and Sam was perched on a small ottoman that was proving to be far more decorative than functional.

"Are you sure this will hold me?" he asked, a glass of Chardonnay in one hand and a plate of cheese and crackers in the other. He was holding them aloft as he tried to balance himself on the fabric cube, which appeared to be slowly collapsing beneath him.

"Just don't put your full weight on it, and you'll be fine," Sadie advised.

"Jesus," Sam muttered, and stood, leaving a dent in the crushed orange velvet. "I'll just stand."

"Do whatever you want, but shut up," Sadie said, and pointed at Olivia. "You were saying?"

"Um. Where was I?"

"Cade's penis," Sadie said helpfully while Amanda choked on her wine.

"Right. His penis is good."

"You are so bad at this," Sadie said with a sigh.

"Sadie," Amanda said warningly while Olivia hid her smile in her wineglass. "It's not our business unless Olivia wants to share."

"Okay, fine. I'll accept 'good'," Sadie said, putting air quotes around the words just in case anyone missed the sarcasm dripping from them. "You don't happen to have any pictures, do you?"

"Sadie," Rebecca and Amanda said at the same time.

Olivia burst out laughing. "Sorry, no."

"I'm working with amateurs," Sadie muttered darkly.

"Olivia," Amanda began with a warning look for Sadie, who rolled her eyes and sipped her wine. "You don't owe us any information, and we're not going to push you if you don't want to share. But we're your friends, and we worry about you, and, well, we would like to know if the consensual non-consent play is going well."

"It is. I mean, we just got started, and we haven't done that much yet—"

"What exactly have you done?" Sadie wanted to know, then sighed when Amanda nudged her. "You know, if you want to tell us."

"Well, we did a date-rape scene last Friday night," Olivia put in, squirming in her seat at the memory. "That was hot. And we've done some somnophilia—"

"Is that like him fucking you when you're asleep?" Rebecca wanted to know.

"Yes." Sadie waved a hand at Rebecca without looking away from Olivia. "Hush."

"And yesterday, when I got home from work, he jumped me in the entry way, dragged me up the stairs by my hair, tied me to the bed, and ate my pussy until I almost passed out."

"Nice," Sadie said.

"Are you just doing rape fantasy, or are you putting the consensual non-consent into other areas, too?" Sam wanted to know.

"What do you mean?" Rebecca asked, her forehead wrinkling in a frown. "CNC is rape fantasy, isn't it?"

"That's only one part of it," Amanda explained.

"We're focusing on that for now," Olivia said. "But both Cade and I wanted a D/s element, and though we haven't done any scenes that aren't focused on the rape fantasy element yet, we set up safewords for that."

"You don't have a safeword for the CNC scenes?" Rebecca asked, her gray eyes wide.

"We do," Olivia hastened to assure her. "Although some people don't, because the whole point of CNC is to not have control."

"How is that safe?"

Olivia shrugged. "Different strokes, right? But I wanted one, so we have one. Actually, we have two. But one of them is more like a false safeword."

"A false safeword?" Sadie frowned.

Olivia nodded. "It hasn't come up yet, but if we're in a scene and I say 'red', that's a safeword he can ignore."

"What's the point of a safeword you ignore?"

"Well, if you say 'no' in a scene, that can be ignored. It's part of the role-play, right? That's why nobody picks 'no' as a safeword."

Sadie nodded. "Okay, I'm with you."

"So making 'red' an ignorable safeword adds another layer to the CNC. But if I say 'safeword', that's the stop button."

"'Safeword' as a safeword," Sam mused. "That's kind of awesome."

"Wait." Rebecca held up a hand. "If you say 'red' in a public scene, you know that's going to bring the DMs running."

Amanda nodded. "That's a good point."

"Yeah, that's a problem," Olivia mused, then shrugged. "I don't think we'd do a rape fantasy in public. It's such a hard limit for most people, we wouldn't want to inadvertently violate anyone else's boundaries."

"Smart," Sam said.

Sadie leaned forward and picked up the half-empty bottle of wine from the coffee table. "What else do you have planned?"

"*I* don't have anything planned," Olivia said with a laugh. "And Cade is a vault, so I have no clue what's on the agenda. Except...he gave me a list."

"A list of scenes that he wants to do?"

Olivia shook her head. "A list of other Doms that may or may not participate in a future scene with us."

Sadie topped off her wineglass and wiggled with avaricious delight. "Now we're getting to the good stuff."

Olivia took a deep breath. "One of my fantasies is a…well, it's a group sex thing."

Sadie nodded, her eyes glued to Olivia. "I'm with you."

"Kind of like an interrogation," Olivia continued.

"Less with you, but go on."

Olivia chuckled. "The details aren't important, but he made a list of all the Doms he knows and asked me to eliminate anyone I absolutely wouldn't want to have involved."

"*All* the Doms he knows?" Amanda raised an eyebrow. "That's a long list. Cade knows everybody."

"I know. I didn't even recognize some of the names." Olivia sighed and leaned back in her chair, feeling remarkably relaxed. This sharing business was actually kind of nice. "It's a lot harder than I thought it would be."

"How so?"

Olivia tilted her head back to look at Sam, still leaning against the wall. She opened her mouth to answer him, but then Sadie said, "Oh, for God's sake," and stomped out of the room.

Amanda stared after her. "What the hell?"

"Wait for it," Rebecca sighed, and Sadie came marching back into the room with a small stool in her hands.

"Here." She plunked it down in front of Sam. "Happy now?"

Sam eyed the stool carefully, as though he was assessing its structural integrity. "Will this one put me on my ass too?"

"It's my makeup stool," she said. "I sit on it every day. Park it and shut up."

"Excuse me for not wanting to get dumped on the floor," he grumbled, and sat. "You were saying, Olivia?"

"It's hard, because the all the ones on the list that I trust are, well, taken."

"Like who?"

Olivia looked at Amanda. "Like your husband."

Amanda's eyes widened behind her glasses. "Oh."

"And Nick," she went on, and Rebecca blinked in surprise. "And a few others, like Simon and Isaac and Mark."

"Married, engaged, married." Sadie pursed her lips as she ticked them off. "Isn't there anyone single on the list?"

"Well, there's Jack." Olivia frowned. "But I can never get a read on him. He always looks pissed off."

"That might be the sadist thing," Sam offered.

Sadie waved a hand. "Nah, that's just Jack. He has resting dick face."

Sam laughed, choking on his wine. "Good one. Collette's going to love that."

"Hey." Sadie pointed at him. "What's said at submissive wine night—"

"Stays at submissive wine night," Sam finished. "I know the rules. I won't tell her you're the one who said it."

"Like she'd believe it was anyone else," Rebecca said drily.

Sam sighed. "Fine, I won't tell her."

"Jack's a good guy," Amanda put in. "But if you're not comfortable with him, you should take him off the list."

"I'm not sure if I am or not." Olivia waved away the question of Jack. "I just know the ones I *am* comfortable with are out of the question."

"Why?"

Olivia looked at Rebecca. "What do you mean, why?"

Rebecca leaned forward. "The question isn't whether or not they're available to you, but whether or not you'd be comfortable with them, right?"

"Right," Olivia agreed slowly.

"Then, that's the criteria you need to use to evaluate the list." Rebecca shrugged. "The rest is up to Cade, isn't it?"

"I guess so. But you're my friend." She looked at Amanda. "Both of you. I wouldn't want you to think...well..."

"She doesn't want you to think she's lusting after your man," Sadie put in.

Olivia nodded when both Rebecca and Amanda turned to her. "What she said. I feel weird enough as it is."

Amanda frowned. "Why do you feel weird?"

Olivia shrugged, uncomfortable. "I always feel weird. CNC tends to freak people out."

"Hang on." Sam leaned forward. "I can't speak for anyone else, but I'm not freaked out."

Sadie raised her hand. "Me neither."

"I don't want to play with rape fantasies, but it doesn't bother me that you do," Amanda said, and Rebecca nodded.

"Really?" Olivia fiddled with the hem of her T-shirt. "You don't think I'm weird?"

"Hella weird," Sadie said, and Olivia blinked. "But, honey, we all are."

"I'm a male submissive," Sam pointed out. "You think I don't get shit about that from the toxic masculinity set?"

"I spent last weekend in a dog cage in my basement," Amanda put in. "I peed outside and ate out of a bowl."

"I dress up like a schoolgirl," Sadie said.

"I call my boyfriend 'Daddy'," Rebecca continued, and shrugged. "You think that's not weird, try saying it in Ikea."

Sadie's jaw dropped. "You didn't."

Rebecca nodded. "When we went to look at bookshelves for the office. He didn't like the ones I wanted, and I said "but, Daaaaaddeeeeee" and a woman the next aisle over tripped over a couch."

Sadie was laughing so hard she had to put her wine down.

"See?" Amanda spread her hands. "None of us qualify for 'normal'."

"You wouldn't be upset if I left James on the list?" she asked. "Or Nick?"

Rebecca shook her head. "Nick being on the list doesn't bother me at all. I like that you trust him. Whether or not he'd do it would be something we'd have to talk out between us."

"Same here," Amanda said. "That's a conversation for James and me to have. It's not your responsibility."

Sadie picked her glass back up. "I want to hear about some of these other fantasies."

"Well." Olivia set her empty glass aside and rubbed her hands on her thighs. "I have a home-invasion fantasy."

"Like, a masked intruder?" Amanda nibbled thoughtfully on a wedge of cheddar. "That could be hot."

"And an abduction fantasy, but that's tricky."

Rebecca's eyes were still the size of saucers. "How so?"

"Well, he'd have to kidnap me from someplace I wasn't expecting, like from the parking garage at the hospital or the store, and that's…"

"A felony?" Sadie put in.

"Right."

"He might know some people who could help him pull that off," Amanda pointed out, and everyone laughed.

"You seem really happy," Amanda said.

"I am. I am happy," Olivia realized, and smiled.

"Well." Sadie raised her glass, and the others followed suit. "Here's to being happy."

* * * *

Olivia walked into the kitchen at Cade's a few hours later, her abs sore from laughing all night. She'd had so much fun. No one was freaked out by her CNC kink — no one had referred to her as the 'rape fantasy girl', one of the less offensive nicknames she'd been given when she'd first come on the scene — and everyone had been so supportive of her relationship with Cade.

It was nice to have friends who didn't judge.

She set her purse on the counter, then picked up the folded piece of paper with her name on it in Cade's distinctive scrawl. She flipped open the note. *Helping a friend with something, be home late. Don't wait up. -C*

"Bummer," she murmured, and looked down at the cat, who'd wandered in to sit at her feet. "Looks like it's just you and me tonight, Phoebe."

Shaking off the disappointment she felt at his absence, she scooped up the cat. Phoebe set up a rumbling purr, appearing content to be held for now, and Olivia headed for the stairs. She'd treat herself to a soak in the tub, then break out one of the in-case-of-emergency books on her e-reader. If she tired herself out enough, maybe she'd be able to fall asleep without wishing Cade was beside her.

An hour and a half later she closed her e-reader app and yawned. She was curled up on the velvet chaise on the third floor, the room softly lit by the glow of her Tiffany lamp. Her tablet was backlit, so she didn't need the light to read, but the glass shade threw slashes of jewel-toned light on the creamy walls and gave the room a cozy, dreamy feel. It was pretty, and made her feel somehow less alone.

Her eyes had grown too heavy to read, so she set the tablet on the table and tugged the knitted throw up to her shoulders. She knew she should get up and go downstairs to sleep — there was a big comfortable bed with a fluffy duvet and million-thread-count sheets waiting for her, but the bed felt lonely without Cade, and it wouldn't be the first time she'd fallen asleep on the chaise. She smiled as her eyes drifted shut. Maybe, she though hazily as sleep crept in, he'd find her up there and wake her up in some deliciously perverted way and make her forget she was ever lonely.

She didn't know how long she'd been asleep when the noise jolted her awake. She sat up, disoriented, the throw falling away from her shoulders. There was something different, something not quite right about the room, and even though she was too fuzzy to make sense of it, a thin trickle of fear wound its way into her gut.

She rubbed her hands over her face, then tossed the throw aside, barely noticing when it slithered to the floor. She looked around the room, listening hard for a repeat of the noise that had woken her, but everything was quiet. She could hear the quiet tick of the small clock on the bookshelf, and the swishing sound that was the lilac bush planted outside brushing against the house. It had taken her the better part of a week to stop jumping every time she heard it, but she was so used to it now that even on windy nights it didn't register as alarming.

But something had. She tilted her head, ears straining and heart pounding, as she scanned the room for anomalies. The door was still open, the way she'd left it, so Cade would know she was there when he came home. The bookshelves were undisturbed, books and knickknacks where she'd left them. The prints and photos still hung on the walls, though she looked them over twice, since the muffled thump of a frame hitting the floor could absolutely have been the noise that woke her.

But everything was where it should be. The books, the knickknacks, the pictures on the wall, her tablet on the table by the lamp —

She froze. The lamp was off. She hadn't noticed at first, because the moonlight streaming in through the wide window was bright enough to light the room, but the glass shade was dark, its jewel tones muted.

The small trickle of unease turned to a flood.

She curled her hands into fists, wishing she still held the tablet. It would have made her feel better, even though it wouldn't make much of a weapon. But it was on the table next to the darkened lamp, too far away for her to reach quickly.

Her heart pounded so hard she could hear it, and a copper taste filled her mouth. She realized dimly she must have bitten her tongue, or her cheek, but she couldn't feel it. There was no room for pain, not with her brain screaming *get out, get out now* so loudly it drowned everything else out.

She stared at the door, open to the short run of stairs that led to the second floor. Her phone was still in the bathroom, perched on the edge of the sink where she could reach it from the tub, a lifeline too far away to be useful. If she could get there, and lock the door behind her, she'd be safe.

From what or whom, she didn't know. But she was suddenly terrifyingly certain that someone was in this room with her, and the longer she sat there trying to figure out what to do, the more danger she was in.

She didn't give herself time to think it through. One second she was sitting on the chaise, starting at the out of reach tablet, and the next she was running for the door. But she'd forgotten about the throw on the floor, and her bare toes got tangled in the knitting. She didn't fall, but she staggered, costing her precious seconds, and just as she reached the open door, hard hands yanked her back.

She opened her mouth to scream, but the sound was cut off when something slapped over her mouth. She clawed at it, the distinctive smell of leather filling her nostrils as hard fingers bit into her cheeks. Her hair was yanked back, hard and high, and pain screamed through her scalp. She automatically went to her toes to ease the pressure, practically dancing en pointe as he dragged her back into the room. She stopped dragging at the hand over her mouth and flung her hands back, fingers curled into claws, and aimed where she thought his head would be.

She met nothing but air, but there was harsh breathing in her right ear, so she adjusted course, aiming for the sound. She made contact, but instead of skin or hair met a thick, slick cloth. Her nails skidded across it harmlessly, and before she could try again, she was flung face down across the chaise.

She landed with a grunt, her knees hitting the floor as her torso fell across the long end of the chaise. It knocked the breath out of her, disorienting her for precious seconds, and before she could gather her wits, he was on top of her, hard thighs bracketing her hips, leaning into her to pin her down. She bucked, fighting for the space to get her hands out from between her chest and the chaise, but he just pressed down harder, his greater weight and size combining with her ungainly position to keep her in place.

"None of that, now," he said, the words guttural with a distinctly English lilt. His hand pressed into the middle of her back, holding her down when she bucked again.

Her cheeks hurt so much from the earlier press of his fingers she'd hadn't realized he wasn't holding her anymore. "What do you want?" she ground out, her face throbbing, fear a sharp taste in her mouth.

The quiet snick of a knife reached her ears a second before she saw the blade, inches away and gleaming in the moonlight, and she froze.

"I thought that was obvious, darling," he purred in a gravelly voice. "I want you."

She held herself still when he laid the flat of the knife against her cheek, the metal so cold against her heated skin that she shivered. Her heart was pounding, pumping blood through her body so fast and hard she could feel her pulse in her fingertips, in her toes, in the bruises forming on her face.

In the suddenly needy flesh between her thighs.

He dragged the knife down her cheek. It slid across her skin slowly, almost teasingly, and she fought not to flinch. In other circumstances, she might have described it as a gentle caress. But the blade was thin and sharp, and there was nothing gentle about this man.

"I have money," she managed, forcing the words out. He was pressing her so hard into the chaise that she couldn't draw an easy breath, and she knew she'd soon be too lightheaded to fight. "Cash, and my debit card. You can have it all."

He laughed softly, so close his breath danced over her face. His voice was like smoke over gravel, somehow soft and harsh at the same time. He fisted the hand planted between her shoulder blades, gathering the thick terrycloth of the robe she'd put on after her bath. It pulled across her arms and shoulders, digging in painfully, the tough fabric holding fast.

"Sorry, darling, but money's not what I'm after. Hold still now," he said, and lifted the knife from her cheek.

She didn't have the breath to gasp when the knife sliced through the robe, nor the wit to fight when he shifted his weight to pull her up and yank the ruined fabric from under her. When she was forced back down, his knee in her back to keep her pinned this time, she was naked.

"So soft," he said calmly, almost conversationally, Cade's familiar voice all but buried in the accent. The cold kiss of the blade slid over her shoulder, down her ribs and waist to her ass. "I'd hate to have to hurt you, beauty."

"Then let me go," she wheezed, wasting precious air.

"Not going to happen," he said with a chuckle, and reached underneath her.

She struggled as he yanked her arms out from under her, bucking and twisting as best she could, but he had her thoroughly pinned. He forced her arms to bend at the elbow and swiftly secured her wrists, and she recognized the feel and the weight of terrycloth. The belt from her robe, she realized, automatically flexing her wrists to test the strength of the tie.

"It's adorable that you're trying," he mused, and the mocking lilt had her seeing red. His knee lifted from her back, giving her one glorious moment of freedom, and she used it. Quick as a snake, she rolled to the side, bringing her legs up hard, and her knee connected solidly with his stomach. She felt a surge of grim triumph at his muffled *oof* and scrambled to her feet when he curled in on himself. But she must not have connected as solidly as she'd thought, because she only made it one running step before he was on her again.

He didn't cover her mouth this time, and the scream she let out when he yanked her back by her hair could've shattered glass. Then she was face down on the chase again with him full length on top of her, the rough denim of his jeans scraping her bare legs as his hot breath bathed the side of her face.

"Fucking cunt," he muttered, twisting his hand in her hair and yanking so hard tears sprang to her eyes. Her neck was arched so far back that her ears were all but touching her shoulder blades, but still, she couldn't see him. He was a shadow, a specter in a black hood and leather gloves, and she was at his mercy.

"Cunt," he said again. Spittle hit her temple, and she flinched. "I was going to take it easy on you. Pet you a bit, make you feel good. But that's done now, innit?"

He dragged her up by her hair, maneuvering her on the chaise so fast the room spun. Her scalp was screaming, the pain bringing hot tears to her eyes, and when she managed to blink them clear she was flat on her back with her head hanging over the edge. He was kneeling, thick, denim-clad thighs filling her vision, and all the spit in her mouth dried up when he reached for his zipper with one black-gloved hand.

"But you just couldn't be nice," he went on in that London-fog voice, the metallic whisper of the zipper underscoring the sneer. "So we'll do this the hard way."

Denim parted, peeling away under the pressure of the hard cock behind it. He was blocking out most of the moonlight, but she could see he was naked under the jeans, no underwear to slow him down. Then his cock was free, filling her vision, and incredibly, her pussy clenched in response.

He slapped his penis on her cheek and she tried to jerk away. But he still held her hair in one leather-clad fist, so all she got for her efforts was more pain. She closed her eyes, but nothing could block out the sensation of him hot and heavy against her cheek.

He dragged his cock over her face, up her cheek and across her forehead. It left a sticky trail over her skin, and she clenched her jaw so tight it throbbed.

He used his grip on her hair to force her head back even farther so she was almost upside down. "You're going to suck me off, darling," he said softly, slapping the broad head of his cock against her firmly closed lips. Little drops of pre-come spattered across her mouth and chin like hot embers. She tried to jerk away again, but he held her easily in place, his sinister chuckle ringing in her ears.

She froze when she felt the cool, keen edge of the blade against the curve of her breast. "And if I feel even a hint of those pearly whites…"

He let the threat hang in the air, the knife speaking for him, then he pushed the head of his cock against her mouth again. "Open."

She kept her mouth stubbornly closed. But the knife pressed harder, the point of it digging into her nipple, and with tears of pain and despair stinging her eyes, she parted her lips.

"Wider," he demanded, the knife moving slightly against her skin. There was a bright stab of pain, followed by a warm, wet trickle over her skin. He'd cut her, she realized with a dull sort of shock, and opened her mouth.

"There's a girl," he said with mocking approval, and unceremoniously shoved his cock to the back of her throat.

She immediately gagged, choking and coughing, her jaw flexing to try to expel the intruder. Then a loud crack rent the air and pain, sharp and sweet, exploded in her breast.

He'd slapped her, and fresh shock mingled with the pain as she continued to gag and gasp.

"Teeth, darling," he reminded her in a sing-song voice, and slapped her again, her breast bouncing under the blow. She struggled to open her jaw wider, tears streaming into her hair.

"There we go." He pulled back slightly, giving her a moment to pull in a ragged breath before shoving back in again. It was slightly easier this time, but she still gagged, spit flowing from her mouth in an embarrassing flood.

"Hitting you seems to make you work harder," he observed, a cackling sort of amusement in his tone. He slapped her other breast this time, the one he'd cut, and the pain was so intense she cried out. But his cock was lodged in her throat, so all that came out was a watery gurgle, her throat working around him, and he groaned.

"Fuck yah, more of that," he said, and slapped her again. He set up a rhythm—thrust in, slap a breast so her throat worked around the sensitive head of his cock, pull out, and repeat. Over and over, until tears and spit were running down her face and pain was a constant companion. Her chest throbbed lightly where he'd cut her, and she wondered vaguely if she was still bleeding. Her neck hurt from being held in the hard arch, her scalp sang from his fist in her hair. Her bound hands were pinned painfully under her, and her back ached from the uncomfortable angle.

Her body was a symphony of pain, and somehow the worst hurt of all was the deep, empty ache in her pussy. She was wet and throbbing, every nerve ending lit up and begging. If she'd been alone, her hand would've been tucked between her thighs, working the slick, needy flesh to orgasm. With her hands tied, the only thing she could do was rub her thighs together to get the friction she needed, but she didn't dare, lest he notice her arousal.

There was no way he wouldn't. She'd shaved in the bath, making sure the plump mound and soft lips were free of every last strand of hair. There was nothing to shield her, nothing to keep the evidence of her arousal from view. Her pussy would gleam wet in the moonlight, her thighs would be slick with it.

He would notice, then she'd be in real trouble.

Olivia's throat rippled around the head of his cock, and Cade gritted his teeth. It felt fucking amazing, and he was half tempted to forget the rest of the script and just fuck her throat until he came all over her face. He could make it work with the use-and-discard-themed scene he had planned, but it meant she wouldn't get to come.

In their long email discussions about the kinds of scenes she wanted, being forced to orgasm against her will came up over and over again. The fear turned her on, she'd told him, but she couldn't push through it to come on her own. She wanted to be forced to enjoy it while every instinct she had was screaming at her not to.

She coughed around his cock, a thick, ragged sound. He couldn't see her face, buried as it was under his balls, but he was watching everything else with a keen eye. Her legs were shifting restlessly, her thighs gleaming with wet, and even with only the moon for light he could see the lips of her pussy were swollen and slick. Every time he shoved his cock into her throat her hips jerked, and her thighs grew wetter.

Her nipples were bone hard, her breasts red from the repeated slaps of his leather-covered hands. He eyed the small cut on the inner curve of her right breast critically. It had stopped bleeding almost immediately, though each time he slapped that breast, it opened up and bled a bit more. It was little more than a deep scratch and would heal cleanly. He doubted it would even scar, but if it did, there would be only a thin, silvery line as a memento of the evening.

Her thighs shifted restlessly, reminding him that he still had work to do.

"What's this, then?" he drawled, forcing his voice into the English accent she'd confessed she loved, using the cover of the words to fold the knife closed and lay it aside. He kept one hand on her breast and ran the other down the center of her body, enjoying the convulsive ripple of her abdominal muscles as he forced his cock deeper into her throat. She let out a muffled whine as his fingertips grazed the top of her mound, and she slammed her thighs together.

His laugh was pure perverted delight. "I don't think so, darling," he admonished, and delivered a stinging slap to one thigh. "Open your fucking legs."

She stubbornly kept them closed, and he smacked her again, leaving a bright red handprint on her left thigh to match the one on the right. She jerked with the pain, another thin whine vibrating around his cock, but her legs remained firmly together.

"Easy way or the hard way," he reminded her, and slowly, carefully, pushed his cock deeper, not stopping until he felt her lips on his balls.

She panicked, her torso twisting on the chaise as she fought for freedom, for air. He silently counted off the seconds in his head. He couldn't stay there long, not without major risk, and he was just on the verge of pulling free when her thighs fell apart.

"Good girl," he said, masking his relief with a guttural laugh, and yanked his cock out of her mouth.

She coughed and retched, dragging in great gulps of air as he rose and circled the chaise to stand on the other side. He didn't bother to mask his delight when she picked her head up to glare at him through watery eyes, her face coated with tears and spit. The hood he wore would hide most of his expression, but he didn't mind if she saw him grinning.

"You bastard," she choked out, her voice strained and raw, and tried to kick him. He dodged her bare foot, laughing even though her heel had some dangerously close to his dangling balls. Not wanting to have to dodge another one had him reevaluating his plan.

He rolled her onto her belly, ignoring flailing legs and muttered curses, and parked himself on her ass again, facing her feet. "One minute, darling," he said cheerfully while she bucked and jerked under him. "I just need to take care of something, then we'll get on with it."

He retrieved the coil of rope he'd placed under the chaise that afternoon and looped it around her ankle. Working fast—she was really kicking, though she was beginning to tire—he bent her leg, bringing her heel as close to her butt as he could and quickly wound the rope around her upper thigh. It wasn't too tight or too restrictive, but it would keep her from racking him in the nuts.

Satisfied with the improvisation, he repeated it on the other leg, then stood up to admire his handiwork. "There, now, where was I? Oh yes. Here."

She jerked when he shoved a hand between her thighs. "Get your fucking hands off me."

"You must really like the hard way," he commented gleefully, and abandoned her pussy to beat her ass for a few minutes.

He peppered her butt with blows, making sure to spread them around. Her ass was glowing red within minutes, but he kept going. She was still spitting curses at him and struggling to get free, surprising him with her endurance. So he kept at it, watching her butt jiggle and jerk and the dark spot on the chaise under her get bigger.

"You fucking asshole," she finally groaned, and sagged against the chair, panting.

"Aw, darling," he crooned, and stroked a gentle hand over her bottom. He could feel the heat pumping off her skin through the leather gloves, and nearly stripped them off so he could feel that burning glow against his bare skin. But he wanted to stay in character, so he'd just have to settle for feeling the heat against his groin when he fucked her.

He checked his watch, calculating. Thanks to her energetic struggling, they'd been at this for a while now, and they both had to work in the morning. If he wanted to make sure she got good aftercare — and he did — he needed to hurry things along. Which suited him just fine — he'd been hard as a rock since he'd crept into the room, and he was more than ready to get on with it.

"I told you," he said, pushing her thighs apart and climbing between them. They were at the very edge of the chaise and he didn't have a lot of room, but he'd make it work. He leaned forward, planting one hand between her shoulder blades as much for balance as to hold her down, and took his cock in the other. "Easy way or the hard way."

She lifted her head and twisted around to peer at him over her shoulder. Her face was still wet, her eyes puffy from the tears, and her hair had come free of its loose braid to lie, ratted and matted, around her face. But her eyes were glittering bright with fear and excitement, and her lips curved in a defiant sneer. "Fuck you," she snarled, and he laughed.

"Oh no, darling." He grinned and pushed his cock against the hot, wet opening of her cunt. "Fuck you."

He drove into her, plowing through the tight, slick clench of her pussy until he was fully seated, his groin pressed against her burning ass. He held still, a task made all the harder by the soft rippling of her sheath. Part of it was adjustment—he was big, and though she was slick with arousal, it was still a tight fit. But she was also much closer to coming than he'd realized.

He pulled out slightly, making her gasp and twitch under him, then pushed back in, rolling his hips to grind against her ass. A cry escaped her lips before she choked it off, and he grinned.

"Why, darling," he drawled. "Are you enjoying yourself?"

She laughed, a short burst of sound that made her tighten around him for a brief, agonizing moment. "You're revolting," she said, the disdain clear even as she shuddered and pulsed around him.

"Revolting, am I?" He rolled against her ass, panting a bit as he held on. He was close too, close enough his balls were drawing up, his spine tingling. "What's that say about you, then, if I'm revolting, but you're about to come?"

"I'm not," she protested, her voice so thin it was barely a whisper. Need and lust mingled with despair, twisting her expression before she buried her face in the cushion.

"Oh, yeah, you are." He picked up the pace, slamming into her harder and faster, grinding her into the chaise. He shoved her legs farther apart, adjusting the angle to make sure her clit hit the chaise with every thrust. "Your pussy is sucking at my cock—excuse me, my revolting cock—like it's desperate."

He leaned closer, lifting his hand to her hair so he could yank her head up and back. He bit her neck, his teeth clamping down when she jerked against him, then whispered, "Are you desperate, luv?"

"I hate you."

"Manners," he tsked, dark joy blooming inside him at the pleading note in her voice. She was so close, he just needed to push her over the edge. "That's gratitude, for you. Here I am, working so hard to get you off, and you throw it back in my face."

"I don't want an orgasm from you."

"I don't think your pussy got that memo," he said, jerking her head back and slamming into her harder. "I can feel it squeezing me, trying to suck the come right out of me. Do you want my come, pretty girl? Is that what you want?"

"Don't you *dare* come inside me," she choked out, and he laughed.

"I'll come wherever the fuck I want," he said, taking the accent deeper. "And you can't do a thing about it."

"I hate you," she sobbed out.

"I know." He was fucking her quickly now, short, hard jabs as his own orgasm rushed forward. "Say it again. Scream it while that sweet pussy comes all over my revolting cock."

"I hate you!" she screamed, and shattered.

He let himself off the leash, hammering into her while she jerked and spasmed and cried underneath him. Her cunt had gone fist tight with her orgasm, and he forced his way through the clutching spasms, racing now for his own pleasure. It hit him like a brick to the back of the head, pleasure so bright and sharp his vision dimmed. He shouted in triumph as he filled her up, her cries music to his ears.

When he was empty, he yanked her head back again, grinding his still hard cock inside her. "There now, what do you say?"

She choked out a laugh, her eyes soft with pleasure as she tried to work up a sneer for him. "Fuck you."

"Nah, that's not it." He jammed himself against her ass, grinning when she winced. "Try again."

"You're revolting?"

He swallowed the laugh, lifting off her just enough to deliver a sharp, heavy slap to her already bruised ass. "One more try. What do you say when someone gives you an orgasm?"

She panted beneath him, watching him with liquid eyes. "I'm not saying 'thank you'."

"You've got no manners at all, do you?" he mused. He flexed his hips, sliding his still hard cock even deeper, and her eyes went wide with shock.

He grinned. It would take him a few minutes to be up for another round, but there was plenty to do while they waited.

Chapter Ten

The summer slid by in a haze of work, friends, and kinky sex. Cade finished up the job he was supervising in Oklahoma City and picked up another in Austin, so he was gone a few days a week. Though she missed him, and the house felt lonely without him, she liked the way he made up for lost time too much to complain.

They were working their way through the list of fantasies she'd given him that first week pretty quickly, and she loved every minute of the elaborate role-play scenarios he constructed for her. But she was surprised to find that it was the everyday stuff she loved most. Waking up with him inside her, being grabbed and bent over the table in the middle of dinner. She would fight or beg, depending on her mood or how he directed her — she was getting pretty good at discerning how he wanted the interaction to go from the tone of his voice, or a few well-placed words — and the result was that she walked around most days with a dreamy smile on her face.

Even the D/s aspect of their relationship was clicking right along. She'd chafed a bit at those daily updates at first, especially when he was in town. It felt unnecessary—why text or email when she could just tell him what was going on? But after a while it just became part of her routine, and she found she liked having the extra connection. He didn't always answer her messages, but she'd learned to tell him if she needed feedback, and he always gave it. And as time went on, she found herself texting him more, not less, filling him in on the minutia of her day, good, bad and everything in between.

His other D/s rules had taken some getting used to as well. He'd instituted a no-underwear rule, though he graciously allowed her to wear panties to work, and it hadn't bothered her as much as she'd thought it would. So far, the punishment for forgetting the rule was to have the offending pair of panties used as a gag for an impromptu scene, and she was tempted to 'forget' at least once a week.

Perhaps the most difficult of his rules to get used to had been the no-masturbating-without-asking rule. It wasn't that he said no a lot—in fact, it was rare for him to say no at all—but it was the asking itself that she found difficult. It was one thing to give him control over her body in a scene or during sex, but to give it to him when she was alone? Her instinctive resistance to the idea had shocked her, but curiously, he hadn't seemed surprised at all. If she didn't want to ask permission, he'd informed her in his calm, sure way, that was fine. But the rule was in place, and violations would be punished.

She hadn't thought it would be a big deal. After all, they were fucking almost every day, anyway—it wasn't like she was orgasm deprived. But then a two-day work trip to Austin had stretched to more than a week, and on day six with no end in sight, she'd broken down.

She'd asked him over text message early in the morning, before work. The mornings were the worst, because he often woke her with sex, and she'd gotten used to starting her day with him inside her. So she'd forced herself to type the words, feeling anxious and oddly humbled while she waited for his answer.

When the phone had jangled with an incoming call instead of the soft chime of her text alert, she'd answered almost hesitantly. "*Hello?*"

"*Good morning,*" he'd rumbled. "*Are you missing me, fofa?*"

He'd sounded so good, his voice heavy and rough with sleep and arousal. She'd closed her eyes and buried her face in his pillow — it still smelled like him — so she could pretend he was next to her.

"*Yes,*" she'd whispered, all her needy, desperate want poured into the word.

"*Then go ahead and make yourself come for me,*" he'd replied, and she had.

Somehow, getting herself off while he listened from his hotel bed several hundred miles away was the most intimate thing they'd done so far.

By the time she'd been living in his house for six weeks, she felt like she'd been there for years, and the thought of leaving made her unbelievably sad.

She said as much to her friends at lunch one day.

"Well, of course you don't want to leave," Rebecca told her, sympathy in her wide gray eyes. "Why would you?"

Olivia shrugged. "We've never talked about making it permanent, so I assumed at some point, I would."

"That man thinks the sun rises in your pussy," Sadie said around a mouthful of tuna melt.

Amanda shoved her glasses up and rolled her eyes. "Nice, Sadie."

"Am I wrong?" Sadie glanced around the table, nodding triumphantly at the chorus of murmured nos. "Trust me. He's not going to ask you to leave."

"Have you guys talked about the future at all?" Rebecca wanted to know.

"Not specifically," Olivia admitted. "But we make plans, you know? Like, one of his favorite bands is coming to town in November, and he already bought tickets for us to go together. And he wants to have a holiday party this year and asked if I'd help plan it. Stuff like that."

"Sounds to me like he's thinking long-term," Amanda said.

"Me, too," Olivia confessed, and abandoned her fries for the chocolate milkshake. "I just wish we could have a 'this is where we are, this is where we're going' conversation."

"Why can't you?"

Olivia glanced at Rebecca. "I'm scared of it."

"Been there," Rebecca murmured.

"Done that," Sadie finished.

"Things are going so well, you know? I don't want to rock the boat. And besides," Olivia said, and set her milkshake down with an annoyed snap. "He's the Dom, dammit. Isn't this his job?"

"Technically, yes," Amanda allowed. "But he's not a mind reader, and you're not a doormat. You need to be able to tell him what you want."

"I know, I know." Olivia looked around the table at her friends, grateful for their sympathy and understanding. "I just don't know what that is, exactly."

"Do you want to keep living with him?"

"Yes."

"Do you want to keep being his submissive?"

Olivia let out a slow breath. "Very much yes."

"Do you love him?" Sadie wanted to know.

"I do," Olivia replied, and pressed a hand to the butterflies that had taken flight in her belly. "Oh God, I think I might throw up."

"Yep," Rebecca said with a laugh. "That's love, all right."

Amanda reached over to pat Olivia's hand. "Just breathe, sweetie."

"Is he a good roommate?" Sadie wanted to know. "Like, does he leave dishes and clothes and whatever scattered around?"

Olivia shook her head. "He's neat and organized, almost more than me. My biggest complaint is that he keeps the house so damn cold I can almost see my breath."

"Nick does that, too," Rebecca put in. "Or he would, if I hadn't claimed control of the thermostat when I moved in."

"I should've done that." Olivia wrinkled her nose. "I've been wrapping myself up in this giant wool cardigan I've had since college so I don't freeze to death. And it doesn't bother him. He just walks around shirtless all the time."

"That doesn't sound like a hardship," Sadie quipped.

Olivia's lips twitched. "It's not. Especially since his favorite thing to wear around the house are these thin gray sweatpants—"

"Wait." Sadie raised her hand. "Are you saying...it's sweatpants season?"

Olivia nodded, a wide grin breaking over her face. "It's sweatpants season."

"Oh, please tell me you have a picture."

"Hang on." Olivia dug her phone out of her pocket, Sadie leaning forward eagerly as she flipped through her camera roll. She found the photo she wanted almost immediately, because she'd just taken it Sunday morning. Cade had gotten up early, and she'd come downstairs to find him in the kitchen, sipping a cup of coffee and reading the news on his tablet in nothing but a pair of gray sweats. She'd been struck silent for a moment, and when she'd gotten her voice back the first thing she'd said was *Can I take your picture?* He'd looked startled for a moment, then he'd given her that slow, sexy smile and risen from his stool to pose for her.

She looked at the photo for a moment, all golden skin and thick muscles and the gray sweats that rode low on his hips and left almost nothing to the imagination. Then she passed her phone to Sadie.

"Ho-lee shit," Sadie breathed, staring at the screen. When she finally lifted her head, there was admiration and a touch of jealousy in her eyes. "You lucky bitch."

"God, look at that smile." Amanda crowded up to Sadie to look at the screen. "And the bedhead. Damn."

"I know," Olivia sighed dreamily. "Right after I took that picture, I jumped him."

"I don't blame you," Amanda said reverently.

"Oh, the smile." Sadie's eyes narrowed on the screen. "Shit. I would've jumped him twice."

"I remember that smile," Rebecca said when she took the phone.

"And the dick," Sadie quipped, ducking when Rebecca reached across the table to swat at her head. "What? It's true."

"Don't make it weird," Rebecca admonished, handing the phone back to Olivia.

"You're the one who banged her man." Sadie grinned and ducked again.

"He wasn't mine when she banged him," Olivia pointed out with a laugh, and tucked her phone away. "Besides, her boyfriend's name is on my boyfriend's list of potential group sex partners. Talk about weird."

"You finalized your list, then?" Amanda asked.

"Oooh, who made the cut?" Sadie wanted to know.

"Nick and James," Olivia said, "but as previously stated, I'll cross them off if you're not okay with it."

"Not your responsibility, remember?" Amanda said.

"Just putting it out there."

"What did you decide about Jack?" Sadie asked.

"I left him on the list, which might have been a huge mistake. Sadists scare me."

"Yeah, but you like to be scared," Sadie pointed out, and grinned when Olivia wrinkled her nose. "When is this big group sex thing going to take place?"

"I have no idea. That part, thank God, isn't up to me. But he asked me to email him the list by tonight."

"Is he out of town again?"

"Yes."

"Oh my God, you look like your puppy died," Sadie said with a laugh.

"I miss him," Olivia said, and tried to wipe the sad pout off her face. "And my vibrator died this morning."

"Well, that's easily fixed." Sadie pulled out her wallet and dropped some money on the table. "Let's get out of here and go sex toy shopping."

"Cade's going to make me video chat him tonight if I buy a new vibrator," Olivia mused.

"Then we better find you a good one," Sadie decided. "Amanda? You in?"

Amanda laughed and pulled out her own wallet. "I don't have anything else to do. Rebecca?"

"Fine, but I have to call Nick first."

"No Doms allowed," Sadie admonished as Rebecca lifted her phone to her ear. "This is strictly a submissive shopping party."

Olivia looked at Amanda. "I was just going to order a replacement online."

"This will be faster," Amanda said as Rebecca tried to keep Sadie from grabbing her phone. "And more fun."

Olivia pulled out her own phone to text Cade a head's up. *Going vibrator shopping with Sadie. Be afraid.*

It took him ten seconds to send a reply, and she laughed when she saw the message.

Buy two, and be available for a video chat at eight o'clock so I can see what you bought.

"What?" Amanda asked, and Olivia turned the phone.

Amanda scanned the message and laughed. "Looks like you know him pretty well."

"Yeah." Olivia read the message again, just because she could. "I do."

"Just enjoy it, Olivia," Amanda said quietly as Rebecca and Sadie continued to bicker. "And when the time is right, tell him what you want. You won't get it if you don't ask for it."

Olivia nodded and tried to ignore the voice in her mind that whispered, *But sometimes the answer is no.*

* * * *

Two nights later, Cade was hanging out in James' basement for the monthly Tops & Doms meeting. He'd missed the last couple due to work, and was enjoying the opportunity to catch up with his friends. The gathering was informal, a chance for those who identified as Tops or Doms to get together and talk about their kinks, their relationships, and the unique challenges of both. There was a Bottoms & Submissives group as well that met at the same time, though in a different location. In fact, it was being held at his house tonight, with Olivia playing hostess.

He was glad to see her venturing out into the community a bit more. Though she still had that quiet core of reserve, she'd begun to socialize more freely, and seemed to have formed a close bond with several of the submissives in the scene. She often made plans with Rebecca, Amanda and Sadie when he was out of town, and he knew her texts on those days would be full of joy and laughter.

He liked seeing her happy.

"Cade, bid's to you," someone said, and he looked up to find the other players at the table waiting expectantly.

He looked down at his hand. Garbage. He tossed in his cards and stood. "I'm out."

He walked to the bar James had set up on the other side of the pool table and poured himself a soda, then glanced around the room. The three men he'd wanted to talk to tonight were all here, and had all agreed to hang back after the gathering was over to talk. He just had to get through the next few hours of socializing first, so he carried his drink back to the poker table for the next hand.

Three hours later, the last guest had been shown the door, and it was just Cade, Jack, Nick and James left in the basement. They gathered around the abandoned poker table, all eyes expectantly on Cade.

"First, thanks for being here," he began. "I know this is a big ask, and that you're all willing to consider it means a lot."

"Honored to be asked," Jack said, his hand wrapped around a lowball glass.

Nick nodded. "Same."

"Three for three," James put in. "Knowing you have that kind of trust in me as a Dom is a helluva compliment."

"It's well deserved," Cade replied, and it was. Each of the three men in front of him were, in his mind, the best of the best. Good, thoughtful, caring Doms who could help him bring Olivia's fantasy to life while helping to keep her safe.

"I've talked it over with Amanda," James went on seriously, and Cade knew what his answer was. "I'm sorry, but the CNC...I can't do it."

"Fair enough," Cade said agreeably. He didn't fault his friend for turning him down. It was a big ask, and James had to do what was right for him.

"I had a talk with Rebecca," Nick said, and Cade held his breath. Out of all the men present, Cade was the closest to Nick, and the one he wanted on board the most for this scene. "She wants me to clarify a few things, and she has some conditions, but as long as those are met, she's cool with it. I'm in."

Cade's breath left in a whoosh, and he felt almost giddy with relief. "Thank you."

"I'm in, too," Jack put in, tapping his finger against the glass he held. "Will three be enough?"

Cade nodded. "Three will work just fine. James, how do you feel about being involved in a hands-off capacity?"

"I could probably do hands off," James mused. "What do you have in mind?"

Cade leaned forward and explained, in great detail, his plan for the abduction, torture, and gang rape of his girlfriend.

Chapter Eleven

Olivia blinked at the light streaming through the windows. She'd slept later than usual, even for a Saturday, but she'd gone out with Sadie the night before. She'd intended only to meet her friend for a drink, but Sadie had wanted to go dancing, and four hours later she'd let herself into the house with sore thighs and abs that ached from laughing.

If she hadn't had to go to bed alone, it might have been a perfect evening. But Cade was still in Austin, and wasn't due back until Sunday morning, so she'd pulled one of his T-shirts out of the hamper and worn it to bed, just so she could smell him.

She closed her eyes and tried to go back to sleep — *hello, Saturday* — but gave up with a sigh only after a few moments. Her bladder knew she was awake and was demanding attention, so she slid out of bed and yawned her way into the bathroom. She managed to do her business with her eyes mostly closed, not wanting to wake up any more than she had to, and was already back in bed when she realized it wasn't empty.

"Morning," Cade rumbled when she squeaked in surprise, and skimmed his mouth over her cheek to nuzzle behind her ear.

"What are you doing here?" she gasped.

"I live here, remember?" he mumbled into her neck, and angled his head to nibble her collarbones.

"I thought you weren't coming in until tomorrow," she sighed, arching her neck to give him more room.

"Change in plans." He slid his tongue under the collar of her shirt, then pulled back to frown. "Why are you wearing my shirt?"

"I got cold," she explained, sliding closer and hooking one leg over his hip. He was naked, his skin warm and smooth against hers. This was a much nicer way to wake up, she thought dreamily, and did her best to burrow into him.

His hands slid under the hem of the T-shirt to stroke over her bare ass, his hands rough on her skin. "You don't feel cold to me."

"Because I'm wearing your shirt," she breathed. She lifted her head, seeking his mouth, and sighed when he gave it to her.

The kiss was slow and deep, a sleepy exploration that was no less devastating for its languidness. His kisses were usually marked by a desperation bordering on violence, as those were the kinds of games they enjoyed playing. Sometimes he was playful and teasing, and outside of a scene he was often tender. But this kiss was like being slowly devoured and absorbed, as though he wanted to suck out her very soul. It demanded her utter and complete surrender, and she gave it without hesitation.

He pushed her to her back, his larger body covering hers easily, and grasped her hands to pull them up over her head. He held them there in one big hand, using the other to pet and stroke while he continued to drink from her in those deep, drugging kisses. Her limbs felt heavy and her head light, all her worries and cares floating away as desire, thick and rich and wonderfully familiar, took over.

His mouth left hers, pressing gentle kisses over her cheeks, her chin, her closed eyelids. "Cade," she murmured, sighing again when his lips returned to brush over hers.

"I missed you," he whispered, and she smiled without opening her eyes. He shifted, his pelvis coming to rest against hers, and her legs, already parted to make room for him, widened in response.

"Did you miss me?" he asked, his voice hitching as he settled against her, his bare cock against her bare pussy. He was already hard and she was already wet, but he merely pressed against her, skin to skin, pulse to pulse.

So much it hurt, she wanted to say, but she couldn't seem to make her mouth form the words. She lifted her knees, bringing them high so they bracketed his ribcage, opening herself up even more.

A low rumble sounded deep in his chest, vibrating against her breasts, and she opened her eyes. He was staring down at her, his eyes liquid and dark, so deep she thought she might drown in them.

"Cade," she whispered, and lifted her hips. The slick slide of his cock against her pussy made her breath catch in her throat. "Please."

"Please, what?" he whispered, so close his nose brushed hers in a sweet caress.

"Fuck me."

"Oh, baby." His hips flexed, his cock pushing through the soft, wet folds of her cunt once again. "There's nothing I'd like more."

"Then do it," she said, a moan catching in her throat as his cock brushed her clit.

"I need you to do something for me first."

He thrust against her again, dragging his cock over her so slowly and thoroughly that her toes curled. "What?"

He nuzzled her mouth, flicking his tongue against her bottom lip. "Tell me where they are."

"Where what are?" she breathed, still lost in the sensation of his cock between her thighs and his warm, hard body pinning her to the mattress.

He stopped moving. "You know what," he said, his voice no longer soft and cajoling. It held an edge now, sharp with impatience and something else, something meaner. "I can't help you if you don't tell me where you hid them."

She opened her eyes, blinking to bring him into focus. A mixture of determination and resignation had turned his eyes to flint, one eyebrow raised in question. The first shimmer of awareness that something was going on slipped into her mind, and goosebumps broke out on her skin.

She tried to bring her arms down, but his hand tightened on her wrists, holding her in place. A glimmer of fear flickered to life inside her.

"What are you talking about? I didn't hide anything."

He shook his head, a cynical glint in his eye. "Last chance, babe," he said, and something in her cringed. He never called her babe. He called her fofa, and sometimes baby, but never babe. He said it now with a mocking kind of sneer, distorting the endearment so it held no hint of affection. It made the hair on her arms stand up, and her heart began to pound.

"I don't know what you're talking about," she said, keeping her voice steady with effort. She yanked her arms, twisting to try to escape his grip, but he just leaned his weight into her.

"Okay," he sighed, disappointed and resigned. "Just remember, you brought this on yourself."

"What—" she started to say, then jerked when three men in masks walked into the bedroom.

She recoiled, a scream caught in her throat. Part of her realized this was a game, a scene that Cade had obviously arranged. They'd talked about this particular fantasy at length, going over what she wanted and didn't want out of its enactment. She'd told him she didn't want to be able to tell who they were, and she couldn't.

They were dressed identically in black jeans, black boots, and long-sleeved black T-shirts. Black gloves, the kind her hairdresser wore while doing a color job, covered their hands. They wore black hoods, and their faces were covered by skeleton masks.

It was like having the grim reaper times three staring down at her, and her scream ripped loose.

Cade slapped a hand over her mouth, cutting off the sound almost immediately. She began to thrash under him, twisting her body and pulling at her arms to try to get free. He held her down easily, one hand on her wrists and the other over her mouth, his weight pushing her into the mattress. He spared her one exasperated, head-shaking glance, like she was disappointing him somehow, then turned to the men.

"You search the house?" he asked, and his voice was so cold she shivered.

The biggest of the three men nodded. "Nothing," he said, voice muffled by the mask. "She tell you?"

Cade shook his head while she struggled beneath him. "She's playing innocent."

One of the other men, leaner than the others, snorted. "Thought you were the great seducer, bruv," he said, his Cockney accent so thick she could barely understand him. "You losing your touch?"

"Fuck you," Cade said mildly. "You bring the stuff?"

"We got it," the big one answered with a nod. "How d'you wanna do this?"

"Tape," Cade said, and Big produced a roll of duct tape. He ripped off a length, handed the roll to Cockney, and stepped up to the bed.

Cade moved his hand off her mouth, but before she could let out so much as a squeak, Mr. Big slapped the tape on. He pressed down hard, gloved fingers biting into her cheeks, and helpless tears sprang to her eyes.

"Aw, she's crying," he said mockingly, a hint of southern drawl in his voice. "Should've given 'em up, bitch."

"Save it," Cade said shortly. "Get her hands. You two, grab a foot. And watch it, she's feisty."

Olivia bucked hard as all three men moved in. Big took her hands in one of his, planting the other in the center of her chest to hold her down as Cade levered himself off her. She struggled against his hold, muffled noises coming from behind her makeshift gag as she tried to break free.

"She thinks she's got a chance to get away," Cockney said with a low chuckle, and firm fingers closed around her right ankle. "It's cute."

The third man spoke for the first time, his accent pure Texas. "Don't underestimate her."

"Nah, she won't give us no trouble," Cockney said, and his fingers loosened on her ankle just enough. Olivia kicked out, and her foot hit something solid.

"Mother*fucker*," Cockney wheezed out in a very un-Cockney voice, and there was a hard thump.

"Jesus Christ." Cade stood at the side of the bed, hitching a pair of sweatpants over his hips. He regarded the man on the floor with amusement. "I told you to be careful."

"She tagged him in the balls," Tex said, choking on a laugh. He managed to grab her loose foot, pinning it to the bed with its mate. She jerked her legs, trying to kick out again, but he held fast. "Heel strike. Nice shot."

Big let out a low chuckle. He was bent over her slightly, one knee planted on the bed as he held her down. He was close enough she that could see the details of the mask, made of molded plastic or rubber, with eye holes and a small open space between the skeletal teeth. Both areas were covered with some kind of mesh or film to let in air and light while keeping the wearer hidden from view.

He cocked his head, twisting around so she was staring into the void where his eyes should be. "You got something to say, Princess?"

"Mmfph," she said from behind the gag, her *fuck you* smothered by the duct tape, and snapped her head up, aiming for his nose.

He reared back just in time, so all she got for her troubles was a sore neck. "Oh yeah, she's a live wire," he drawled, the words dripping with a sort of sinister glee that had fear rising like bile in her throat.

"Let's get her downstairs. I've got everything set up." Cade spared her a glance. "Better wrap her hands and feet so she doesn't kill one of you."

"Good idea," Big rumbled, and shifted so he straddled her, still holding her hands pinned to the bed. "You wanna get the tape so I don't get my face clawed off?"

Cade plucked the duct tape from the floor where Cockney had dropped it and peeled off a length, the thick sound ripping at her nerves. He deftly wrapped her wrists together, ignoring her muffled pleas. She might have been a mannequin for all the attention he paid her.

With her hands effectively bound, he moved to her feet, winding the tape around her shins just above her ankles. It tugged at her skin, pulling and pinching, adding a hint of pain to the fear.

Cade moved off the bed and passed the tape to Tex. "Here, hold on to this. I've got zip ties downstairs, but we may need more of it."

Zip ties? Oh, God.

Cade glanced at Big. "Can you handle her, or do you need help?"

"I've got her," Big assured him, then turned back to Olivia. She knew he was looking at her, but she couldn't see his eyes. It threw her off, disoriented her, and panic built once again as he lowered his face to within inches of hers.

"If you give me any trouble," he said, the soft, southern cadence of the words made hard by the ice in his tone, "I will fuck you up in ways you cannot even begin to comprehend. Starting with that sweet pussy I smell."

She shrank back into the pillow, trying to put as much distance between them as she could. He followed her down, filling her nostrils with the scent of plastic and a hint of spicy cologne. The combination turned her stomach, and she fought back a wave of nausea.

"I will hurt you in ways you can't imagine," he went on, so much menace in the softly spoken words that she lost her breath. "Then I'll do it some more. I will create holes in your body where there were none and I'll fuck them so hard you'll wish you were dead. One hint of a struggle from you on this trip down the stairs, and you're done for.

"Nod if you understand me," he said, and she obeyed without hesitation.

"That's a good little bitch," he mocked, and pushed off the bed. He bent, grabbing her wrists and pulling her up, then put his shoulder to her belly and hoisted her up.

"Ready," he said, and walked through the door.

Olivia tried not to touch him on the trip down the stairs, but he was walking fast, and she was bouncing around so much she felt motion sick. She didn't want to throw up with duct tape over her mouth, so she grabbed on to the waist of his jeans to steady herself.

He grunted when she made contact, but didn't slow down, so she assumed she wasn't going to be punished for it. She tried to pay attention to what they were saying, but she was too disoriented. She couldn't hear Cade—he must have walked out first—but the other two were behind her. Tex was giving Cockney shit for having let down his guard, and Cockney was grumbling about revenge.

She'd never been so scared in her life.

She tried to calm down, to regulate her breathing as they walked through the house. She couldn't see much with her hair hanging down, only Big's legs and the floor were visible to her. She heard the squeak of hinges, then they were going down another set of stairs, dimly lit and steep, and a faintly musty smell tickled her nose.

They were taking her to the basement.

"Over here," Cade called, and she twisted her head to try to find him.

"Keep your fucking head down," Cockney snarled, and rapped her on the back of the head hard enough to disorient her.

"Easy," Cade snapped. "You gonna be able to do this without getting personal?"

"The bitch racked me in the nuts," Cockney ground out, and she noted dimly that his accent was fading in and out. "It's fucking personal."

"Go back upstairs," Cade told him. "You can keep watch."

Olivia kept her head down, not wanting another hit, but she could see Cade's bare feet through the curtain of her hair, standing nearly toe to toe with another pair of black combat boots at the foot of the stairs.

"I want my shot," Cockney protested.

"You're not going to get it," Cade said in a voice like ice. "Go back upstairs, and keep fucking watch."

"Fine," Cockney muttered. "But if she doesn't spill her guts, I get to kill her."

"Yeah, yeah," Cade muttered. There was the stomp of heavy footsteps on the wooden stairs, then the basement door slammed.

"That guy is all hat and no cattle," Tex observed. "Where'd you find him?"

"It's not important—we'll deal with him later," Cade said, and his feet reappeared in Olivia's vision just as Big drew to a halt. "Put her on the bench."

"You're the boss," Big grunted, and heaved her off his shoulder.

For a moment it felt as though she was flying through the air, and her hands scraped against Big's shirt in an instinctive bid to stop herself. She managed to grab a fistful of fabric, and her forward motion pulled it free of his waistband. She caught a glimpse of tanned skin and dark ink before she lost her grip, then she was dropped on her butt so hard her teeth snapped together.

"She get you?" Cade wanted to know.

"Nah, I'm good." Big shoved her hair back, his gloved hand slick against her face, and gave her head a little push. "Trying to scratch me, huh? That seem like a good idea to you?"

She didn't say anything—what was the point?—but her mind was working overtime, trying to think of who she knew, who she'd left on the list Cade had given her, who had tattoos like that.

It had to be Jack.

She'd never seen him without a shirt, but she'd seen the ink on his forearm and hand a hundred times, thick black lines and splashes of color. They suited him, suited the vibe he gave off, edgy and polished at the same time. Jack was a sadist, and somehow the tattoos fit that as well, evidence of the close personal relationship he had with pain.

"Nothing to say now, bitch?" he jeered, and pulled a knife out of his boot. She shrank back, but one of them was already behind her, preventing her escape, and Big grabbed her wrists and yanking them forward.

"Hold her the fuck still, or I'll nick an artery and she'll bleed out before we get what we came for," he ordered, and hard hands grabbed her arms.

Cade's hands. She recognized the callouses on his palms and the faint scent of peppermint. She tried to look at his face, but he was behind her, straddling the bench she sat on, and her hair was in the way.

There was a whisper of steel as Big cut through the tape holding her wrists together. With Cade still holding her arms, Big ripped it off, dragging a muffled cry from her as it took skin and hair with it. It hurt enough to bring tears to her eyes, and when she could see again, Big was buckling leather cuffs around her wrists.

There was another slicing sound, and she looked down to see Tex on his knees next to her, freeing her feet. He ripped the tape off quickly, bringing a flood of fresh tears. She battled them back as soft leather was wrapped around her ankles.

"Ready?" Cade asked.

"Go," Big replied, and Cade looped his hands under her armpits and jerked her backward until her back hit what felt like the straight back of a dining room chair. She looked down and saw she was sitting on a weight bench, lightly padded and covered with black vinyl, the adjustable portion upright to force her back straight.

Big still held her wrists in his hands, but now he passed the left one to Cade. They raised her arms out and up, dual clicks echoing as they fastened the cuffs to something. She couldn't see much—her arms were stretched wide and slightly behind her, and the bench prevented her from turning around—but she guessed it was part of the workout equipment. She jerked her arms, testing. It held fast, not even wobbling, but her breasts swung under the T-shirt with the motion, and they noticed.

"Nice tits," Big commented, and she flinched away from the oily satisfaction in his voice. "Nice legs, too. Spread them."

She shook her head fiercely, her hair falling into her eyes again and obscuring her vision. There was a loud crack and pain seared her thigh. "I said fucking spread 'em."

She shook her head again, tears spilling from her eyes when he hit her again, the bright red handprint on her left thigh matching the one on her right. But she kept her legs resolutely closed, muscles quivering as she clenched them tight.

"We don't have time for this," Cade growled from beside her. "Grab the left."

Big wrapped long fingers around the top of her calf and dug into the back of her knee. Her leg jerked, an involuntary spasm that released the tension in her muscles, and he jerked her leg to the side as Cade did the same with the right.

"That's good, hold her there," Tex said, and working quickly with a length of rope, attached her ankle restraints to the base of the same structure her hands were secured to.

Big took a step back, and though she couldn't see his face, there was no mistaking his satisfaction when he said, "That's more like it."

Tex stepped back, shorter than Big by a few inches, and crossed his arms over his chest. Muscles bulged in his arms, straining the fabric covering them, a sight she would've appreciated under different circumstances.

"She's a looker, Cade," Tex remarked. "How come you always get the assignments with pussy perks?"

"Good clean livin'," Cade said, and the others laughed as he came to stand beside them, all three of them with their arms crossed, looking at Olivia as she stared back at them and tried not to panic.

Her arms were stretched so far out she could already feel the strain in her shoulders, and her legs were only marginally more comfortable. The oversized T-shirt was long enough to cover her to mid-thigh, even with her legs spread, and she sent up a prayer that they'd leave it in place. If they stripped her, she'd have no defenses at all—and they'd surely see how wet her pussy was.

"Aw, hell," Cade said suddenly, and every cell in Olivia's body went on high alert.

"What?" Tex asked.

"Should've stripped her before we got her secured," Cade said, jerking his chin at the Dropkick Murphys shirt she'd liberated from the hamper to wear to bed. "I really like that shirt."

"With this score, you can buy ten of them," Big told him. "Hell, you can hire the fuckin' band to play at your birthday."

Cade frowned and rested his hands on his hips. He was shirtless, the sweatpants riding low on his hipbones. His erection was clearly visible, the soft fabric leaving nothing to the imagination, and her pussy pulsed in response.

"I'm going to ask her one more time," Cade said, still frowning. "Maybe I won't have to cut it off."

Big shrugged. "It's your show."

"I'm going to be disappointed if she talks now," Tex drawled, his hand dropping to his crotch. Olivia's eyes went wide when he cupped the bulge in his jeans. "Things are just starting to get good."

"Relax," Cade drawled, and stepped forward. He crouched in front of Olivia, resting a hand between her thighs. She was sitting almost on the edge, only a few inches of black vinyl between her pussy and the end of the bench. His fingers brushed her thigh, twitching in a subtle stroke as he reached up with his other hand and ripped the duct tape from her mouth.

Her face stung like she'd been slapped, and she let out a howling scream. Her eyes burned with unshed tears, but she refused to let them fall. "Asshole," she managed, panting for air through her raw, tight throat.

He balled the duct tape in his fist and threw it to the side. "Sticks and stones," he said with a smirk. "Where are they, Olivia?"

She was breathing too fast and starting to hyperventilate. She forced herself to slow down, counting each breath until they were coming easier and the panicked, can't-get-air sensation had abated. "I still don't know...what you're talking about."

"The diamonds," Big said, and her gaze darted to him. He was tapping his hand on his thigh, clearly impatient. "Where the fuck are the diamonds?"

"Diamonds?" She looked back at Cade and shook her head. "I don't have any diamonds."

"Olivia, I don't think you understand just how badly this could go for you if you don't give us what we want. That guy?" He jerked a thumb behind him at Big, still tapping his thigh rhythmically. "He's not as patient as I am, and not nearly as nice. He's handy with a knife, doesn't mind blood, and your big 'help me, Daddy' eyes aren't going to work on him."

Olivia bit her tongue so hard to hold back the whimper that she tasted blood.

"They might work on him," Cade went on, jerking a thumb over his other shoulder at Tex. "But not in a good way."

"It's a good way for me," Tex called out cheerfully, and both Cade and Big chuckled.

"Good way for him," Cade amended, his commiserating grin fading as he turned back to Olivia. "But it won't be good for you. I like you, Olivia. I don't want to see you get hurt."

The little flare of hope in her chest died when his eyes hardened. "But if you don't tell me where you hid them, I can't help you."

She stared at him for a moment, her heart pounding in her ears as she struggled to gather her scattered thoughts. He was giving her an out, a way to safeword without safewording. If she made up a location — under the bed, in the cookie jar, the glove compartment of her car — the scene would end, Tex and Big would leave, and it would be just the two of them again.

They could go back to bed and pick up where they left off, with lazy sex and cozy snuggles. All of this would go away, like it had never been.

She looked at the two hooded men in front of her. The big one was probably Jack, though that was just a guess. She thought the other might be Nick, but she didn't know that for sure either. The only one she was sure of was Cade, crouched in front of her, waiting for an answer.

He'd done this for her. Recruited help, formulated a plan because she'd told him that was what she wanted, what she needed. He was trying to give it to her, and nothing had ever made her feel more cherished. More loved.

She sucked in a breath, looked him square in the eye and said, "I don't know where any diamonds are."

There was a flare of emotion in his eyes—triumph and satisfaction and pride—then it was gone, his gaze cold and hard once again as he pushed to his feet.

"All yours, man," he said, and Big stepped forward, the knife in his hand.

Cade did his best to appear relaxed and bored as Jack stepped forward and grabbed the neck of Olivia's T-shirt. He hadn't realized he'd be sacrificing his beloved Dropkick Murphys shirt for the cause, but he liked that Olivia had worn it to bed. She would've had to dig it out of the hamper—he'd worn it the day before he'd left for his trip to Austin—and the thought of her sleeping in his shirt warmed him from the inside out.

Maybe I can sew it, he thought as Jack's knife slid through the banded neck.

Olivia flinched away from the blade, and Cade had to remind himself to stay put. Jack was holding the shirt well away from her body, and the man knew what he was doing with a blade. He wouldn't nick her unless she moved unexpectedly, and she was too smart for that. He hoped.

He held his breath as the knife moved through the worn cotton like it was air, jerking through the hem with the slightest of hitches. Jack folded the blade and pocketed it, then flicked the two halves of the shirt aside.

"Pretty titties," Nick drawled beside him in a less-than-subtle twang. He'd asked his friends to try to disguise their voices somehow for this scene, knowing it would make it scarier for Olivia if she couldn't figure out who they were, and Nick was playing it up for all he was worth.

"Whatcha gonna do to them titties?" Nick called out.

"Whatever the fuck I want," Jack said, his own southern accent more subtle. He extended a hand and wiggled his gloved fingers. "Gimme my bag."

Cade kept a close eye on Olivia as Nick grabbed the duffel bag and carried it to Jack. Her nipples were hard and she was shivering, but he didn't think she was cold. Her pussy was wet—he could see it glistening from his position ten feet away—but she'd been aroused before the scene had started, so he wouldn't attribute that to her precarious position just yet.

Jack crouched and unzipped the bag, and her eyes narrowed as she watched him rummage through the contents. Cade had been involved in the selection of every single implement in that bag, and they'd planned the order of use meticulously, so he didn't have to look to know that Jack was pulling out nipple clamps, a small, flexible leather paddle, a trio of super sharp knives, and a handful of zip ties.

And—he remembered when her eyes went comically wide—a ball gag.

Jack held it up so the red rubber ball dangled from his fingers. "Cade, she a screamer?"

Cade pursed his lips as he pretended to think about it. "Yeah, but the basement is pretty well insulated. Noise shouldn't be a problem. Besides, if she's gagged, she can't tell us where the diamonds are." *Or use her safeword.*

"I want to hear her scream," Nick said, his voice appropriately menacing despite the ridiculous twang.

"I don't like distractions while I work," Jack growled. Which was a lie, of course. There was nothing a sadist liked more than hearing the fruits of his labor.

"We've got a goal," Cade reminded him.

"Fine." Jack tossed the gag aside with a flick of his wrist and stood. "But if I accidentally gut her, it ain't my fault."

Cade rolled his eyes, pleased with the way Olivia shrank back against his adjustable weight bench when Jack stepped forward, tapping the small paddle against his palm. The slap of leather hitting the glove was loud, almost as loud as the hitch in Olivia's breathing.

"All right, sugar, let's get started," Jack said, and Cade heard the delight under the guttural words.

Olivia heard it too, and lifted her chin in a show of bravado that was belied by the quiver in her lip. "Don't touch me."

"I don't think you quite understand the nature of your predicament, baby doll," Jack drawled. He leaned forward, pushing his face into hers, forcing her to turn her head to avoid contact. He grasped her chin and yanked her around so they were nose to nose.

Her eyes darted past Jack to skim over Nick, finally landing on Cade. He met the naked plea in their green-gold depths with a shrug. *Sorry, baby, out of my hands.*

"Look at me, bitch," Jack ground out, and Olivia's eyes jerked back to his. He lifted the paddle and skimmed it over her cheek, pressing harder when she flinched. "You're not in charge here."

He dropped his hand from her chin and leaned back. With the paddle still pressed to her cheek, he slapped the inside of her right breast with his open hand.

She let out a choked cry as her breast bounced, and he smacked the left breast before the echo of the first hit had fully faded. Twin marks bloomed almost immediately, bright red against her pale golden skin. Her nipples, already puckered tight in the cool basement air, drew even tighter, and Cade couldn't be sure, but he thought her pussy got just a little bit wetter.

"She marks up nice," Nick noted, and stepped forward. He stopped when he was a few feet away. "Do it again."

Jack obliged, slapping the outsides of her breasts this time so his handprints circled the soft globes.

"I like that," Nick said, and reached out to trail a gloved finger across the marks. "Nice and warm."

Jack grunted. "Get behind her and work her nipples for me, will you? I want to make sure these clamps aren't going to fall off."

"Sure thing, buddy," Nick said cheerfully, and ducked under her outstretched right arm to come up behind her.

"Don't," she gasped, jerking uselessly as Nick reached around her body. His big hands covered her breasts and squeezed, hard enough to have her flesh spilling through his fingers. Cade kept his eyes on her face, watching carefully as Nick began a harsh massage to bring more blood to the surface—and intensify sensation.

"Yessir, these are some pretty titties," Nick crooned softly. He shifted his grip, pinching her nipples between his fingers to twist and pull. She arched forward, trying to ease the tension, but he only laughed and pulled harder, stretching her nipples out so far that her breasts were elongated.

He held them there for a moment, then let them go abruptly so they bounced. Nick brought both hands down hard and fast, smack, smack, smack, then grabbed her nipples again—harder and redder now—and did it all over again.

When he was satisfied that they were hard enough to hold the clamps—and Olivia was fighting back tears—Nick cupped her breasts almost tenderly and offered them to Jack. "Here you go. Two nipples, no waiting."

Jack wasted no time, applying the clover clamps to the bases of her already swollen nipples and tugging to make sure they were on securely. Then he tugged again—Cade suspected for the joy of watching her arch and cry out. The diabolical nature of clover clamps meant the harder he pulled, the tighter they got, and when he finally let the chain connecting them fall to dangle between her breasts, Olivia was no longer holding back her tears.

Cade stepped forward and laid a hand on Jack's shoulder in a pre-arranged signal, and Jack immediately stepped to the side. Cade crouched down, waiting until Olivia's watery eyes focused on him.

Her breath shuddered out, her lips swollen and marked where she'd bitten them. She stared at him, fear and pain and lust swimming in her beautiful eyes, the silvery tracks of her tears painting her apple cheeks.

He kept his eyes locked on hers, though his peripheral vision was working overtime. Her breasts were heaving with every labored breath, the soft flesh quivering lightly. Her nipples were a bright cherry red in the clamps, and Jack's hand prints were still visible.

"What about those diamonds, babe?" he asked, forcing his voice to casual indifference. He hadn't intended to give her another out this fast, but Jack was quickly ramping up the intensity, and he needed to know she was handling it okay.

She lowered her head for a moment, and he saw her mouth working. Then she lifted her head and stared him dead in the eyes. "Fuck you," she snarled, and spat a glob of saliva and mucus right in his face.

He kept his expression blank as he slowly wiped his face clean with the back of his hand, his narrowed gaze clashing with her defiant one, then pushed to his feet and turned to face his friends. They'd both gone still as stone, and he imagined their faces under their masks would hold shock, surprise, and not a small amount of delight.

With his back to her, he let the grin spread over his face. "All yours, pal," he said to Jack, and stepped aside again.

Chapter Twelve

Olivia had stopped trying to guess what the man she'd dubbed Big was going to do an hour ago.

At least, it felt like an hour. In all reality, she had no idea how much time had passed since they'd strapped her to this weight bench. There were no windows in this corner of the basement, so she couldn't tell how bright it was outside, and as far as she knew, Cade didn't have a clock down here.

She couldn't tell by her captors, either. No one so much as glanced at a phone or a watch, though the one they'd made go upstairs to stand guard had poked his head in at some point, just to see if it was his turn yet, he'd said.

But it wasn't. It was still Big's turn, and he was an evil motherfucker.

"I should've kicked *you* in the balls," she gasped, and flinched when he struck her inner thigh with the zip ties.

"You think?" Big said casually, and hit her again.

Fucking zip ties, she thought as pain layered over pain, the sting of the most recent blow a sharp counterpoint to the deep throb of all the ones that had gone before. He held a bundle of about fifty of the little plastic strips in his hand, and when they'd first emerged from the Duffel O'Sadism at his feet, she'd been confused. She was already tied securely, arms and legs spread wide, so she'd assumed they were just for scare.

She'd been wrong.

He wielded them like a short, mean, cat-o-nine tails, and her body bore the marks. Thin red welts decorated her inner thighs, her belly, her breasts. The tender undersides of her arms had been treated to a round, before he'd moved on to the bottoms of her feet. They'd had to adjust her bindings for that, and each ankle was now tethered to a fifty-pound kettlebell. Ironically, they'd had to use some of the zip ties to link the ankle cuffs to the handle of the weights, to the irritation of the sadist known as Big.

He'd looked down at the diminished bundle in his hand, annoyed, then decided having less meant he'd have to do more.

More had apparently meant 'hit Olivia harder'.

He was working her inner thighs again now, stinging little slaps that were coming dangerously close to her pussy. The closer he got, the more agitated she got, until she was squirming uncontrollably, watching those plastic snakes climb her thigh. On the next slap, one strand caught the edge of her labia, and she reacted on pure instinct.

"No, no, no," she chanted, her breathing coming fast and hard. She tried to close her legs, but the kettlebells attached to her ankle cuffs wouldn't let her, and she tried to scoot backward, but she was already as far back as she could go. She couldn't stand up because her legs were stretched so far out she couldn't even plant her feet, and she couldn't bring her arms down because they were still tethered to the weight rack behind her.

There was no escape.

Big ignored her attempts to get away and struck the other thigh, again coming so close to the juncture of her thighs that one zip-tie caught the edge of her labia, and stars exploded in her head.

"Don't!" she cried, the plea ripped from her lips.

He paused, angling his head toward hers. She couldn't see his face, only the skull mask, impassive and unchanging. She didn't have a clue what was going through his mind, and that scared her the most.

"Please don't," she said again, her chest heaving. Pain was everywhere. In her nipples, where the clamps still held them tight and every breath bought fresh hurt. In the welts across her breasts, her arms, her thighs. In her shoulders and arms from being stretched out, in her hips from her legs being spread. There was so much of it that it was hard to concentrate on any one area, but she knew without a doubt that all of it would fade like yesterday's lip gloss if he slapped her pussy with those zip ties.

"Please don't, what?" Big asked. His voice was muffled by the mask, but the slow, southern drawl—and the threat—came through loud and clear. He dropped his hand to softly drag the fistful of plastic across her lower belly. The ends brushed over the top of her mound, a tickling tease, and she flinched.

"Please don't hit my pussy," she managed.

"Tell me what I want to know," he countered, and dragged the fistful of ties lower.

She bit her lip to hold back a cry of pleasure, and of despair. She was so wet, so swollen, that the faint scratch of plastic felt like a lightning bolt. The ties bumped over her clit, a dozen tiny flicks, and she was so sensitive that each one felt like a hammer blow. She wanted to come so badly she could taste it, but oh God, she didn't want him to hit her pussy with those instruments of torture.

If she told them where the nonexistent, totally made-up diamonds were, everything would stop. No zip-tie pussy whip, but also, no orgasm. Sure, she could give herself one, and no doubt Cade would jump her bones later, but the rest of the game would go away.

But if she didn't tell them where the not-real-diamonds were, the game would go on. And she would absolutely get her pussy whipped by zip ties.

"It's a simple question, princess," Big said, and wiggled the zip ties between her legs. A groan was ripped from her throat, and her hips rolled. God, that felt so good, and if he'd just keep petting her like that, this would be a no brainer.

But he wouldn't. She knew pain would be the price to pay for her orgasm, and it scared her.

But she couldn't say no to it, either.

She looked over at Cade, the only face she could see. He was a few feet away, leaning against the wall as he watched Big work her over. He hadn't moved, hadn't spoken since she'd spit in his face, but he hadn't taken his eyes off her once.

She wanted to see his eyes when she gave her answer. And she needed to be looking at him when she suffered the consequences.

"I don't know anything about any diamonds,"

Out of the corner of her eye she saw Big raise his hand, the white plastic ties gleaming for a moment in the harsh overhead light, then his hand fell and pain like she'd never known screamed through her body.

The first blast faded, leaving her tender, brutalized flesh throbbing, then he hit her again, and it was worse, because this time she knew what to expect. His hand fell a third time, not giving her any chance to recover after the last, and tears blurred her vision as she cried out.

But she didn't look away from Cade.

"How come he gets to have all the fun?" Tex complained.

Cade shrugged, his eyes never leaving Olivia's. "Tag in, if you want. I think her ass could use some attention."

"Now we're talking." Tex stepped forward, rubbing his gloved hands together. "Step aside, partner. I want at that ass."

"Figures you'd step in now I've got her warmed up good and proper," Big grumbled, but he obligingly stepped aside.

"You look a little worse for wear, there, darlin'," Tex said, unclipping her ankles from the kettlebells. She drew her legs together, wincing as her stiff muscles protested and her welted thighs flexed.

Tex chuckled at her obvious attempt to protect her battered pussy. "Don't you worry, sugar," he rumbled, and reached for her right wrist. "I'll give that pretty pussy plenty of recovery time."

"Not too much time," Cade said, and her gaze darted back to his. "We're running close."

Close to what? Olivia wondered, then hissed in discomfort when Tex freed her arms. Her shoulders were stiff and sore from being stretched out, and she tried to roll them to loosen them up. But then Tex was scooping her up, and when Big adjusted the bench to lie flat, put her back down on her hands and knees.

They reattached her wrist and ankles to the legs of the narrow bench, Big's hand on her back to hold her down while they worked. Then he sat down in front of her, powerful thighs straddling the bench. She tried to lean back, wanting as much distance as possible between them, then let out a short scream when he hooked a finger in the chain dangling from her nipple clamps and yanked.

"Get down here," he ordered, and pulled again. She went hard to her elbows, but he kept pulling, forcing her down so her face and shoulders rested on the bench. When her cheek was plastered to the vinyl, he released the tension on the chain and shifted his grip to the back of her neck.

"All ready for you, pal," Big announced.

"Thanks, buddy," Tex said cheerfully, and Olivia nearly jumped out of her skin when a broad hand stroked over her upturned rump.

"This is a nice ass," he said admiringly, squeezing both cheeks hard. "You had her here yet?"

"Once," Cade said, and her mind flashed on the morning when he'd surprised her in the kitchen, riding her down to the floor and fucking her ass with his hand over her mouth to muffle her screams. "It's good ass."

"Looks like it." He squeezed again, then brought his hands down simultaneously in a hard spank that echoed in the unfurnished space. "Before I fuck it, though, I'm gonna give it some color."

Olivia closed her eyes and tried to breathe, forcing her muscles to relax and her thoughts to clear. The fear was there, like an oily film over her mind, but Cade was watching. Cade would keep her safe.

It was her last thought before the paddle fell, then she couldn't think at all.

Cade wanted to get his hands on her so bad he could taste it. Nick had been working her ass for several minutes with his hands and the leather paddle, and both cheeks were glowing bright red. She'd gone from startled yelps to long, liquid moans every time he made contact, and instead of jerking forward to try to avoid the blows, her hips were now rolling back into them.

He glanced at Jack, straddling the bench in front of her. With her head down she wasn't able to see him, and he'd pushed back his mask. *Sub space,* he mouthed, and Cade nodded. It was time to head for the finale, then he'd need to see about getting some food and water into his girl.

He waved a hand to get Nick's attention, and gave him the wind-it-up signal. Nick nodded, and while he peppered Olivia's tenderized ass with a series of harsh blows, Cade strode over to crouch at Olivia's head.

He ran a finger over her lips, parted and damp, and her eyes fluttered open. Jack lowered his mask, though Cade doubted she could see him from this angle. Her eyes were wide and unfocused and sheened with tears, and if he didn't know any better, he'd say she looked high. He supposed she was—high on endorphins, the pain and pleasure making happy chemicals flood her brain. He knew they wouldn't have long before they faded, and he wanted to make sure to finish the scene when she was still enjoying them.

"You're not going to tell me where to find those diamonds, are you, babe?"

Her eyes shone as her lips curved in the faintest of smiles. "What diamonds?" she asked, her voice ragged and low.

"Then you're of no use to me," he said mildly, and watched her eyes flare in alarm as he turned to his co-conspirators. "We'll have to get rid of her."

"Hey, we deserve something for all this effort," Nick protested from behind her, right on cue.

"Good point." Cade pretended to consider that he watched a myriad of emotions stream across Olivia's face. Fear, gratitude, lust, affection. It was all there, laid bare for him. "What do you say, boys? Anal train for our troubles?"

"Works for me," Jack put in.

"That's what I'm talkin' about," Nick crowed, his accent twangier than ever. "But I want that pretty porn-star mouth first."

"That seems only fair," Cade said, and pushed to his feet. "Have at it."

Olivia's eyes were wide, tracking him as he stepped back, so she didn't notice Jack scooting back or Nick coming around the other side. Nick shoved a hand in her hair and dragged her up, turning her head toward him. He already had his cock out, and he shoved it in her mouth without ceremony.

"Fuck," Nick growled, the curse mingling with Olivia's gurgling cry. Nick pulled back, giving her a second to catch her breath, then shoved deep again. Cade had told them how to face-fuck her, how she liked to gag and choke and feel like she couldn't breathe, to be forced to take and hold it deep, and Nick was following his instructions to the letter. By the time he pulled back, his cock glistening with spit, Olivia had drool running down her chest and a puddle had formed on the bench in front of her.

"I can't wait anymore," Nick declared, and shoved her head towards Jack. "Hold her still while I tap that ass, will ya? Or better yet, let's spit roast her."

"I can get behind that plan." Jack jerked her head around to face him, bending down to drawl menacingly, "You bite my dick, princess, and I'll slit your throat and jerk off with your blood. You get me?"

Olivia nodded, her chest still heaving as she tried to catch her breath. "Yes."

"Yes, what?"

"Yes, sir."

"Good girl." With one hand still holding her hair, Jack began to work open the buttons on his jeans with the other.

"Hey, Cade, do I need to suit up for this?" Nick called. He'd moved to stand behind Olivia's upturned ass, a condom already on and lubed.

Cade grinned. They'd talked at length about how this would go, and condoms were non-negotiable. Olivia had agreed to forego them with him, and he didn't feel as though he could give that permission on her behalf. But he'd thought it might make for a nice mind fuck, and judging by Olivia's wide eyes, he'd been right.

"Nah," he called back, and watched her eyes flare with panic. "She likes it raw, don't you, babe?"

She shook her head frantically. "No, don't," she began, but she never got any further, because Jack shoved his cock into her mouth and cut off the flow of words.

"Shit, that's a sweet mouth," Jack ground out, pulling Olivia's head down so far her face disappeared into his open fly. She choked and coughed, her shoulders hunched. She sucked in air when he let her up, then choked again when he shoved her back down.

Then Nick pressed his cock to her asshole, and she froze.

"No, you don't, princess," Jack drawled. He fisted both hands in her hair and began moving her up and down on his cock, the *gluck, gluck, gluck* sounds of a sloppy throat fuck filling the room. He kept her moving as Nick penetrated her from behind, providing a distraction from the burning pressure, but she still tensed.

"Loosen the fuck up," Nick snarled, and landed a heavy smack on her already bruised ass. "There's a good slut. Damn, you weren't kidding about this ass. It is *prime*."

"Don't come in her," Jack ordered, keeping up the no-condom pretense. "I don't want to be swimming in your fucking jizz when it's my turn."

"Aw, come on." Nick started fucking her with long, slow strokes, his hands clamped on her hips. "It's just extra lube."

"I want friction," Jack replied, still working her mouth on his cock. She wasn't coughing as much now, having relaxed into the rhythm, but the little gurgle she made whenever he slipped into her throat was hot as hell.

"Fine," Nick said, his voice strained as his hips picked up speed. "I'll come all over this pretty ass. Make a Jackson Pollack painting of her."

Jack chuckled. "That's a picture I'd put on my wall."

"Fuck, yeah." Nick grunted, slapping into Olivia's ass so hard it sounded like he was beating her again. "Goddamn, I think she's coming."

Cade had already seen the signs of impending orgasm in the way her hands had fisted on the sides of the bench, in the set of her shoulders. He hadn't set out to make her orgasm part of this scene, figuring there was enough going on. But he wasn't surprised to see her belly flex and her thighs tighten, or to hear the long, liquid moan that spilled from her lips as she jerked and shuddered between his friends.

"Oh yeah, honey, squeeze me with that ass." Nick thrust hard, driving through the vise-like grip of her asshole. Her spasms had barely ended when he gave a hoarse shout, yanked himself free, stripped off the condom, and came all over her upturned ass in long, heavy spurts.

He stood there for a moment as though he was admiring his artwork, then tucked himself away and stepped back. "Thanks, sugar," he said, delivering a parting slap on the outside of her thigh. "Who's next?"

Cade jerked his head at Jack, who nodded and dragged Olivia's mouth off his dick. "Me," he announced and stepped to the rear of the bench.

Cade slid into Jack's place, his sweatpants already shoved down. Olivia's head had fallen forward when Jack had let her go, so he gathered her hair in his hands and tilted her face up.

She was a wreck. Her face was covered in spit and tears, her hair matted. Her mouth was swollen and red, her lower lip bruised from her own teeth and the face fucking. Her cheeks were flushed, her eyes glassy with pain and shining with joy.

She'd never looked more beautiful to him.

"Hey there, babe," he said, staying in character. He didn't have to grab his cock to aim it at her mouth — the damn thing was drawn to those pouty, puffy lips like a divining rod to water. He just pulled her down, letting the engorged tip bump into her chin, and she opened her mouth like the eager little victim she was.

Her lips slid down his shaft, wet and warm and tight, and he let out a hiss. "Fuck, so good," he ground out, pushing slowly deeper. Jack was behind her, lining up his latex-covered cock with her asshole, and Cade didn't want to be too far in her throat when he speared into her.

Go slow, he mouthed over Olivia's back, and Jack nodded.

She tensed when he made contact, her hands clenching so hard on the bench that her knuckles went white. She let out a muffled groan, her throat spasming around the head of Cade's cock as Jack pushed past her natural resistance to slide deep.

"Fuck, that's good asshole," Jack ground out. His cock was thicker than Nick's, and she would be swollen from the fucking she'd already received, so Cade imagined she was even tighter than usual.

"Right?" Nick chimed in. He'd disposed of the condom and pushed his mask back, then taken Cade's place against the wall. Now that Cade was in the middle of the scene, Nick would act as DM. "She got so fucking tight when she came, I thought she was going to rip my dick right off."

"Yeah?" Jack pulled back, added more lube, then slid forward again, a little easier this time. "I wanna feel it."

Nick was watching Olivia carefully for signs of distress, or the gesture that would serve as her safeword while she was unable to speak. "Good luck with that," he sneered, his derisive tone in direct contrast to his vigilance. "You'll be lucky if she stays conscious at this point."

"Oh, that's not going to be a problem," Jack drawled, and slapped her tender ass. "Will it, princess?"

She let out a muffled scream when he hit her again, his laughter all but drowning her out. "Fuck yeah, she tightened right up when I did that."

"Her throat, too," Cade told him. "Keep hitting her."

"My pleasure," Jack drawled.

He began peppering her ass with slaps, light ones that would nevertheless feel like lightning strikes on her already brutalized flesh. She jerked each time, letting out whines and pleas when Cade's cock wasn't in her throat, garbled groans when he was. They worked her in tandem, one thrusting in while the other pulled out, so she was never empty.

Jack shoved his mask back, his beard damp with sweat. "I wanna come, dammit."

"So? What's the problem?" Nick wanted to know, still vigilant.

"I want to feel her ass squeezing my cock," he ground out, his eyebrows raised in question as he looked at Cade. *That going to happen?*

Cade shrugged. He'd never subjected her to this level of pain before, so he wasn't sure how she'd react. "Try hitting her pussy," he suggested out loud.

Olivia couldn't speak with Cade's dick in her mouth, but they all clearly understood the long and desperate "Noooooo."

"Sounds like a yes to me," Cade chuckled, and jerked his chin at Jack. *Do it fast.*

Jack nodded his understanding and reached around Olivia's hip. She jerked wildly when he made contact.

"Fuck, y'all, she is soaked. Maybe we should've fucked her cunt."

Cade held Olivia's head steady when she tried to pull free. He let her come off his cock — well, mostly — but Nick and Jack had both pushed back their masks, and he didn't want her to see them. "You would've had to suit up for her pussy," he pointed out.

Jack sighed in mock resignation. "I guess I'll just have to make do with this." And he slapped her pussy.

She screamed, the sound unobstructed without Cade's cock in her mouth, and her head flew back. Cade had a moment of panic that she'd see Nick, and quickly gestured at him to lower his mask. But her eyes were closed, her mouth open as her body shuddered and jerked.

"Again," Cade said, and her eyes opened just as Jack obliged.

Her eyes were wide, pain and pleasure lighting them up so the gold flecks all but glowed. She stared at him as the orgasm tore through her, everything she was feeling there for him to see. Pain, pleasure, despair, triumph. It was all there, and she offered it up to him unhesitatingly.

It was his. *She* was his. All he had to do was take her.

Overcome with love and lust and a thousand other feelings he couldn't name, he kissed her, stroking his tongue into her mouth while she moaned and shook and came, wanting to be part of her pleasure so badly he almost forgot about his own.

She sagged a little against him as Jack shouted, and he knew his friend had pulled out to add his come to the canvas of her ass. Cade broke the kiss and scrambled up from the bench, nearly tripping in his haste, and caught the lube Nick tossed him one-handed. He coated his cock, then tossed the bottle aside and stepped around Olivia's upturned ass.

She was nearing the end of her rope — they'd have to call the scene in a few minutes, for her safety. But he wanted to finish it.

The sight of her red and bruised ass, covered with the come of two men, brought his need to boiling point, and he shoved his cock into her quivering asshole without ceremony.

"Shit, fuck, shit." She was still coming, faint little flutters battering his cock as her orgasm wound down. It wouldn't take long for him to come — he could already feel it gathering in his gut, in his balls. He knew she was probably done, that another orgasm was likely out of the question, but there was one thing that might push her over again.

Or it might be so painful that she'd pass out.

Either way, it had to be done.

Teeth gritted to hold off his orgasm, he caught Jack's eye. "Clamps," he ground out, the wit for subterfuge abandoning him, and Jack understood.

Dropping his mask back in place, because there was nothing to keep her from looking at him now, Jack once again straddled the bench in front of Olivia. She didn't seem to notice him at first, but when he reached underneath her for the clamps still on her nipples, she jerked away from him so hard that, if he hadn't been sitting on it, she might have toppled the bench.

Jack laughed, the delighted, evil chuckle of a sadist. "Brace yourself, princess," he advised. It was all the warning she got before he released the clamps.

She screamed with such agony that Cade would've stopped to check on her if they'd been alone. But Jack was there, keeping watch, and so was Nick, and before the scream had even faded away her asshole clamped down on him so tight it felt like a velvet vise, and he realized she was coming again after all.

He emptied himself into her, the pleasure nearly buckling his knees, and he barely had the presence of mind pull out and jerk the last of his come onto her battered ass while the rest of it dripped out of her red and swollen asshole. He staggered back, barely noticing when Nick came around and aimed a phone — Cade's phone, as previously agreed — at the sight.

Cade almost told him not to bother, that the image would live in his brain in vivid technicolor for as long as he drew breath. But he wanted to show it to Olivia, to let her see how beautiful and amazing she was.

Nick took a couple of photos, then handed the phone to Cade. "I don't think we're getting those diamonds, y'all."

"Guess not," Cade replied, his voice ragged and raw. He hitched up his sweats and stepped to the side, his eyes on Olivia.

"What do you want to do with her?" Jack asked and rose from the bench, following the script they'd laid out. The plan was for Cade to offer a derisive and snide 'It's been fun, see you around' and pretend to leave the basement with the others before releasing her.

He opened his mouth to say his line, but staring at his love, dazed and half-conscious on his workout bench, the come of his two friends painting her ass while his dripped out of her, they just wouldn't come.

"I'm going to keep her."

Chapter Thirteen

"Here, fofa. Take a drink."

Olivia forced her eyelids open and tried to focus. "Cade?"

"I'm here." A hand brushed against her cheek, and it felt so warm and solid she leaned into it. "I need you to drink, Olivia."

"Tired," she murmured, and nuzzled his hand. Her whole body hurt, but it was a dull, distant throb, like being poked through a layer of cotton wool. "Heavy. Why do I feel so heavy?"

"You need water, and food," he told her, and poked at her mouth with a plastic straw. "Come on, baby, take a sip for me."

"Okay," she sighed and opened her mouth. The second the water hit her tongue she realized she was parched, and tried to suck down as much as she could.

"Easy," he warned her, and pulled the straw away before she was ready. "Take it slow, okay? Can you eat something?"

"Food." She sat up a little straighter at the idea, and sniffed the air. "I smell…"

"Steak," he said, and sat next to her. They were in the living room, tucked in a corner of the sectional. She was wrapped in the comforter from his bed, snugly warm, while he still wore nothing but his sweatpants.

"Hi," she said softly, unable to keep the dreamy smile from her face. He looked so good, and she felt so good, and all she wanted to do was feel good with him for the rest of her life.

"Hi, yourself," he said, and smiled back. "How do you feel?"

"Um." She looked down, as though she could see through the layers of cotton and down to assess her body. "Sore."

He brushed her hair back, his touch gentle. "Where?"

"Everywhere, I think," she said, shifting a bit, and winced. "And my butt. Wow."

"Wait until you see it," he said. "But in the meantime…"

"Ooooh." Her eyes went wide at the plate in his hands. Slices of rare beef lay next to salted baby potatoes and grilled asparagus. The scent hit her nose again, and her stomach rumbled. "Who made that?"

"A concerned friend," he said mysteriously, and she would've questioned him further, but her stomach rumbled again, and she abandoned the interrogation as he picked up a slice of beef in his fingers. "Open up."

She obeyed, moaning with pleasure as the flavor hit her tongue. "More, please."

"Lie back," he instructed, and when she'd leaned back into the corner of the sofa, scooted up beside her.

She began to fight her way out of the comforter, intent on freeing her arms so she could take the plate, but he stopped her with a hand on her arm. "What?"

"Stay wrapped up," he told her, and picked up another slice of beef. "I'll feed you."

She opened her mouth automatically, like a baby bird, her eyes wide as she chewed. She hadn't quite gotten her equilibrium back from the scene, and she would normally attribute the fluttery, off-balance feeling to that. But he was feeding her, taking such sweet care of her after he'd debauched her so thoroughly, and she couldn't hold back the tears.

"Uh-oh," he said, and reached out to set the plate on the ottoman. "Talk to me, fofa."

She shook her head frantically, burrowing into his arms. "Nothing's wrong," she insisted on a wail. "I don't know why I'm crying."

"It was a heavy scene." He pressed a gentle kiss to her hair. It only made her cry harder. "Are you having trouble with anything specific?"

She shook her head, rubbing against his broad chest. "I don't think so. I'm just…"

"Overwhelmed?" he suggested.

"Yeah." She hiccupped. "I'm sorry."

"Nothing to be sorry for," he assured her, and tilted her head back with gentle hands. "Let's get some food into you, all right? That'll help."

She sniffed and nodded. "Okay."

"There's my girl," he murmured. When more tears spurted out of her eyes, he just cuddled her close and held a baby potato to her lips.

He fed her the whole plate, holding her tight all the while. He gave her the water to hold, reminding her to take periodic sips, and by the time both plate and glass were empty, she felt more like herself.

Well, herself in love. Because if there'd been any doubt in her mind before, it was gone now. She was head-over-heels, no-more-calls-we-have-a-winner, I-understand-love-songs-now, in love with Cade Hollis.

He tilted her face up to eye it critically, and she smiled at him. Maybe it was the post-scene buzz, but acknowledging her feelings for Cade wasn't sending her into the panic she would have expected. Instead, it felt...good. Right. Like a warm blanket on a chilly night, or an ice-cream cone on a blistering summer day.

Like it's what's supposed to happen.

"You look better," he decided.

"I feel better," she said, snuggling closer.

"I'm glad," he said, and there was something in his voice that had her peering up at him.

"What's wrong?"

"Nothing." He shook his head and smiled, but his eyes were troubled. "I'm still processing, too."

Top drop, she realized, and shifted the blanket so she could put her arms around him. "Anything you want to talk about?"

He tugged gently at a lock of her hair. "Mostly I just want to know that you're okay."

"I am." She tilted her head back to see his face. "I really am. The only thing I wasn't okay with was being fucked raw—"

"They were wearing condoms," he assured her hurriedly.

"I figured that out," she said with a smile. "Other than that, Big and Tex were great."

"Big and Tex?" His face creased in a grin.

"That's what I was calling them in my head," she said, then frowned. "Wait. What happened to Cockney?"

"You mean, the one you racked in the nuts?" His grin widened. "He stayed up here as security, just in case. And he made the steak."

"Did I kick him that hard?" she wondered.

"Yeah, you did. He was still walking funny when he left. But he was always going to be security."

"Oh." She bit her lip. "Are you going to tell me who they were?"

He cocked his head. "Do you want to know?"

"Honestly? Yes and no. I mean, I do want to know, but I don't want it to be weird the next time I see them."

"They won't make it weird."

"I'm not worried about *them*," she muttered, and he laughed.

"I'm happy to tell you if you want to know," he said, and dropped a kiss on her forehead. "In the meantime, let's go get a bath."

A bath sounded heavenly. He got up, and she started to scoot to the end of the sofa, intending to follow. But he bent and scooped her up, blankets and all, and carried her to the stairs.

"You know," she said, twining her arms around his neck. "I could really get used to this kind of Saturday."

"Me, too, fofa." He started up. "Me, too."

* * * *

By that evening, Olivia was feeling like herself again. They'd spent the day lazing around, watching movies and playing board games, and Cade had only left her side to bring her more food, or a thicker blanket, or his beloved University of Oklahoma sweatshirt, marvelously soft from a thousand washings. The strangely hollow feeling that always plagued her post-scene had almost completely disappeared.

Apart from a few lingering worries, it was a perfect day.

"Why are we fast-forwarding though half of this movie?" Cade asked as *Julie & Julia* zoomed past on the screen.

"Because I only like the Julia parts," she told him.

"Why didn't you pick a movie you like all of?"

"Because this one is my comfort watch."

"You mean, half of it is your comfort watch."

"Yeah." She leaned her head against his shoulder and watched him frown at the screen. She'd been debating with herself all day, and though part of her didn't want to know, she knew it would take up too much real estate in her brain if she didn't. "Jack was Big, wasn't he?"

He hit pause on the remote and looked down at her. "Do you want to know?"

"Yes. And no."

He turned so they could see each other clearly. "Can you explain that?"

She struggled to put her feelings into words. "I'd like to keep it as part of the scene, you know? Preserve the mystery. But I'm already pretty sure who all of them were, except Cockney, and I'm starting to get anxious about it. And not good anxious."

He stroked his knuckles across her cheek. "Yes, Jack was Big."

She nodded. "And Tex?"

"That was Nick."

"I thought so, but…"

"The accent?"

"Yes! It was so over the top, I just couldn't picture grumpy Nick getting so into it."

Cade laughed. "I think he enjoyed the departure from his usual Big Daddy persona."

"And how," she muttered, rubbing her sore backside, and smiled when he laughed again. "And Cockney?"

"That was James."

She stared at him in horror. "I kicked James in the balls?"

"Baby, you drilled him. He had to crawl into the bathroom to puke."

"Oh, my God." She buried her face in her hands, horrified. "I broke James. He didn't even get to participate in the scene!"

Cade was laughing as he pulled her hands away from her face. "He was never going to participate, not directly. He was here for security, in case anyone came by the house while we were in the basement, or if I needed an extra set of eyes on you."

She blinked. "He was never going to be in the scene?"

"He wasn't comfortable with the CNC, but he wanted to help out."

"Oh. That's so sweet," she said, then closed her eyes in despair. "And I kicked him in the balls."

"Trust you to go off script," he said, clearly amused, and she opened her eyes to glare at him.

"How am I supposed to ever look Amanda in the eye again? I broke her husband!"

"I promise, he'll survive to fuck another day."

"I feel terrible," she grumbled, burrowing her face into his neck as he gathered her in.

"You shouldn't. It worked perfectly with the scene, James is going to be just fine, and now the rest of us have something to razz him about."

"You promise?"

"I swear, we are absolutely going to give him shit about this for the rest of his life."

She pulled back to look at him, and he grinned at her unrepentantly. "I meant, do you promise he isn't broken?"

"I promise, he isn't broken."

"I still feel bad," she sighed.

"Aw," he murmured, and brushed a kiss over her cheek. "I should make you feel better."

She squirmed when he nibbled on her jaw. "Yeah?"

"Yeah." He kissed his way down her neck, his beard soft against her skin. He pushed aside the sweatshirt to get to her collarbone. "Much better."

"Mmm." Her eyes drifted closed as sensation swam in, warm and sweet and unrushed. "What did you have in mind?"

She felt his lips curve against her skin in a slow smile, and her breath hitched as she waited for his answer. But the slamming of the back door brought him up with a jerk.

"Filho, where are you?" a lightly accented voice boomed.

"Oh, God," he groaned, and dropped his head to her neck.

"Cade?" Olivia pushed at his shoulder, but he didn't budge. "Who is that?"

"I brought you some leftovers, since you couldn't be bothered to come to dinner. At least this way I know you won't starve."

"Is that your mother?" Olivia whispered, horrified.

"Yes," he sighed, and lifted his head. "Apparently she didn't believe me when I said I had plans tonight."

"You have to get off me." She planted both hands on his chest and shoved hard. He didn't budge. "Cade, she's going to come in here."

"I know." He sounded mournful, but there was a glimmer of mischief in his eyes. "Maybe if we're making out, she'll get the hint and go away."

"Your sister brought the baby with her, who you haven't seen in months. It would be nice for Lucas to remember he has an uncle."

"That does not sound like a woman who takes hints," Olivia told him, starting to panic. "Why haven't you seen your sister's baby?"

"He's six months old—he doesn't do anything yet. Besides, I saw him at the baptism in April."

She dodged when he tried to kiss her. "You cannot kiss me while your mother is here."

"Why not?" He slid a hand in her hair to hold her still. "She's seen me kiss people before."

"None of them were me," she managed to get out before he caught her mouth. She struggled, trying to worm free, but that only made him laugh. "Cade!"

"So, this is why you can't come to dinner with your family?"

Olivia froze in horror. "Oh, God."

"Show no fear," Cade whispered against her lips, clearly enjoying himself, and she would've smacked him if she'd been able to get her arms free.

Then Cade leaned back, and Olivia got her first look at his mother. She was small, barely over five feet, and dressed in a pair of stylish pink capri pants and a fitted white T-shirt. Her hair was golden-brown, like the lighter streaks in Cade's hair, and long enough for the braid she wore to drape over her shoulder. She wore little makeup save the lipstick that matched her pants, and had the same golden skin and coal-dark eyes as her son.

She stood next to the sofa, arms crossed and foot tapping in disapproval, and what did Cade do? He grinned. "Hi, Mamãe."

She rolled her eyes, clearly not impressed. "This is how you greet your mother?"

Cade rose and wrapped his arms around her, then pressed a kiss to each of her cheeks in turn. "Better?"

"Better," she allowed, then slapped a hand on his bare chest. "Why are you lazing around half dressed?"

"It's hot," he said, and she rolled her eyes again.

"It's freezing in here. Look, this poor girl is huddled under a blanket. Go turn the air conditioning down."

"No," he said easily. "If I leave, you'll start interrogating my girlfriend, and I like her too much to let you run her off."

"Girlfriend, is it?" She turned her dark gaze, speculative now, on Olivia, who barely resisted the urge to pull the blanket over her head. "If she's your girlfriend, why haven't I met her?"

"Because you're scary," he said bluntly.

"Sem vergonha," she said, shaking her head at him. "Introduce me before I disown you."

"Only if you promise to be nice," he said, and let out a laughing *oof* when she smacked him again. "Ouch. You've been working out."

"Filho," she said warningly, and Cade held up his hands in a gesture of surrender.

"Fine. Mom, this is Olivia, my girlfriend. Olivia, this is my mother, Mercedes Hollis. Please don't let her run you off."

Olivia, who'd been charmed by the byplay in spite of her embarrassment, suddenly found herself the center of attention. "Um. It's nice to meet you, Mrs. Hollis."

"Please, call me Mercedes. Mrs. Hollis is my mother-in-law, God rest her evil soul."

"She's been dead for ten years, Mãe."

"And I asked God to rest her soul, didn't I?" Mercedes sniffed, then turned the full force of her personality on Olivia. "So, Olivia. How long have you known my son?"

"About a year and a half," Olivia began, then blinked when Mercedes turned and whacked Cade on the back of the head.

"A year and a half you're dating this woman and I don't hear about it?"

"We've only been dating a couple of months," Olivia hastened to explain.

Mercedes scowled and smacked him again. "Two months you're dating and I don't hear about it?"

"She's got you there," Olivia pointed out, and bit her lip when he turned his scowl on her.

"I like her," Mercedes declared, and sat down next to Olivia before Cade could stop her. "What do you do for a living, Olivia?"

"I'm a physical therapist," she replied, and shot Cade a warning look when he sat down next to her. He ignored it and pulled her into his arms again.

"And how do you know my son?"

"Ah…" That one gave her pause. She couldn't very well say *we belong to the same BDSM club.*

"Mutual friends," Cade stepped in smoothly.

"I see," Mercedes murmured, eyes sharp, and Olivia resisted the urge to squirm. "And where is this relationship going?"

"It was going to the bedroom before you showed up," Cade said.

"Cade," Olivia groaned.

"What? It was."

"You're embarrassing her," Mercedes said, a glimmer of amusement in her eyes.

"Am I embarrassing you, fofa?" Cade asked cheekily.

"Yes," she hissed, and turned to apologize to his mother. But Mercedes was staring at her son in shock, and to Olivia's horror, tears glimmered in her eyes. She turned to Cade. *Do something,* she mouthed.

"Mom?"

"I'm fine." Mercedes gave them a brilliant smile and stood. "And I've overstayed my welcome. Olivia, it was lovely to meet you. I hope I'll see you again soon."

"It was nice to meet you, too." Confused, she glanced back at Cade, who merely patted her hand in reassurance and rose to his feet.

"I'll walk you out," he said to his mother, and wrapping an arm around her shoulders, walked with her into the kitchen.

Cade waited until they were in the kitchen to speak. "Tá tudo bem, Mãe?"

She took his face in her hands. "You called her 'fofa'."

"Yeah." He'd known she'd catch the significance of that. "That's who she is."

She sighed and gathered him in her arms. "She loves you?"

"She does." She hadn't said it yet, but he knew she did. He hoped she did.

"You'll marry her."

The non-question made him smile. "Yes, I'll marry her."

"In the church?" she said hopefully.

"Let's not get carried away," he said, and she eased back with a sigh.

"I'm happy for you." She kissed his cheeks. "Bring her to dinner soon, yes?"

He nodded. "Yes. Te amo, Mãe."

Her eyes filled again. "Te amo, meu filho," she said, and, blowing him a last kiss, slipped out of the door.

He walked back into the living room, his hands in the pockets of his sweats, unsurprised to find Olivia waiting with worried eyes. "She's fine," he said, before she could ask. "She just got a little emotional."

"Why?"

He sat beside her. "I think it's a mom thing," he said vaguely.

"Oh. She seemed nice."

"She is. She's also pushy, overbearing, and a pain in my ass."

"You love her," she said, her eyes softening.

"Yeah, I love her. She wants me to bring you over for dinner."

Her face lit with cautious joy. "Like, a family dinner?"

"You up for that?"

"Sure. I'd like to meet your family."

"Then you will," he said easily. "But in the meantime…"

"In the meantime?"

"I was in the middle of something before my mother interrupted."

"Oh, were you," she said, squealing when he pushed his face into her neck to nuzzle. "Remind me what that was again? I forgot."

"With pleasure," he murmured, and set about reminding her very thoroughly indeed.

Chapter Fourteen

"And the next day, he took me to dinner at his mother's."

"Whoa. Meeting the mom, big step." Sadie pulled a chair from the stack and set it against the wall. "How'd that go?"

"It was nice. A little nerve-wracking," Olivia admitted. She set a chair next to Sadie's and reached for another. "I don't have a lot of experience with big families, and I was still feeling sort of fragile from the scene the day before."

"I'll bet." Sadie frowned at the circle of chairs they were creating. "What kind of a demo is this again?"

"Wax play. Why?"

"Just wondering if we need to leave a splash zone."

Olivia pursed her lips. "No splash zone, but Simon said he'd be opening it up for audience participation, so we should leave some extra room."

"Maybe one more row then," Sadie decided, and grabbed another chair. "Anyway, you were fragile?"

Olivia placed her chair to start the next row. "I always am after a big scene."

"Me, too. It takes me a while to recalibrate."

"But dinner was nice — excellent food — and no one got in my face too badly. Oh, and get this. His whole family calls him 'Cage'."

"Really? Why?"

"Apparently, in Portuguese the d and e together make a soft g sound, like in judge or fudge. And while his mom and dad had agreed to name him Cade, his mom hadn't seen how it was spelled until it was on the birth certificate. The first time they took him to Brazil to visit her family, everyone called him 'Cage', and it became a sort of running family joke."

"That's funny. Does he hate it?"

"He doesn't seem to. Why?"

"Bummer. It would've been fun to torture him with that."

"You have a death wish."

"Nah, just a maim wish. Besides, he's not going to do anything to me. He's too besotted with you. Which reminds me, have you told him you love him yet?"

Olivia winced. "No."

"Why not?"

Olivia placed the last chair and straightened with a sigh. "Is it bad that I'm scared?"

"God, no." Sadie let her chair drop with a thump. "Being scared of scary shit is smart, and what's scarier than love?"

"Tell me about it."

"However," Sadie went on, nudging her last chair into place, "if you let being scared keep you from getting something you want, that might be bad."

"Dammit."

Sadie slung an arm around her. "You're a brave bitch, remember."

"I hate being brave." Feeling sulky, Olivia dropped her head to Sadie's shoulder.

"Girl, same," Sadie said with feeling, and Olivia laughed. "Look. Do you trust him?"

With my life. "Yes."

"Does he make you feel safe?"

Olivia thought of the way he took care of her after every scene, the way he made sure her car had a full tank of gas and she got enough protein in her diet. The way he touched her constantly, in small, seemingly insignificant ways. The way he carried her to bed when she fell asleep during a movie, and the firm way he corrected her when she forgot one of the rules.

"Yeah," she finally said, her voice tight with emotion. "He does."

"Then my guess is, you can trust him with this."

Olivia lifted her head to smile at her friend. "You know, you're pretty wise for a brat."

"I have hidden depths," Sadie drawled. "Don't tell anyone."

"I'm a vault," Olivia vowed, laughing as they turned to walk out of the demo space. Then she froze. "Oh, shit."

"What?" Sadie looked up at the man standing in the doorway. "Oh, shit. Is that Kyle?"

"Yeah." Olivia wiped her palms on her thighs and wished she hadn't chosen this outfit. The corset paired with nothing but panties and stockings made her feel pretty and sexy, but at the moment, she wished she'd chosen armor instead of lingerie. "I haven't seen him since we broke up."

"You don't have to talk to him," Sadie said, keeping her voice low as Kyle looked around the room. "Where's Cade?"

"He's helping James set up the fucking machine. Oh, hell, he's coming over here. Don't leave, okay?"

"Not going anywhere," Sadie promised, and grabbed Olivia's hand.

She held on to it, grateful for the support, as Kyle approached.

He looked good, she noted absently. The summer tan went well with his blond hair, and he looked fit in his leathers. He stopped a few feet in front of her and nodded. "Olivia."

She raised her chin. "Kyle."

"Kyle," Sadie drawled, and smirked when his gaze flickered to her. "What brought you crawling out of your hole?"

His eyes narrowed. "Good to see you, too, Sadie."

Her response to that was a derisive snort, and Olivia had to bite her lip to keep from smiling.

After a tense, five-second staring contest, Kyle looked back at her. "Do you have a minute to talk?"

"No, she doesn't," Sadie interjected with a saccharine smile. "So if that's all—"

"Excuse me, do you mind?" Kyle said, his tone so condescending that Olivia squeezed Sadie's hand tighter to prevent her from killing him.

"Yes, as a matter of fact I do mind," Sadie said, acid dripping from her words. Her eyes had narrowed to slits. "You were a colossal dick to my friend, and she doesn't owe you anything."

Kyle gave up all pretense of politeness and glared at Sadie, his jaw clenched so hard Olivia could hear his teeth grind. "Someone," he said softly, "needs to put you in your place, little girl."

Sadie, who despite her slutty Catholic-school uniform could never be mistaken for a little girl, stepped forward without hesitation. "Give it your best shot, dickhead."

"What's going on, here?" a new voice said, and Olivia sagged with relief as Jack stepped forward. He was wearing the reflective vest that indicated he was on dungeon monitor duty, and Olivia had never been so glad to see anyone in her life.

"Sir." She straightened a little as he turned his dark eyes on her, an automatic response to the authority he wore like a cloak. "Sadie and I were setting up for the wax play demonstration. We were just finishing when Kyle came in."

Jack's gaze flicked to Kyle, still locked in a staring match with Sadie. It might have been funny if not for the distinct possibility of bloodshed. "Why does Sadie look like she wants to rip his throat out?"

"Because I do," Sadie declared.

"He said he wanted to talk to me, but I asked Sadie not to leave me alone with him. And she kind of…"

"Went bulldog," Jack finished, a twinkle lighting his gaze before he turned to look at Sadie. "Sadie, step back."

"No," Sadie said, never taking her eyes off Kyle.

"Sadie," Jack snapped, his voice like a whip, and the warning in it sent alarm skittering up Olivia's spine.

Sadie turned her glare on Jack. "She asked me not to leave her alone. I'm not leaving."

"I'm not asking you to," Jack told her evenly. "But you're scaring Olivia. Take a step back."

Sadie stepped back, her gaze going from feral to concerned when she turned to Olivia. "Sorry, sweetie. You okay?"

"I'm okay," Olivia assured her, breathing a quiet sigh of relief when Sadie grabbed her hand again. "Thanks."

"Anytime," Sadie said with a meaningful look at Kyle.

Jack cleared his throat. It was hard to tell with the thick beard, but he looked like he was trying not to smile. "Kyle. We haven't seen you around in a while."

Kyle gave Jack a short nod. "Jack."

"Come on out to the bar. I'll buy you a drink."

"I appreciate that," Kyle said, flicking his gaze back to Olivia. "But I need to talk to Liv."

"That's not going to happen, Kyle," Jack told him, his gaze steady.

"Please," Kyle said, still watching her. "Five minutes."

"Listen, motherfucker—" Sadie began, but stopped when Olivia squeezed her hand.

"I'll talk to you," she told him. "But I want Cade here."

Kyle hesitated, then nodded. "All right."

Olivia turned to Jack, who was frowning at her. "Do you know where he is?"

"He's still helping James." His gaze flicked to Sadie. "I don't suppose you'd be willing to go get him."

"I don't suppose."

"Fine." He slipped a small two-way radio from his belt. Cell phones were banned in the play space, but all the DMs carried a radio in case they needed to call for help. He stepped away and spoke quietly into it, keeping one eye on Sadie. When the radio crackled, he slipped it onto his belt and came back. "Kody will find him and let him know."

"Thank you."

"No problem."

The four of them fell silent as they waited. It wasn't exactly an awkward silence, but it wasn't comfortable either. Sadie was glaring at Kyle, Kyle was looking at Olivia, and Jack was looking at Sadie with exasperation tinged with amusement.

"Sadie, stop glaring at Kyle," he said.

"I'll stop glaring at him when he stops glaring at Olivia," Sadie countered.

"I'm not glaring at her. I'm looking at her," Kyle muttered, his face twisted with annoyance.

"Stop looking at her, then."

"Where do you want me to look?" Kyle snapped.

"Up your ass," Sadie shot back. "Maybe you'll find your brains up there."

"Jesus," Jack muttered, and this time Olivia was sure he was smiling. "Sadie, give it a rest."

"It's fine," Olivia told her, trying not to laugh, and sighed with relief when Cade came through the door.

"Thank God," Jack said, and took a step back. "Sadie."

"What? I told you, I'm not leaving."

"It's okay," Olivia whispered as Cade reached them. "I'm covered."

"I'll step back," Sadie said grudgingly, and gave Olivia's hand a squeeze before letting go. "But I'm staying in the room."

Jack nodded at Cade. "We'll be over here," he said, and dragged a reluctant Sadie away to stand with him against the far wall.

Cade laid a hand on Olivia's shoulder, warm on her bare skin. "Fofa?"

"I'm okay," she assured him.

He nodded, then turned to Kyle. "Kyle."

"Cade."

"You know better than to pull something like this."

"I just want to talk to her, Cade." His gaze flicked to her neck, where a thin strip of leather circled her throat. "I didn't know you'd collared her. I would've come to you first if I had."

Cade nodded, and Olivia relaxed slightly. It was a serious breach of protocol to approach a collared submissive without the permission of their Dominant, and if Kyle had circumvented Cade on purpose, it would've added a layer of insult to an already tense situation. That he hadn't seemed aware of their relationship was strange—she'd been wearing his collar at parties for months now, and their relationship wasn't a secret. But Kyle hadn't been around since they'd broken up, so it was possible he'd been out of the loop.

Cade stroked her shoulder, drawing her attention. "It's up to you."

She glanced at Kyle, waiting patiently, then back at Cade. "I can talk to him."

"Do you want me to stay with you?"

"I'd really like to talk to her in private," Kyle began.

Cade's head whipped around to stare at him, and Kyle shut his mouth with a snap. "This will happen however Olivia wants it to, or not at all."

Kyle hesitated slightly, then nodded.

Olivia laid a hand on Cade's arm, wanting to soothe. The hard glitter in his eyes told her his temper was on a short leash. "Can you wait with Jack and Sadie?"

"If that's what you want." He pinned Kyle with a look. "You have five minutes, and you keep your hands to yourself."

Kyle nodded. "Understood. Thank you."

Cade squeezed her shoulder in reassurance, then crossed the room to stand next to Jack.

Olivia looked up at Kyle, her fingers linked together in front of her as she waited for him to speak. The flash of anxiety that she'd felt when he'd walked into the room had faded, leaving her feeling strangely...fine. Her belly wasn't in knots. Her shoulders were relaxed. She felt calm and at ease, partly because had three sentries standing guard, ready to spring into action if she appeared at all distressed. But mostly, it was because whatever Kyle had to say, however he felt, it wasn't her problem anymore.

"It's good to see you," Kyle finally said.

It was on the tip of her tongue to return the sentiment, but she wouldn't have meant it, so she merely nodded.

"You're doing okay?" he asked, and jerked his head toward the wall where her sentries waited. "With Cade, I mean?"

She gave in to the urge to look over at him. He was leaning back against the wall, his arms crossed over his chest and a scowl on his face as he watched them. He caught her eye and gave her a slow wink, then went back to scowling at Kyle.

"I'm great," she said honestly, and looked back at Kyle. "Is that what you wanted to know?"

"Partly," he admitted, and a faint flush stained his cheeks. "I never checked up on you after you left. I'm sorry about that."

"Just about that?" she said drily, was surprised to see his blush deepen.

"I'm sorry about all of it," he said. "The contract, the ultimatum. I hope you can forgive me."

She already had, she realized, but that didn't mean she was going to let him off the hook. "Then tell me why."

He nodded. "That's fair. Can we sit?"

She fought back impatience and nodded, leading the way to the rows of chairs. She sat and waited for him to take the chair across the aisle. A good three feet separated them, which suited her fine. He leaned forward, his elbows on his knees, and looked down at the floor. "I couldn't do it."

She frowned, confused. "Couldn't do what?"

"Consensual non-consent. Some of it was fun," he went on hurriedly, as though he wanted to get the words out as fast as possible. "The somnophilia, for one. I liked that. And the lighter scenes. But the role-play you wanted to do, I just…I just couldn't."

Olivia felt like she'd been hit with a shovel. "But you told me…"

"I know." He lifted a hand to rub at the back of his neck, guilt and remorse twisting his face. "I did want to try it, in the beginning. I wasn't lying to you."

He shrugged when she just stared at him. "I didn't think it would give me so much trouble. I mean, it was consensual. I knew that. But it felt real, and I didn't like myself when I was doing that kind of stuff."

"Oh," she said softly, her heart twisting in realization. "Oh, Kyle."

"I just couldn't be that guy," he went on, staring at the floor now. "I wanted to be, for you. I thought I could."

So many things made sense now. "And the contract?"

He gave her a sheepish smile. "Last ditch effort. I thought it would help. Like if we had that level of D/s, if I had control over everything, it would make me feel better about..."

He trailed off, then shrugged again. "I think I knew it wouldn't work, you know? We're just not compatible that way. We have enough other kinks in common that I could ignore it for a while, and I liked you so much. I really wanted it to work."

"I did, too." She said it automatically, though now that the words were out, she didn't know if they were true. "Kyle, why didn't you just tell me?"

"I couldn't. Hell, I could barely admit it to myself. You know what I felt when I came back that night and you were gone?"

She shook her head.

"Relief. A little guilt, a little disappointment. But mostly relief, because I didn't have to pretend anymore."

She blew out a shaky breath. "I'm so sorry you felt like you had to be someone you're not."

"It's not your fault."

"I wish you'd talked to me about it," she began, then stopped when he shook his head.

"We just would've broken up sooner." He sat up straight, his gaze locked on hers. "You need something I can't give you. Believe me, I tried."

"I know," she said softly. "I know you did."

"Anyway. I just wanted to say I'm sorry."

"Thank you. I appreciate it."

He glanced back at Cade, still leaning against the wall, watchful. "Are you happy with Cade?"

She hesitated, not wanting to add to the sadness lurking in his eyes. But he'd asked, and he deserved the truth. "Yes, I am."

He nodded. "He likes those dark places, huh?"

"Yeah."

"He keeps you safe?"

"He does." *Safe and warm and loved.* "It's working really well."

"I'm glad," he said, and it sounded as though he meant it. "You deserve someone who can give you everything you need."

"So do you, Kyle."

His smile was sad. "I'm trying to figure out what that is."

"I hope you do."

"Thanks. Well." He stood up. "My five minutes are about up, I guess."

"Yeah." She stood as well and took a step toward him. "Thank you."

"For what?"

"For braving the gauntlet over there," she said, nodding at the trio across the room.

"Yeah, well." He lowered his voice. "Don't repeat it, but I'm more scared of Sadie than either Cade or Jack."

She laughed, a little surprised that she could. "I won't tell."

"Thanks." He paused for a second, then bent down and kissed her cheek. "Be well, Liv."

"You too," she said softly.

He gave her a last, sad smile, then turned, nodded at Cade, and walked out.

"Good riddance," Sadie said clearly, hurrying ahead of Jack and Cade to reach Olivia first. "Are you all right?"

Olivia nodded, blinking back tears. "I'm fine. He just wanted to apologize."

"Oh." That knocked a little of the wind out of Sadie's sails, though she still scowled at the empty doorway.

"You're upset," Cade said, his hand warm and solid on her back.

"A little sad," she offered with a tremulous smile. "Thanks for being here, all of you."

Jack nodded and wrapped his hand around Sadie's arm. "We'll leave you alone."

"Hey," Sadie protested as he began to pull her toward the door, scrambling to keep up with his long strides. "You know, I can walk without help."

"But can you stay out of trouble without help?" Jack asked drily, and towed her out through the door on her gasp of outrage.

"They should just do it already," Olivia observed.

"Jack and Sadie?" Cade laughed. "That's a match made in hell."

"Stranger things," she murmured, and laid her head on his chest with a sigh.

"Talk to me, fofa." His arms came around her, his warmth seeping into her chilled skin. "Do I need to kick Kyle's ass?"

"No." She gave a half laugh that sounded more like a sob. "He apologized, like I said. Explained why he did...what he did."

"Do you want to talk about it?"

"Not now. Later, maybe."

He was rubbing her arms, trying to chafe some warmth back into her. "Do you want to go home?"

She shook her head. "No, but I don't think I want to play tonight."

"That's fine," he assured her.

"I'm tired," she said, her voice thick with tears and confusion. She didn't know why she felt so unbearably sad.

"Tell me what you need, amor," he murmured against her temple.

"This." She wrapped her arms around his waist and closed her eyes. "Just this."

* * * *

Later, curled against him in the dark, she told him what Kyle had said. "Was it my fault?"

"No." Cade's arms tightened around her. "No, it wasn't. Kyle is the one who made the choice to lie, to pretend. He put you both in a terrible position."

"Maybe I expected too much from him." She lay with her cheek on his chest, staring at the moon though the window. "He told me when we met, he'd never done CNC before."

"But he told you he was interested, and willing," he reminded her. "You had no reason to doubt him."

"But I should've seen it." She twisted to look up at him in the dark. "Shouldn't I have noticed that something wasn't right?"

"I don't know," he told her. "I wasn't there."

"I should have," she said again, and turned back to the window. "But I wanted the consensual non-consent so badly, and I just...couldn't see past that."

"I'm sorry, fofa."

"Me, too," she said softly, staring at the moon. "Me, too."

Chapter Fifteen

"Hang on." Sadie set down her drink. "Let me see if I've got this straight. You think that you were so focused on how much you wanted the CNC stuff that you didn't see the problems with your relationship with Kyle before it was too late?"

Olivia nodded. "Right."

"And now you think you're doing the same thing with Cade?"

"Kind of."

Sadie picked up her drink, drained it, and signaled the waitress for another. "I'm going to need more alcohol for this."

"Look, obviously Kyle wasn't the right guy for me."

"Obviously."

"But I thought he was," Olivia continued. "Because he fit all the criteria. We had chemistry, our kinks were compatible—"

"Except they weren't," Sadie pointed out. "Because he lied."

"But I didn't know that." Olivia frowned. "Where was I?"

"I can honestly say I have no idea." Sadie nodded her thanks to the waitress as she delivered another shot. "Have a drink. Maybe it'll come to you."

Olivia eyed the shot of tequila in front of her, then shook her head. "No, thanks."

"Okay, then," Sadie said, and knocked it back. "Shit, that burns. You were saying?"

Olivia rubbed her head. "I don't remember."

"Can I tell you what I think is going on?"

"Yes, please."

"You're in love with Cade, and it's freaking you out—perfectly normal reaction, by the way, everyone does it."

"Gee, thanks."

"And your jerk of an ex showing up with his half-assed apology is also messing with you."

"I really think it was a sincere apology," Olivia protested.

"It's still messing with you. These are two separate freak-outs, but you've smooshed them together in your mind, so now they're all tangled up together, and you think they're linked."

"But they are linked."

Sadie sighed. "Don't make me do another shot."

"Look, all I'm saying is, I thought I was in love with Kyle, because I'd convinced myself we were a perfect fit. And that turned out to be a big lie."

"Because he was a big liar," Sadie pointed out. "Do you think Cade is lying to you about liking CNC?"

Olivia frowned. "No."

"Do you think he's lying about liking you?"

"No. But what if I've convinced myself that he fits me when he doesn't?"

"You've lost me again."

"I mean, he definitely fits me kink-wise," Olivia went on, trying to gather her scrambled thoughts. It made sense in her head, but it was coming out all wrong. "But what if he doesn't fit me otherwise, but I've convinced myself he does, because I don't want to lose the kink?"

Sadie stared at her. "That's the most absurd thing I've ever heard in my entire life."

Olivia sighed. "I'm not explaining this well."

"Oh, you've explained it perfectly. But it's codswallop."

Olivia blinked. "Codswallop?"

"My gran was English. Her favorite saying. It means 'bullshit'."

"I know what it means," Olivia muttered.

"Good, because that's what it is. You guys fit so well it's almost nauseating. You're just scared."

"I don't think I'm *just* scared," Olivia began, but Sadie ignored her.

"Which, as I said, is a perfectly normal reaction. Everyone does it. But that's no excuse for being a ninny."

"Another word from Gran?"

"No, that's my Aunt Muriel. Look, you love Cade, right?"

"I think so," Olivia said, hedging her bets.

"And he loves you," Sadie went on. "Your kinks are compatible, and that's no small thing considering what they are."

"Which is my point," Olivia said triumphantly.

"Your point is crap. I'm telling you, as an outside observer, you and Cade fit. You fit so well you might as well be a jigsaw puzzle. In fact, you're a perfect fit, and it's both inspiring and depressing."

"Why depressing?"

"Because it's, Liv," Sadie said, deadly serious for once. "It's so fucking rare to find someone who genuinely likes you and loves you and wants to fuck you up in the exact way you like to be fucked up. Most of us will never get that. We'll have to settle for just a little less. And that's okay, that's life, but I swear to God if you fuck this up by pigeon-pecking it to death, I'm going to be so fucking pissed at you."

"I don't want to fuck it up," Olivia said, suddenly near tears. "I'm just scared it's not real."

Sadie reached across the table for her hand. "I know. I know you are. I'm sorry, I shouldn't have yelled."

"It's okay." Olivia sniffed. "But maybe, no more shots."

"Deal." Sadie leaned back. "You know, I'm not the person you should be having this conversation with."

"I know. That scares me, too."

"That, I understand perfectly. Wanna get some pie? This place has pretty good desserts."

"I want cake," Olivia decided. "Chocolate cake. If I'm going to eat my feelings, it should be chocolate."

"You're a wise woman," Sadie said, and signaled for the waitress.

* * * *

Olivia knocked on the door and waited. He was expecting her—the doorman had called up—but she was nervous. She'd intended to drive home after dropping Sadie off, but instead she'd found herself searching for a parking space downtown. And now she was standing in the hallway of this fancy-pants building in the Old Post Office District, waiting for Jack to open the door.

Then it swung open and there he was, in a pair of black cotton pajama pants and nothing else, his hair down around his shoulders and all his tattoos on display.

"Hi," she said, and gave a weak little wave. "Sorry to drop by unannounced."

"Is everything okay?" he asked, his dark eyes flicking over her as though he was searching for an injury, or possibly a clue as to why she was darkening his doorstep at almost midnight on a Tuesday.

"Oh, sure," she said, feeling silly. "I was having drinks with Sadie, and I—"

He stepped out and looked down the empty hall. "Where is she?"

"I took her home. It's just me."

"Come on in." He stepped back, opening the door wider, and she hurried past him before she lost her nerve.

The door shut behind her and she moved farther into the room, taking in the high ceilings and exposed duct work, the gleaming wood and the floor-to-ceiling windows that put the city on display like art. "Wow, some place."

"Thanks. Have a seat."

"Okay." She chose the leather couch that looked like it probably cost more than her car.

He moved to a bar cart by the enormous window and pulled the stopper from a crystal decanter. "Want a drink?"

"Oh, no thank you. I'm driving, so…no thank you."

"Is Cade still in Austin?"

"Until Friday. I'm not interrupting anything, am I?" she asked, suddenly horrified that she might have barged in on him when he wasn't alone.

He shot her an inscrutable look and poured two fingers into a glass. "If you were interrupting something, I'd have told the doorman to send you away."

"Right. Of course. Sorry." She clutched her purse in her lap and tried to remember why she'd thought this was a good idea.

"What's going on, Olivia?"

"I'm trying to figure something out," she blurted, before she lost her nerve. "And I could really use an unbiased opinion."

He sat down in the chair across from her, drink in hand. "What do you need an opinion about?"

She hesitated, wondering how much to tell him. Sadie had seemed to get bogged down in the details, and while she always thought it was best to have as much information as possible, maybe he didn't need the full story. Especially since she didn't seem to be capable of articulating it clearly.

"Olivia?" he prompted.

"Sorry." She took a deep breath. "Did Cade tell you what Kyle said to me the other night at the club?"

"No."

"Well, damn. That would've made this easier."

"Is Kyle bothering you?" Jack asked, sitting up a little straighter.

"No, nothing like that," she hurried to reassure him, but he didn't relax, and she sighed. "Okay, here's the thing. Kyle basically apologized for the way things ended between us, and he told me why he did what he did with the slave contract and the ultimatum."

Jack waited a beat. "Do you want to share that reason with me?"

He was awfully polite for a sadist. "Because he was trying to give me what I wanted, even though he didn't want to."

Jack frowned. "Wait, are you talking about the consensual non-consent play?"

"Yes. When we first met, he said he was interested, and he was, but when we started to get into it, he realized it wasn't for him."

"And he didn't tell you that."

"No," she said, relieved that he understood. "He said he kept trying, but it wasn't getting better, and he thought if we had a Master/slave relationship—"

"It would help," Jack finished with a frown. "Damn."

"Looking back, I can see the signs were there. And I ignored them, because I wanted it to work so badly. I forced him into a role that didn't fit him."

"Kyle put himself there," Jack corrected. "This wouldn't have happened if he'd been honest with himself—and with you. It's his mistake, Olivia, not yours."

"But what if I'm doing it again?"

"What do you mean?"

"I mean with Cade." He was looking at her so intently she dropped her gaze to the rug. It was abstract, splashes of color on a white background, and far easier to look at than his stern expression. "What if I'm forcing him into a role he doesn't want?"

"Do you really think he's faking how much he enjoys doing consensual non-consent play with you?"

Jack asked, and the words were full of such unbridled amusement that she looked up.

"No," she said, taken aback by the grin on his face. She'd never seen him smile like that before, and good gravy. He was hot when he was brooding, but he was incendiary when he smiled. "That's not what I meant."

"What did you mean then?" He tilted his head, amusement still curling his lips.

"I meant, what if…" She struggled to find the words, growing frustrated when they didn't come. "I'm in love with him," she finally blurted out.

"I know," he said simply, and she blinked.

"You do?"

"It's obvious, Olivia," he said, not unkindly, and chuckled when she fell back against her chair with a wail. "What's the problem, sugar? Do you not want to love him?"

"It's not that," she muttered, staring at the exposed duct work in his ceiling. It was painted black, which suited her mood.

"Do you not want him to love you?"

"I do want that," she said, and sat up. "That's the problem."

He spread his hands. "You've lost me."

"What if I'm putting him in the boyfriend role just like I was putting Kyle in the Dom role, and it doesn't fit him?"

He stared at her for a full five seconds, then said, "That's the most asinine thing I've ever heard."

"Now you sound like Sadie," she muttered.

"Normally that would make me reevaluate, but I'll make an exception." He set his drink on a low table next to his chair. "Cade doesn't do anything he doesn't want to do, Olivia."

"Yes, but—"

"If all he'd wanted from you was a rape fantasy, he didn't have to move you into his house. Which, I'll remind you, he did before play was on the table."

"I know—"

"I don't think you do," he said, and she closed her mouth with a snap. "I don't think you have any idea how that man feels about you."

"Why are you mad?" she asked before she could think better of it.

He stared at her for a moment, his expression shadowed and unreadable. Then he sighed. "Do you know how rare what you two have is?"

He sounded like Sadie again, and she almost told him that just to see him twitch, but he was talking again before she had the chance.

"It's a kind of magic," he was saying, "a gift that most of us just don't get."

"What if it's not a gift to him?" she managed.

He shook his head, his hard eyes softening. "He's the only one that can answer that question, isn't he?"

"I was afraid you were going to say that."

"You're a smart, capable woman, Olivia," he said, and she blinked at him in surprise. "He'd be a fool not to love you."

"Um. Thanks?"

"You're welcome."

"I should go," she began.

He rose to his feet. "Stay there while I get a shirt and some shoes, and I'll walk you down."

"Oh, you don't have to," she said, then froze when he pinned her with a glare.

"Yes, I do. Where's your car?"

"Um. In a lot down the street."

He shook his head like he was dealing with a small, disobedient child, and pointed a finger at her. "Stay there. I'll drive you to it, then follow you home."

"Jack, I appreciate it, but…"

"If you leave this room before I get back, I will paddle you raw."

"You already did that," she reminded him.

That grin appeared on his face again and she went a little breathless. "You won't like it this time," he promised, and headed for the stairs.

She sat back in the chair and watched him go, thinking that black pajama pants season was almost as good as sweatpants season.

Chapter Sixteen

Cade let himself into the house on Saturday afternoon with a sigh of relief. The jobsite in Austin was finally straightened out, though the construction manager and three crew members who'd decided to cut corners on supplies and line their pockets with the savings were now filing for unemployment. There was more work to be done, but that was a worry for next week.

The house was cool and quiet, and he felt a stab of disappointment. He'd told Olivia he'd be home late, but part of him had hoped to find her waiting for him. He'd missed her this week, and as his schedule had been so unpredictable, they hadn't managed to connect by phone more than a couple of times. She'd sent him her check-in texts, as usual, but it hadn't been enough. He wanted to hear her voice.

He shook off the disappointment and headed for the stairs. He needed a shower, then he'd find out where his girl was. She'd likely made plans her with girlfriends for the afternoon, and while he wouldn't interfere with her time with her friends, he wanted her to know he was home.

Or maybe not, he mused, heading into the bedroom. He had some ideas for a new home-invasion scene he'd been wanting to put into play, and since she wasn't expecting him, the timing was perfect.

Buoyed by the thought, he dropped his duffel by the closet and headed into the bathroom, then drew up short.

Olivia was in the tub with bubbles up to her chin, her hair piled on top of her head and her eyes closed. The cat, curled on the bathmat, looked up with a meow.

"Well, hello," he drawled, expecting her to pop open those gold-flecked eyes and smile at him. When she didn't, he frowned.

"Liv?" he called, raising his voice slightly, but she still didn't react, though the cat came forward to wind around his feet. "Hey, Phoebe. You watching over our girl?"

Phoebe meowed, shedding all over him, then pranced out of the room, no doubt to see if he'd left any offerings in her food bowl. "Joke's on you," he called after her, then turned back to Olivia in time to see her eyes pop wide.

She screamed and sat up so fast water sloshed over the side of the tub. "Jesus, Cade! You scared me to death!"

"Sorry," he said, realization dawning as she pulled a pair of wireless earbuds from her ears. He could hear the music from across the room. "Guess you didn't hear me."

"Guess not," she said, setting the buds next to her phone on the floor and tapping the screen to stop the music. "When did you get in?"

"Just now," he said, and leaned over to give her a kiss. "I caught an earlier flight."

"Oh."

He sat on the edge of the tub. "You sound disappointed."

"I'm not," she assured him, then grimaced. "Okay, kind of. I had a whole thing planned."

"Yeah?" He stroked a finger over her shoulder, tracing her tattoo through the bubbles that clung to her skin. "What kind of thing?"

"A thing," she said, then huffed out a breath when he just stared at her. "I hadn't worked out the details yet."

"Maybe I can help," he offered, dipping his fingers lower to skim her breasts. Her skin was soft and flushed from the bath, her nipples delightfully puffy. If he had anything to say about it, they wouldn't stay that way long. "I'm a pretty good planner."

"You can't plan your own surprise," she said, her breath catching as he gently pinched a nipple. "Besides, I don't know if you'll like it."

"I'll love it," he promised. "As long as we don't have to go anywhere tonight."

"No, it's a home surprise."

"Good." He shifted to leaned down and put his lips on her shoulder. "Because I missed you, and I'm planning to make up for lost time."

"You can't," she told him, and to his amusement, nudged him back.

"I'm sorry, I must have misheard you," he said, hiding his enjoyment under a layer of chilly politeness. "It sounded like you said, 'you can't'."

Panic made her eyes widen. "I didn't mean it like that."

"Good, because that would be against the rules, wouldn't it? Unless I'm hearing a safeword?"

He waited a moment, and she bit her lip, her eyes wide and her pulse pounding in her neck. When she didn't say anything, he nodded. "That's what I thought. Stand up."

Slowly she rose to her feet, water sluicing down her body, little patches of bubbles clinging to her skin. He took his time looking her over, from head to toe and back, and smiled when she trembled.

He rose from his perch and grabbed the bath towel waiting on the counter. "Come here."

She stepped out of the tub and stood quietly as he dried her off. He rubbed briskly, and when he tossed the towel aside, her skin was glowing a rosy pink. He grabbed the back of her neck in a hard grip and dragged her out of the bathroom. She stumbled beside him but he didn't slow down, and when they reached the bed, he shoved her onto it. "Get on your back."

She scrambled to obey, her hair falling out of its loose topknot to spill into her eyes, and she shoved it aside to watch him warily. He started to strip, his movements deliberate and violent, his gaze locked on her face. "Hold on to the headboard and spread your legs."

He dropped his shirt to the floor as she obeyed, holding the headboard so hard her knuckles went white. But her legs didn't part fast enough for his liking, and he brought his palm down without mercy on the tender skin of her thigh.

"I said spread your fucking legs," he said, and smacked her again.

Breathing hard now, she obeyed, pushing her feet out to the corners of the bed. She could spread them wider, but that would do for now.

"Don't move," he ordered. He peeled off the rest of his clothes, then climbed onto the bed between her knees and shoved two fingers into her cunt.

Though she was damp, she was far from ready, and she let out a cry of shock and pain. Her legs instinctively tried to close against him, but he pinned her thighs down with his knees and fucked her with his fingers until she was moving her hips in time with his hand.

He dragged them free and wiped them on her thigh, then caught her legs behind the knees and shoved them back. Her eyes were wide, her lips parted as she panted for breath. Her nipples were no longer soft, but tight with arousal. The rough handling was turning her on like it always did, and after a week of work headaches and missed connections, he wanted to gobble her up in big, greedy bites.

So he did.

He pushed her knees back farther so they all but crushed her breasts, then leaned down and spat on her cunt. Her shocked gasp made him grin, and he did it again, his spit glistening on her bare lips, then shoved his tongue deep.

She bucked against him, and he tightened his grip on her thighs to hold her in place. He'd missed her pretty cunt, and he was going to eat his fill.

He nibbled and sucked, licked and stroked, the taste and scent and feel of her like a drug. The more he had, the more he wanted, a glutton for pussy. She came fast, shrieking and bucking under him, but he didn't stop.

She begged him to, babbling that she was too sensitive, that it hurt, and tried to push him away. But her safeword never crossed her lips, so he simply ordered her hands back on the headboard and shoved his face back into her cunt.

When she'd come again, shaking and pleading, he wiped his face on her belly, rose to his knees, and shoved his dick into her.

She was wet from his mouth and two orgasms, but she was fighting him. "Take it," he ground out, the words so guttural they were barely distinguishable. "Come on, open that slutty cunt and take it. You know you want it. Tell me you want it."

"I don't," she cried, her eyes glistening with tears as he pushed harder.

"You let those tears loose and I'll use 'em for lube," he warned her, pulling back slightly then working himself back in. He sank to the hilt with a grunt and stayed there, grinding against her clit while she spasmed around him.

"Want it, don't you?" he breathed, pulling out and thrusting back in slowly. Her pussy was clinging to his cock now, wet and willing. "Yeah, you want that big dick."

Her eyes flashed, a split second of warning before she let go of the headboard and slapped him, right across the face.

She hadn't pulled it—which he supposed was fair, as he never did—and he swore he felt his teeth rattle as his head snapped around. Delight made him grin into her terrified eyes. "You want to play rough?" he asked, grinding the words out, then grabbed her flailing hands and pinned them on either side of her head. "Bring it on, sweetheart."

She was struggling beneath him now, twisting and bucking to try to dislodge him. He dragged her hands above her head, pinning her wrists in one hand and bracing the other on the headboard. He leaned his weight into her, fucking her harder as the telltale tingle rose in his balls. He was going to come soon, too soon to wait for her. He hammered into her, racing selfishly for his own orgasm, and when it hit and he began coming inside her in long, heavy spurts, she let out a wail that could've woken the dead.

He ignored it, ignored her struggles and her curses, focused on wringing every last drop of pleasure out of his release, and when he stopped moving, still buried inside her, he grinned at the look on her face.

"If looks could kill," he said, and laughed when her eyes narrowed. "What's the matter, sweetheart? Did you want to come again?"

"Get off me," she ground out, furious and aroused and all but spitting at him.

"Sorry, no can do." He swiveled his hips slowly, keeping him half-hard inside her. He wasn't done, not by a long shot. "Never let it be said I left a lady hanging."

"Don't!" she choked out, yanking at her arms when he put his free hand between her legs.

"Don't what, sugar?" he drawled. "Don't this?"

He flicked her clit and she jerked, her cunt clenching around his still embedded cock. "Yeah, you like that. Tell you what, sweetheart. If you beg me, I'll make you come one more time."

She shook her head and yanked at her arms. "No."

He tightened his grip on her wrists, pressing them into the mattress, and flicked her clit again. "Beg me."

"Fuck you."

He grinned at the way her voice caught on the words. "I know you're trying to be defiant, sweet cheeks, and it's admirable. Really. But you just sound needy."

He lowered himself to whisper in her ear, his bigger body pinning her down. "Needy and desperate."

She twisted under him, rubbing her breasts against his chest as her pussy rippled around his dick, which was recovering quicker than he'd anticipated. "Please," she whined.

"Not until you beg. Come on, sugar. Four little words. 'Please make me come'. I know you can do it."

He angled his hips to shove his hand between them. Her pussy was soaking wet now, from her arousal and his come, so he traced his fingers through the puddle and moved them to her clit.

She whined and jerked, her cunt spasming on his cock. At this rate, by the time she got around to begging, he'd be ready to fuck again. He slid his fingers over her clit for the pleasure of watching her flinch, then began to circle it gently. She relaxed, relief coming into her eyes, but he knew that the gentle touch would soon be more frustrating than soothing.

He was counting on it.

Sure enough, she began to squirm under him, trying to press up into his hand. He stilled his fingers when her hips arched up, only resuming the soft, teasing strokes when she subsided. She'd lay still for a moment, quivering with need, until it became too much to bear and her hips surged up again, seeing deeper contact.

Then he'd back off, waiting until she was still again before resuming.

Over and over, the pattern repeated. Her skin grew damp with sweat, her breasts flushed. Her pupils were so big they looked blown, her iris only a thin ring of greenish gold around them. She was so far gone he was having to frequently stop stroking to keep her from going off, and still her lips remained firmly clamped shut.

His own need was ramping up, making it harder to concentrate. Her cunt was so wet it literally squished around his cock, the sound obscene. His dick felt raw, like one big exposed nerve, and even though he wasn't moving inside her, he could feel himself drawing impossibly closer to a climax.

Which he couldn't have until she got off, and she was being remarkably stubborn. He was going to have to take drastic measures.

"You gonna beg or not?" he asked.

"Never," she croaked even as her hips rolled under him, robbing the vow of its punch.

"Oh, you'll beg," he assured her. He pulled his hand away from her clit, grinning when she whimpered in protest. He lifted his hand so she could see it glistening with their combined fluids, then shoved his fingers into her open mouth.

Her head jerked in an instinctive protest even as her lips closed around him and she began to suck.

"That's it," he ground out, forcing his hips to remain still. If he started fucking her, she'd go off like a rocket, and he still needed her to beg. "Suck me clean, baby. All the way, there's a good slut."

He shoved his fingers to the back of her throat, just enough to make her gag. He pulled free and laid his spit-shined fingers on her breast. "Beg."

"No," she wheezed, then let out a scream when he slapped her breast hard, then grabbed her nipple and squeezed.

"Beg," he repeated, and waited for her to shake her head before pinching down hard. Holding her tight, so tight he could almost feel his fingers on either side of the rubbery little nub, he pulled up, stretching her breast into an elongated tear-drop shape. Her groan was pure agony, her back arching up to try to ease the pressure, but with her hands pinned down, she couldn't get high enough.

"Beg," he whispered.

"I hate you," she choked out, her throat thick with tears once more.

"I'm just trying to make you feel good, baby," he crooned. "But I can't do that unless you beg."

"I can't."

"Sure you can." He pulled harder, stretching her breast as far as he dared, then abruptly let go. The sudden release of pressure made her cry out, the cry turning to a scream when he slapped her breast one, two, three times in rapid succession, making sure the edge of his hand caught her nipple squarely on every blow.

"I'm going to make it easy for you," he decided, pitching his voice so she could hear him over her own ragged breaths. "Until you beg me, I'm going to hurt you. When you beg, I'll stop hurting you and make you come."

She moaned. "Please, don't."

He tsked lightly. "Begging me to stop is not one of your options. Pay attention now, because I'm not repeating myself again. Your options are get hurt, or beg to come. Got it?"

Her eyes were wide and pleading. "Why are you doing this?

"Because I can," he said simply, and bared his teeth in an evil grin. "Ready?"

"No," she moaned, but he ignored it and reached for her other breast.

She held out longer than he'd expected, and far longer than he wanted, but finally, when his teeth were buried in the soft underside of her left breast while he repeatedly slapped the right, he heard it. "Please make me come."

He lifted his head, triumph and relief flooding through him. "I'm sorry, what was that? I didn't quite hear you."

She swallowed hard, her cheeks wet with tears. "Please make me come."

"There, now. That wasn't so hard, was it?" he asked, smugly victorious. He levered himself up, letting go of her wrists to plant both fists in the mattress and, without ceremony or finesse, began to fuck her.

The lewd slap of their bodies was punctuated by grunts and moans from both of them as they strained toward each other. Her legs spread wider, her knees rising to clasp his ribcage as her hips tilted up, her body urging him to go deeper, harder. He shifted his weight to one arm, reaching the other hand down between them. This time there were no teasing, gentle circles — he went to town on her clit, rubbing and tugging and pulling until she arched off the bed with a scream, her body taut, then she broke, shuddering and gasping as she came, her pussy milking him with rhythmic pulls, and he let himself off the chain, hammering into her until he found his own release.

His arms gave out and he collapsed on top of her, his cock jerking inside her, her cunt pulsing around him. He wanted nothing more than to curl up and sleep, still buried inside her. But she was crying softly under him, her body still trembling from the aftermath of her orgasm and whatever emotion the impromptu scene had brought up.

He pushed himself up to see her face, wet with tears and so lovely it took his breath. "Hello, fofa."

"You asshole," she replied, and hiccupped, fresh tears spilling from her eyes. She balled up a fist and punched him in the shoulder.

The awkward angle meant she couldn't put much into it, and her fist skidded off his sweaty skin. She cried harder, and he felt the first trickle of alarm. "Hey, hey, what's wrong? Did I hurt you?"

"No," she sobbed, and hit him again. "But I had a plan, and now it's all shot to hell."

He folded his lips to hide his smile. "Aw, fofa, I'm sorry." He kissed her softly, cheeks, lips, eyes. Her cute little nose. "What was your plan?"

"Forget it." She hiccupped again. "It's ruined."

"I bet we can fix it." He carefully rolled them to the side, sighing with regret when he slipped out of her, and cuddled her close. "Tell me what it was, and we'll figure it out together."

"It doesn't count after sex," she wailed, and buried her face in his neck.

"What doesn't count after sex?" he asked, stroking her back to soothe as he frantically wracked his brain. What the hell was she talking about?

"Telling you I love you," she sobbed, and his hand froze on her back.

"What?"

"It doesn't count if I tell you I love you after sex," she repeated. "Everybody knows that."

"Everybody, huh?" he said, fighting to keep his voice even as he resumed stroking. Joy was like a bright, beaming light inside him, bathing everything in a warm glow.

"Yes, everybody." Her breath hitched. "I was going to tell you over dinner."

"Yeah?" He smiled into her hair, so fucking happy he could barely contain it. "What were you going to make?"

"Your mom made feijoada," she replied, sniffling into his shoulder. "And she showed me how to make rice."

"You asked my mom to teach you to make rice?" She was already planning the wedding, he thought wryly.

"Well, I've only ever used a rice maker, and I wanted to do it right."

"That's very sweet," he said softly. "I'm sorry I messed that up."

"We can still eat it," she said grudgingly, and he laughed.

She pulled back to frown up at him. "Are you laughing at me?"

"No, fofa." He kissed her, soft and sweet. "Did I ever tell you the story behind that nickname, by the way?"

She knuckled a tear away. "No."

"It's a pretty good story," he told her, lifting a hand to brush her hair away from her face. "Kind of a family legend. Would you like to hear it?"

He could see confusion in her hazel eyes, but she tilted her face into his hand and nodded.

"You know my mom is Brazilian, right?" He waited for her nod. "Well, she came to the States as an exchange student when she was eighteen. That's when she met my dad. His younger sister was one of her classmates, and they got to be friends."

He paused to tug a strand of hair away from her lips. "Anyway, she and Aunt Amy hung out a lot. Dad was away at college, but he came home for Christmas that year, and that's when they met."

"Was it love at first sight?" she asked, and he chuckled.

"More like hate at first sight. Or at least, deep dislike at first sight. He thought she was stuck up, and she thought he was arrogant. They didn't fight, exactly. My grandparents wouldn't have stood for that. But they got in their little digs. Mom used to cuss him out in Portuguese, until my grandmother caught wind of what she was doing. Gran told her she couldn't use any words they couldn't look up in a Portuguese-English dictionary, so she started calling him 'fofo'."

He paused for a moment. "Portuguese is a romance language, so some words are gendered. Fofa for girls, fofo for boys."

"I took French in high school," she told him, and he nodded.

"Anyway, 'fofo' just means cute or fluffy, so when they looked it up in the dictionary, it didn't seem derogatory. But dictionaries don't generally include cultural nuance, and in Brazil, it's an endearment for little kids, or something fluffy and cute. So using on it an adult man was...let's just say, not complimentary."

"She was mocking the shit out of him," she guessed.

"Oh, yeah." He laughed. "He always suspected something was up, because she was never sweet to him. But he said when she called him 'fofo', she might as well have been spitting sugar."

Curiosity and amusement lit her gaze, her tears forgotten. "How'd he find out?"

"When he went back to school, he went to one of the language professors. She clued him in."

"Was he angry?"

"A little. But he started coming home on the weekends, just to fight with her. And the fighting was starting to feel less like hate and more like fun. When he came home for spring break, it took them three days to get caught steaming up the back seat of my grandfather's Caddy."

He smiled when she let out a gurgling laugh. "When she was supposed to fly back home, they eloped. And she stayed."

She sighed. "That might be the most romantic thing I've ever heard."

"She still calls him 'fofo'," he said, his gut tightening a little, because this was the important part. "And sometimes she's still mocking him. But mostly, when she says 'fofo', what she really means is 'I love you'."

"Oh." Her eyes filled with tears again. "Cade."

"I wanted you almost from the moment we met," he said softly. "And at first, that's all I thought it was. Took me a while to figure out that it wasn't just lust. By the time I did…"

"I was with Kyle," she whispered. "Why didn't you tell me?"

"I didn't want to interfere with your relationship," he said simply. "I still got to be your friend, and that was enough for a while."

"I can't believe we wasted so much time," she said, the tears slipping free.

"I don't think it was a waste," he countered, brushing at her wet cheeks. "I don't think we would've gotten this far, this fast, without those years of friendship behind us."

"I love you so much," she choked out. "Even if you did ruin my surprise."

He lowered his head so his lips brushed hers. "I love you, too, fofa."

"Every time you call me that from now on, I'm going to cry," she told him with a watery laugh.

"Good," he said, and gave her his most sinister stare. "I like making you cry."

"Beast," she accused.

"You love it."

"I really do." She gave such a heartfelt sigh he couldn't help but smile. "I never thought I'd find this."

He traced his thumb over her cheek, gathering more tears. "This?"

"You." Her lips curved in a tremulous smile. "Someone who'd love me, and take care of me, and who would fuck me up in the exact way I like to be fucked up."

"I do love to fuck you up."

"I know." Her breath hitched on a sob. "I'm so happy. Sadie was right."

He shook his head at the change in topic. "Yeah? What was she right about?"

"That this is special, and rare, and I should cherish it instead of pigeon-pecking it to death."

"She said that, did she?"

She sniffed. "Uh-huh. So did Jack. Well, he didn't say pigeon-pecking, but the gist was the same."

He didn't have to feign surprise. "Those two agreed on something?"

"Well, they didn't know they were agreeing."

"That explains it." He laid his lips on hers, savoring the way she curled into him. "What do you need, love?"

"Can we eat later?" She pressed her forehead to his, her eyelashes spiked with tears. "I just want to lie with you like this for a while."

Her eyes were swollen, her cheeks blotchy, and her hair was a wreck. He'd never seen her more beautiful. "Forever, fofa," he told her, folding her close with a sigh. "Forever."

Author's Note

Those of you who are familiar with consensual non-consent probably already know that it's common for people come to it as survivors of sexual trauma. Not everyone who is into CNC is a survivor, of course, but many are, for reasons for that are as varied and individual as the people themselves. I made the deliberate choice not to make that a part of Cade and Olivia's story, simply because I didn't feel equipped, either as a writer or as a survivor, to handle it properly.

Want to see more from this author?
Here's a taster for you to enjoy!

Dark and Deadly:
Show Me Something Good
Hannah Murray

Excerpt

Kit Howard was having a shitty Saturday. Which, when she stopped to think about it, wasn't surprising. The week leading up to it could best be described as 'hellish', so why should today be any different?

It had started out fine—hopeful, even. She'd slept late, a rare treat, and by the time she'd arrived at her favorite coffee shop, the morning rush had ended. She'd snagged the best booth by the window, and with a mocha latte and a cinnamon roll dripping with icing, had settled in to work.

Updating her résumé hadn't taken long—she'd distilled the last two years of ten-hour days and 'other duties as needed' into one short paragraph and a handful of bullet points designed to entice future employers into hiring her. She had an enthusiastic, if somewhat floridly worded, recommendation from her previous boss, which would normally give her a solid leg up in her quest for fresh employment. But since he'd dictated the recommendation to his lawyer from the jail cell where he sat awaiting arraignment on twenty-three counts of embezzlement, tax fraud, and insider trading, she wasn't counting on it.

Still, since it was his fault she was out of a job, it was the least he could do.

The investigators who had descended on the office on Monday morning had confiscated her phone, laptop, and everything in her desk drawer — ignoring her protest that her favorite lipstick and her extra pair of stockings were unrelated to illegal stock tips. Human resources had handed out pink slips to all staff members who had reported directly to the soon to be indicted CFO before the end of the day, cleaning house in an effort to prove to their stockholders that they were on top of the situation, and she'd spent the rest of the week with investigators, answering questions about her boss, his habits, and every single person she'd ever seen go into his office.

They'd done it partly to be thorough — they must have put every piece of paper, email, and financial transaction from the last ten years in front of her over the course of those five days — and partially as cover. None of her co-workers knew she was the one who'd blown the whistle on Arthur and his felonious activities, and she was keen to keep it that way. It would come out eventually, but hopefully by then the world would have moved on to bigger, uglier scandals.

After a week of sitting in a windowless room with investigators and her older brother the lawyer, whose pugnacious and confrontational nature was finally doing her some good, they'd thanked her for her help and returned her lipstick and stockings. Her phone and her laptop were still considered evidence, since she'd used both for work, so she was using her mom's old phone and her sister's old laptop until she could buy new ones.

She could only be grateful that she'd had the forethought to restrict her porn consumption to her personal tablet.

Still, she needed both a phone and a computer, and wouldn't be able to afford to replace either until she got a new job.

She'd worked her way through a half dozen listings — all of them below her previous salary — when she realized she was out of coffee. She glanced up to hail a server and noticed with dismay that the café had filled up. She waited, hopeful one of the two servers bustling about would see her raised hand, but when neither of them acknowledged her after a few minutes, she scooped up her empty cup. Despite the crowd, there was only one person waiting at the takeout counter, so she draped her coat over her laptop and slid out of the booth.

She stood in line, shivering a little when the door opened behind her with a jangle of bells and a gust of frigid air. The café was loud, canned holiday music mixing with the hum of conversation and the clatter of dishes, so when she stepped up to the counter, she had to raise her voice to give her order. She stepped aside to make room for the person behind her, and let her mind wander while she waited.

She needed a new job, and fast. After years of saving up for a down payment, she'd bought a house last summer, and what had seemed like a perfectly reasonable monthly mortgage in July suddenly felt much less comfortable. Even Greta moving out at Thanksgiving hadn't worried her — though she was definitely keeping the thermostat set lower now that her lover's perpetually cold feet were no longer a factor. She'd known that Greta might not always be there to split the costs, and had been careful to only take on as much mortgage as she could afford on her own. But she'd also counted on having a job, and finding out her boss was committing securities fraud only weeks after she'd moved in was a curve ball she hadn't anticipated.

She'd gone over and over her bank accounts this week, and no matter how she crunched the numbers, she only had enough money in her savings to cover a few months of mortgage payments. Thankfully her car was paid off, but she still needed to pay for insurance, and when she added in utilities and the pesky need to eat every day, she calculated her savings would last her less than two months. She could dip into her retirement account, but by the time taxes were taken out and fees were assessed, that would really only buy her another month or two.

She raised her head as her name was called, and took the mug the barista handed her with a smile, well aware that unless her luck changed, this was the last mocha latte she'd be having for a while. She called out a "thank you", tucked a couple of bucks into the tip jar, and turned carefully away from the counter. The foam was right up to the top, and she was concentrating so hard on not spilling any of it on the way back to her booth that she didn't see the man standing in her way until it was too late.

She squeaked and tried to stop, her feet stuttering to a halt on the cement floor only inches before they collided with the boots in her path. But while her body ground to a halt in time to avoid a collision, the liquid in her cup followed the laws of physics and kept going. She watched with helpless horror as coffee gysered up out of the oversized mug to splash across what seemed like an acre of camel-colored wool.

"Oh, damn," she moaned, her heart sinking as her drink—coffee and chocolate syrup, for double the staining power—immediately began to soak into the expensive fabric.

"What the fuck?" a deep voice boomed, and a hush fell over the café as every head turned toward them.

The sudden absence of chatter made the canned music seem unnaturally loud, and it jolted her into action. She turned to the counter, the remaining liquid in her mug—not much of it, thank God—splashing across the surface as she reached for the pile of napkins at the edge. A wad of them in hand, she spun back to her latest catastrophe.

"I am so sorry," she babbled, swiping at the growing stain in an attempt to minimize the damage. Maybe if she could keep it from spreading, it could be dry cleaned, and she wouldn't have to stretch her already groaning bank account to replace the coat. "I'm so sorry, I didn't see you."

"You should watch where you're going," the voice growled, and she winced at the sharp censure.

"I know, I know," she said, still focused on the stain. It wasn't spreading any more, giving her a glimmer of hope. "But my mug was so full, and I was concentrating on not spilling it."

"Nice job," he said sarcastically, and the apology she'd been about to offer—*again*—died on her lips.

She dropped her hand, the wad of wet napkins clenched in her fist. The sharp retort she'd been about to spit out died as she looked up into the most handsome face she'd ever seen. Because that was just the kind of luck she was having this week.

He was tall, with tawny blond hair and pale skin, his cheeks and nose red from the cold. The elegant coat she'd just ruined was draped over shoulders that seemed impossibly broad, the collar turned up to brush the curling ends of his hair. A thick scruff of beard covered his jaw, his generous mouth was currently twisted in annoyance, and she was sure his crystal-blue eyes would be pretty if he wasn't glaring at her like she'd just taken a crap on his shoe.

Sure, because a handsome asshole is just what I needed. Thanks a lot, universe.

"I'm sorry," she said, her tone considerably less conciliatory than it had been. "It was an accident."

He looked down at the stain on his coat, glaring so hard that half his forehead disappeared. "Do you have any idea how much this coat cost?"

She was very much afraid she did. If she had to replace it, she'd be eating ramen and canned tuna fish at every meal for months. "I'll pay for the dry cleaning, of course."

He went from glaring at the coat to glaring at her while the noise level around them returned to normal. "Forget it."

"I insist," she countered, and crossed her fingers over the wet napkins that the stain would come out. "I'll give you my contact information so you can send me the bill."

He shook his head, and she tried not to notice how his hair glinted in the overhead lights like burnished gold. "I don't have time to get it dry cleaned, and I don't want your contact information."

He was being a dick, and her remorse was fading fast, so she took a deep breath and slipped into executive assistant mode. "If you don't have time, you can leave it with me and I'll have it cleaned for you."

He shot her an incredulous look. "You want me to leave my coat?"

"I know an excellent twenty-four-hour dry cleaner. You'll have it back before you know it."

"It's Saturday. And the day before Christmas Eve," he pointed out.

Shit, she thought, and pulled her phone out of her pocket and began scrolling through her contacts. "I'll call the cleaner now, see if they can do a rush job."

"Lady, you're not listening," he muttered, and she paused. "I don't need you to clean the coat."

"I'm the one who soiled it," she pointed out, reaching for reason and calm so she wouldn't start crying, or worse, punch him in his handsome, jerky face. "It's only right that I take care of the cleaning."

"It was an accident," he said, forcing the words through clenched teeth.

"Yes, it was," she said with a broad smile, and thought she saw his cheeks pinken further. "Regardless, I don't feel right about not taking care of it."

"You're not going to let this go, are you?"

She should, she realized. He didn't seem to care, and heaven knew she couldn't spare the money. But something about his attitude had her digging in her heels. "No, I'm not."

"Fine." He shrugged out of the coat and held it out. "Here."

"Thank you," she said, holding on to her smile with an effort. He was wearing a white fisherman's sweater that made his shoulders look even broader, and worn jeans that clung to thick, sturdy thighs. There was a rip right over the left knee, and for some reason, that little slash of skin was fascinating. "I'm sure I'll be able to get it back by the day after Christmas, at the latest."

"Whatever," he muttered, and turned toward the door. He'd taken two steps before she realized he was actually leaving.

"Wait!" She had to raise her voice over the din. "You didn't give me your name!"

"I know," he called without looking back, and with a jangle of bells, walked of out the door.

Dismayed, she watched him go. It had started to snow, and by the time he disappeared around the corner, his gilded hair was covered with a thin layer of white. "Well, shit," she muttered, and looked down at the pile of camel-colored wool in her arms.

"Coffee for Nate," the barista called out behind her.

She looked around. Nobody was approaching the counter. "Um, I'm sorry. Was Nate a tall, blond, white guy wearing this coat?"

The barista, whose name tag read Gem, blinked. "Yeah."

"He, um, left."

Gem continued to look confused. "Without his coat? It's snowing."

"It's a long story," Kit said, figuring it sounded better than *he was so desperate to get away from me he walked coatless — and without his coffee — into a snowstorm.*

"Right." Gem stared at her for another moment, then down at the coffee. "Since he's gone, do you want his coffee?"

"Oh. Um." She eyed the cup. On one hand, it felt weird to take someone else's drink. On the other, hers was currently soaking into the pile of cashmere in her arms, and the someone else was kind of a dick. "Sure, I guess. What is it?"

"Mocha latte," Gem said, holding it out.

It figured that when something finally went her way, it was a measly cup of coffee.

About the Author

Hannah has been reading romance novels since she was young enough to have to hide them from her mother. She lives in the Pacific Northwest with her husband—former Special Forces and an OR nurse who writes sci-fi fantasy and acts as In-House Expert on matters pertaining to weapons, tactics, the military, medical conditions and How Dudes Think—and their daughter, who takes after her father.

Hannah loves to hear from readers. You can find her contact information, website details and author profile page at https://www.totallybound.com

Home of Erotic Romance

Sign up for our newsletter and find out about all our romance book releases, eBook sales and promotions, sneak peeks and FREE romance books!

Printed in Great Britain
by Amazon